nico & tucker

rachel gold

BELLA BOOKS
2017

PUBLISHER'S NOTE

Other Bella Books by Rachel Gold

Being Emily
Just Girls
My Year Zero

Acknowledgments

I have tremendous gratitude for my devoted early editors: Steph Burt and Lin Distel, you fixed so much about the structure of the story. Major thanks to Vee Signorelli whose help with the themes of this story changed the face of the novel for the better. And huge gratitude to Shuvani Roma for ideas, support and magic.

Thank you to:

Alia Whipple for unfaltering alpha reader encouragement.

Elyse Pine, MD, Trans Youth Lead Physician, Gender JOY, Chase Brexton Health Care for detailed help with all the medical information.

Sean Saifa Wall, intersex activist, collage artist and TEDx speaker for input, ideas and great information.

Kim Nguyen for feedback and brainstorming.

My brother, Dan Gold, for loving Thailand, moving there, and sharing his knowledge of Thai culture.

Erica Abbott for answering legal questions.

Ha'Londra Dismond for inventing "soul Thai."

Axel Kohagen for roleplaying Tucker's therapist with me.

Allison Moon for the consent exercise Nico uses later in the book and framing the way I think about sex education.

My writer's group the AoPers: Juliann Rich, Aren Sabers, Dawn Klehr, Vee Signorelli, Eva Indigo, Heather Anistasiou.

Editor Katherine V. Forrest for writing the best editor letters and enhancing the voice of this novel.

A big thank you to a special someone who logged in one of my game accounts to level my character while I finished drafting this novel. And lastly, thank you to the current generation of teens who are going places with gender in the US that my generation barely dreamed of.

About the Author

Raised on world mythology, fantasy novels, comic books and magic, Rachel Gold is the award-winning author of multiple queer and trans young adult novels—including *Being Emily*, the first young adult novel to tell the story of a trans girl from her perspective. She has an MFA in Writing from Hamline University and is an all around geek and avid gamer. For more information visit rachelgold.com.

For the real life Sharani—you're wonderful!
And for all the real life Nicos.

CHAPTER ONE

Nico

Getting out of my house should've been easy. Only my grandmom, Yai, was home and she was used to me sweeping through the house on my way to dance. She sat in the eating nook sipping a cup of tea with a bunch of theater brochures fanned out on the table in front of her. An old radio gave off the low buzz of an NPR talk program. I waved on my way in from school.

Up in my room, I changed into my party clothes and grabbed my duffel bag. I had spare outfits in case I changed my mind during the two hour drive about what to wear. I was giddy nervous because I hadn't seen Tucker in a while and it was Valentine's Day.

Since I'd met her four months ago, she'd been on my radar. When her life got torn apart last fall, we grew closer; she needed somebody to talk to who wasn't at her school.

The more we talked, the more I liked her.

Liked her so much that I decided it would be worth the awkward conversations I had any time I tried to actually date a person. She was very cool on trans issues. I wanted that to mean it would be easy to talk about me too.

Lately Tucker had been sounding like she might be ready for dating. I so wanted that dating to be with me. But I couldn't ask, too jumpy, so I said I'd come up for this party. The queer and trans student group at Freytag University was doing a big Valentine's Day bash.

I'd skipped my last class of the day because I wanted to get to the university early and have dinner with my best friend Ella. When Ella had been outed as a trans girl, the administration put her in a two-room suite with no roommate. Tucker asked to move into the other half of the suite. They were in and out of each other's room endlessly, so Ella would have the most recent intel about this maybe-dating situation with me and Tucker.

And I had to be early because Ella would want me to help pick her outfit, which always took forever. Though, to be fair, choosing what I was wearing took forever too.

What do you wear to show that you're interested and available, but maybe not exactly what the other person is expecting?

I picked orange. Nothing rhymes with it, right? So that's got to say, "Expect the unexpected."

Plus it gave my skin a warm, dark golden color that went well with not wearing makeup. I'd been skewing more into the boy territories of my genderfluid map. Tucker was lesbian. Maybe she wouldn't even like how I looked anymore.

I almost went back upstairs to change my outfit. But I had spares in the bag. I'd be okay.

I dropped my duffel in the hall and turned into the kitchen to see if there was anything worth drinking in the fridge. On the way, I stole a peek at Yai's theater brochures. She now had half the table covered with them and was writing dates and times on a legal pad—planning her spring 2014 theater season attendance.

Her teal sweater was a pretty casual style, but she had on earrings and a necklace like always. I'd caught her in a sweatshirt and earrings before—and they were nice earrings.

"Where are you going?" she asked, putting down her pencil.

"Freytag for that party, remember? I'm staying over."

"Don't you have class now?"

I ducked my head into the fridge instead of answering and heard her gravelly laugh. Yai is completely Thai and completely American and awesome.

Yai met Grandpa Bolden when he was serving in the US Military in Thailand decades ago. She swears that she fell in love the minute she saw him. He never pushed her to Americanize. No matter what people said to him, he made sure that Thai culture had as strong a place in their house as black culture. Their daughter, my mom, loved that about her childhood.

Yai came to live with us when I was nine, after Grandpa Bolden died. I loved having her here. Nobody else combined her level of no-nonsense practicality with a fanatical love of the arts. She was the biggest nerd in my life, except for me.

When I was eleven, she started taking me to the theater. Every year she bought a season ticket to every tiny local theater—even the one in an old garage with a sketchy heating system. She went to every production at least once, and returned to the ones she loved best. She even came to every dance performance of mine. I could gaze out over an audience of queer, trans, nonbinary, genderfluid wildness and there in the middle would be a short, elderly Thai woman her white hair up in a bun.

"How are you doing in this class you're missing?" Yai asked.

"Great, it's Biology, Ella helps me." I leaned against the counter between the kitchen and the eating nook and opened the orange juice. The corner of a theater program caught my eye and I pulled it out of the mail pile. "You missed one."

"They sent me two." She tapped the duplicate on the table in front of her.

I half-heard her answer because an attorney's return address caught my eye. I moved the thin, nasty-looking envelope out from the bottom of the stack. It was addressed to my mom with her full name.

"He was supposed to drop the suit, the shitbag," I grumbled.

Yai clicked her tongue. You were never supposed to disrespect your parents even if they were incredible shitbags.

I held the letter up to the light, trying to see inside. If Yai wasn't watching me, I'd have slit it open. It looked like a single page, not a lot of writing. Probably a court date being moved or a request for information.

My dad had started this lawsuit against my mom and my doctor before I turned eighteen and somehow he was managing to drag it out, even though I was legally in charge of my own body now—and even though he had less than no right after everything he'd done.

He wanted me to be a boy. Or, failing that, a girl. Not a fantastical genderfluid person. He thought it was malpractice or even abuse that my mom and my doctor didn't force surgery on me.

He was the one who had forced surgery on me when I was four. Took me in for "masculinizing genital correction" while my mom and Yai were out of the country. Only Mom's quick intervention kept me from being mutilated from dozens of unnecessary surgeries.

Could I counter-sue him? I should figure out which legal organization to call and ask.

"That's not for you," Yai said firmly. "Put it back. Go have fun with your friends."

"I don't want Mom to have to keep worrying about this. I'll talk to him again."

"It can wait a few days."

I pushed the envelope back to the bottom of the pile and went to kiss Yai's cheek. She patted my arm. Despite what she'd said, I knew the next two hours would be nothing but me obsessing over what to say to my dad.

I wished I could go back to obsessing about Tucker.

CHAPTER TWO

Tucker

Getting up on a ladder to hang anything, no problem. But this much pink was killing my dyke credibility. At least we were doing the setup early enough that Nico wouldn't see me like this. I had pink lights in one hand and pink streamers in the other, trying to pin the lights to the top of the ladder with my knee so I could wield the hammer.

"Cal, this is nuts," I grumbled around the nail I was holding with my teeth.

"It's beautiful," he called up to me. "I'll get the hearts."

Cal had frosted his short blond hair pink. With his face red and sweaty from party prep, the hair made him look like a molding tomato. Despite being built like a football player, Cal had zero endurance.

"There's no room for hearts," I told him, wishing he'd sit down for a few minutes and give us both a break.

"Where's your sense of romance?" he yelled cheerfully, heading back into the house.

Cal shared the bottom of a duplex with a roommate I'd seen twice last semester. The place was effectively Cal's. And it was the heart of the campus queer and trans student group. We had a tiny resource center on the third floor of the student union, but Cal's living room was so much more comfortable. Most of the meetings happened there, and all of the parties.

Like the party last Halloween, just after I'd broken up with Lindy and she…and things got bad. Too bad to think about.

I used to love this house, but now it creeped me out to be inside. I kept seeing Lindy on the back porch inviting me back to her apartment, her tall, skinny frame dressed as some famous painter. I saw Lindy moving through the people in the living room to wait for me out front. I could smell her inside the house. Impossible, I know. It made me choke. When people arrived for tonight's party, they'd fill it up with new memories. I'd be okay. I had to be.

I pounded a nail through a streamer, looped the lights over the nail, moved along as far as I could reach, pounded in another. Climbed down the ladder, moved it a few feet, climbed up again. One nail, another nail, down, move, climb.

The motion calmed me. I liked the burn in my shoulder from the swing of the hammer. The cold air swirled up under my jacket and sweatshirt when I raised my arm and it felt delicious on my sweaty stomach.

Cal handed me a bunch of shimmery pink and red foil hearts on cardboard backing and I didn't even complain. I nailed them at intervals with the streamers. Maybe I could fit a second row of lights along the edge of the gutter. I found a package of picture hanging hooks in Cal's junk drawer and went back up the ladder to see if they'd fit the side of the gutter.

I heard Summer's voice from down the sidewalk before I could make out the words. I was not looking forward to being at this party with her. She was one of the officers in our queer and trans group, angling to be its president next year when she was a senior. As far as I could tell, she wanted to run everything. She was stuffing her resume for law schools and internships.

She wouldn't be happy until she was the first Latina U.S. president. I'd for sure vote for her, but socially we'd been oil and water since last semester. Over the winter break I wasn't even sure I wanted to come back to this school. On top of things with Lindy, the teaching assistant in my Women and Gender Studies class did everything she could to make the class miserable for me. Turns out, Summer was dating her.

I didn't like Summer's politics and I did not trust her.

"…let's say I accept that 'they' is a singular pronoun," Summer's words clarified as she got closer. "Do you say 'how are they?' or 'how is they?'"

She had to be talking to Tesh, who'd come out as nonbinary over the winter break and started using they/them pronouns. Sure enough, I heard Tesh's voice answering her, "Good question. Technically the second one's correct but the first one sounds better."

"You get how this could feel made up to me, right?" Summer asked

"People make up language all the time, *bae*," Tesh told her.

Summer laughed. "Point taken, but if all the girls turn nonbinary or into trans men, who's left to date?"

"So it's over? You're single again?" Tesh asked.

I held very still on the ladder and turned my head to watch. Neither Summer nor Tesh had seen me. The ladder stood at the corner of the house, halfway behind a tall pine tree. They were coming from campus, which put the tree between me and them.

Through the branches, I saw Tesh first, wearing a long, black coat and carrying two grocery bags. Summer had one hand wrapped around Tesh's arm at the elbow and the other holding a heavy bag over her shoulder.

Best friends for the last two years, why they'd never hooked up I didn't understand. They clearly adored each other. Now that Tesh wore drab, masculine clothing, the two of them would be a super cute couple. Summer's bright colors made them seem more solid together, and Tesh's short blue hair emphasized Summer's thick, dark, shoulder-length curls.

Too bad Tesh already had a girlfriend or this could be Summer's moment. They looked happy, heads bent toward each other, chatting and walking in the crisp late afternoon sun.

"Oh yeah, she's not coming back," Summer said. "We're done. I'm glad. She was a lot of work and I'm so busy this year. The LSAT is freaking me out."

"You'll slay it," Tesh told her. "And you'll find someone perfect. Give it time."

They turned onto the walk leading up to Cal's. Halfway along it, Summer tugged on Tesh's arm so they stopped walking. Tesh turned toward her.

Oh God, Summer was going to take her moment anyway. She stared at Tesh with that super intense I'm-going-to-kiss-you-now expression.

Could I scurry down the ladder and run behind the house without them seeing me? It was a creaky ladder. If I didn't stay still as a stone, they'd hear me. From where they were standing now, the tree barely covered me. Maybe if I stayed frozen, they'd never realize I was here.

Tesh looked as frozen as I was. Summer grabbed the front of Tesh's jacket, tugged, and leaned up. Their lips met.

I held my breath. How would Tesh deal with this? Short kiss and push Summer away? Or…

Tesh pressed into the kiss. All three grocery bags hit the ground. Tesh embraced Summer, while Summer's hands went up around Tesh's face and hair.

That was so much. It had been obvious Summer was smitten with Tesh. Summer was pretty easy to read. Tesh wasn't. But damn, that kiss was super clear. They were trying to memorize each other. It wasn't any sloppy making out. Their lips moved together, communicating everything they couldn't say out loud.

They pulled apart, both gasping, hands still on each other.

"I can't," Tesh whispered. The cool breeze carried the quiet words to me. My hand was freezing to the gutter. My face was freezing in shock.

"Please," Summer said, the word more plaintive than anything I'd ever heard from her. She would beg for Tesh if she had to.

I so didn't want to be here for that.

Tesh kissed her, pulled away, said again, "I can't. Not now, just not now."

Picking up one of the bags, Tesh ran into the house. Summer watched Tesh go, mouth open, hands limp at her sides. She was crying. She moved to one of the grocery bags, picked it up and set it down again. Turned back toward the house and then spun halfway back, eyes focusing on me.

Her tear-streaked face went from soft grief to rigid fury. I held up my hands.

"Do you have to be in the middle of *fucking everything*?" Summer yelled at me.

I went down the ladder carefully, shaking with the effort of having stayed frozen so long and the impact of Summer's anger.

"I wasn't—"

"This isn't about you," she yelled.

"I know."

"No you don't. Every fucking thing is about you. You don't get this too. You don't get to swoop in here and…everything I have you take it and twist it."

She spun and walked away, stride heavy with rage.

What was she talking about? I hadn't taken anything of hers. I guess if she thought that Lindy getting expelled had pushed her own girlfriend to leave school, maybe she could justify being pissed at me. But that was messed up.

I needed a hot shower and soup and to tell my roommate Ella all about this because holy crap.

I carried the two grocery bags from the front walk into the kitchen. Tesh was putting the first bag's contents into the fridge.

"Tucker?"

"Found these on the walk," I said.

"Did you see Summer?"

"Heading back toward school. Did something happen?"

Tesh touched their lips, turned in the direction of the school. "I made a mistake."

I burned to ask: which one? Kissing Summer or not kissing her more? Instead I said, "I've got to change for the party, you okay here?"

Tesh nodded and put more pop into the fridge. I about ran back to campus.

CHAPTER THREE

Nico

On the two-hour drive from Columbus up to Freytag, I rehearsed different ways to talk to my dad about dropping the lawsuit. Threaten to countersue? Maybe. Offer him a bribe? If I could ever figure out what he wanted, short of turning me into a man.

Dinner with Ella didn't help. I wanted her to tell me about Tucker, but Ella was all aflutter about her boyfriend—it being Valentine's Day. I offered advice about boys, about friends, about sex. But it felt like we were on different planets and I was shouting across the vacuum of space. We didn't sync up until we were back in her room.

"Help me pick what to wear," she said, standing in front of her closet.

"He'll like you in anything," I told her. "He's smitten."

But before long I was trying on things from her closet while she checked out how bad she looked in my orange shirt. She stuck her tongue out at her reflection, yanked the shirt off and slipped her sweater back on. I was laughing so hard I couldn't catch the shirt when Ella threw it back at me.

"That makes your skin look like three-day-old rice porridge," I said. "Or, wait, like a zombie. I'll bring it up for Halloween."

Hands on hips, she demanded, "Put on a pastel, I dare you."

"I am much too fabulous for pastels, babygirl."

Friends since early high school—we'd dated on and off for two years—we didn't look like we belonged together. Short, delicate Ella looked very high-society white girl and hid her nerd tendencies well. Her closet was full of sweaters. Even my everyday clothes had the feel of costume to them. Plus I was a blend on so many levels. Average for a guy, tall for a girl. I appeared light-skinned next to my mom and medium brown next to my dad. I flowed and danced through the fixed identities around me.

Ella went back to her closet, tucking strands of straight blond hair behind her ear. She said, "I have a dress you might like, if you're in a dress mood. My sister says it's too small for her. But it's too big on me."

I was not in a dress mood. But I wanted to keep playing with Ella. She'd had a tough first semester at college while I was down in Columbus partying with the astrophysics geeks and my theater friends.

She'd come up here already half-outed. Rumors were flying about there being a trans girl on campus. In the dorms—shocking! No one was inclined to believe the trans girl was Ella. After all, she's five-foot-five. And everybody *knows* what trans people look like, right?

They were much more willing to believe that tall, thick-shouldered Tucker was trans. She's not, but we don't hold that against her. We don't hold anything against her because she's fourteen kinds of hot. Not only physically, but smart in this mellow, thoughtful way, calming and deep.

Brave, ridiculous Tucker came out as a trans woman to protect my Ella. She was not ready to get beat up over it, but she was. And she got so wrecked by what came after that she still didn't see how messed up she was.

"Hand over the dress," I told Ella. "Let's see."

I pulled off my chest binder and paused. I didn't have a bra with me. I didn't usually need both a binder and a bra on the same night. The dress was thick enough to wear braless and cut with a sporty, high neckline. I slipped into it.

"That works," Ella said, like she'd expected the opposite.

The mirror showed an athletic girl ready to hit the tennis courts. The dress was a good blue for me, bold and electric with gray side panels. But it was profoundly not my style. I'd grown my hair out a few inches since fall and compensated by dressing more masculine. In this dress I went most of the way to full girlie girl.

"If I ever go through a Serena Williams stage…" I said.

"You'd need to bulk up your arms, you're too skinny."

Ella opened her mouth to say more, but there was a tap on the inside door of her suite and Tucker called, "Are you in there?"

Before I could ask her to wait, Ella opened the door. I grabbed the top item from the pile of clothes on the bed and held it to my chest, even though it was small and lace-edged. I was not ready for Tucker to see my chest. Or me without most of my usual, armoring, fabulous clothing on. Or me in a dress.

"Can I borrow your hot pot?" Tucker asked Ella, and then, seeing me. "Oh hey, hi."

"Hey," I echoed, unable to keep a ridiculous grin off my face.

Every time I saw Tucker she looked more excellent than the last. Her whole wardrobe was faded jeans, T-shirts and sweatshirts that were fraying at the edges. There was something magical about a tall girl with big shoulders where you could see the contours of her skin through the threadbare T-shirt she was wearing.

Plus Mohawk, did I mention? Bleached and starched up in a soft wave above the shaved sides of her scalp.

Her blue-eyed gaze traveled down my body, paused at the line of the skirt, blinked and leapt up to meet my eyes with a question. I couldn't tell what the question was. Could be: wow, you like dresses? Could be: are you really a girl? Could be: do you honestly play tennis?

I held the cloth against my chest tighter realizing as I did that it was one of Ella's camisoles. I could not have been more in the girl spotlight. I wanted to run. Dance away from the blinding cultural certainty of these clothes. I wanted to tell Tucker: *I'm not this, I'm not.*

But she was grinning—at me or at the image of girl she'd superimposed on me?

I knew that expression on her face. I'd seen it on too many people. It was: *oh good, I figured you out.* She saw the curve of breasts in this dress, around the edges of the lacy camisole that didn't cover me. She assumed it meant everything it did not.

She was going to ask me out now, tonight, thinking she knew, thinking we were all okay and I could perform genderfluid all I wanted now that she knew I was a girl. It was an inverted kind of naked: exposed as something I was not. I watched myself being erased.

We'd talked about gender, that I was nonbinary, didn't see myself as either male or female, or rather as a lot of both and more. But she didn't know the whole backstory on that. She didn't know that the physical details of me weren't binary either, weren't what most people think of as male or female.

I hadn't found a way to tell her. I mean, I didn't know when or how. If we never tried to date, never kissed, never seemed like there would be more, was there any reason to tell her? Awkward enough to say "I like you" out loud pre-kissing, but the whole thing: "I like you, now can we talk about my genitals?"

And now so much harder because she thought she knew me. Complex fear. Not the simple physical animal panic of my skin wanting to preserve itself. I've had that; I know what that fear is.

This fear was rooted in the nauseous anxiety that after months of getting to know her, seeing her vulnerable, seeing her messed up insides, I could show Tucker who I am and still have her freak out.

Ella broke the silence between us by saying, "We're trying on costumes for next Halloween. Nico's thinking about going as Serena Williams and I was going to go zombie."

Bless her, she knew how inside-out I felt. She was trying to let Tucker know that I was in another costume.

"*Walking Dead* is so last year," I managed to say, even though my tongue was sticking to the roof of my mouth.

"You're not wearing that to the party tonight?" Tucker asked.

"Nico's eschewing dresses until yo can perfect the guy-in-a-dress look," Ella said and I wanted to hug her. She picked up her hot pot and handed it to Tucker with a pointed stare at the door.

Tucker paused on the threshold. "But I wanted to tell you about Summer…can I talk to you later?"

Ella nodded and made a shooing gesture. Brow furrowed, but smiling, Tucker went back into her room.

"You okay?" Ella asked me as I stripped out of the dress in a hot second.

"No."

"How can I help?"

"You did."

I jerked on the chest binder and tugged it comfortingly into place, back to flat-chested. Then undershirt, bright orange shirt, skinny jeans, guy boots.

"Do you have any non-white girl hair products?" I asked.

"There's a gel that might be yours in the second drawer down. It ended up in the bathroom box and I figured one day you'd have a hair emergency in my room."

"You're an angel. An obnoxious, smirky angel, but I'll take it."

It wasn't the right gel, but it got my hair to settle closer to my scalp, a smidge more masculine. Antidote to the dress.

* * *

We drove the four blocks to the party so I'd be parked there in the morning. I was staying in Cal's roommate's room. I didn't want to have to make the drive back home to Columbus in the middle of the night.

Cal's house was visible from the end of the block: flashing pink lights, pink crepe paper, giant heart decorations. If you'd filled a fire truck with Pepto Bismol and turned the hoses on

Cal's house, you could not have made it any more pink. It was glorious.

I followed Ella into the front hall, carrying my duffel. She veered left, through the combined living room and dining room, heading for the kitchen. I paused, duffel over shoulder, to see if Tucker was there yet.

From a chair near the couch, Summer called to me, "You look pretty tonight. Or is that handsome?"

"Both, darling," I told her and darted the rest of the way down the hall.

A quick left put me in the roommate's room. I dropped my duffel on the bed and cracked the window because unwashed laundry was not my ambiance.

What to do about Summer? I wanted to like her. She was light brown and loud, which I loved. But her obsessing about my gender got old months ago.

Some people got stuck on it. I'd had people say—to my face—that *my* gender bothered *them*.

And if they knew the whole truth…if Tucker knew…

But I was not thinking about that.

I slipped out of the bedroom, hoping the closed door would keep partygoers out of my stuff. A dozen people milled around the dining room table, picking at pizzas and bowls of chips. I grabbed a pop from the buffet.

Tucker turned the corner from the hall and came over to give me a hug. I wanted to hold onto her. We were about the same height but she was heavier than me—not hard to do; I burn calories like a nuclear reactor. She had this unbelievable chest and I wanted to slide my hands up under the sweatshirt and anything else she had on—but I was not thinking about that.

Especially after the whole dress thing.

Okay, yeah, I was totally thinking about that.

She smelled like sawdust and warm metal, and she'd swapped her threadbare T-shirt for one that was fraying at the neck, just visible under a newish university sweatshirt.

So I wouldn't stare, I waved a hand at the living room crowd and asked Tucker, "What's new?"

"Tesh's hair," she said.

Tesh was in the core group of queer and trans students who hung out together at Freytag University. At first I'd thought Ella was nuts to pick this random school in rural Ohio when she could've gone to OSU with me. But now that I'd met Cal, Tesh and some of the other students, it was shaping up to be a cool place.

Last fall, Tesh was all about peasant blouses, skirts, and boots. Now she sported cropped dark blue hair and a men's shirt with a tie. Not like shirts have a sex, unless, you know, assuming buttons are the genitals of a shirt, technically the ones with the buttons on the right side could be male shirts.

The blue of Tesh's hair made her eyes luminous. Her? Maybe it was the whole new presentation that caused Tesh to glow. In addition to the hair and clothes, Tesh was binding. No rise of breasts showed under the shirt.

I perched on the couch arm and leaned toward Tesh so I wouldn't have to shout over the music.

"You look great! I love that hair color."

Tesh grinned. I knew that look. I mirrored it back.

"Pronoun?" I asked.

"They them."

"Awesome."

"What's yours?" they asked.

"I'm sticking with yo and yos for a while," I told Tesh.

I'd been through many nonbinary pronouns, and 'yo' felt good. Short and easy. Plus since it meant "I" in Spanish, it sounded pronouny already.

Tesh said, "Thanks for being around and, I don't know, being you. You helped me figure out some stuff."

I wanted to hear more about that, was going to ask, but Summer huffed from her seat in a folding chair across from Tesh. "Of course you two are best friends now," she grumbled. "They, yo, how many pronouns am I going to have to keep track of?"

Leaning against one of the pillars between living room and dining room, Tucker asked her, "You effortlessly keep track of the personal lives of everyone on campus who's ever had a queer thought, how hard can it be to manage a few new pronouns?"

Summer glared at her so hard I wondered what Tucker had done to piss her off. Hard to imagine Tucker doing anything to warrant that.

Summer asked, "So if you're lesbian and you date a nonbinary person, are you still lesbian or are you, like, a nonlesbian?"

I tried not to stare at Tucker's face, to puzzle out the mixed expressions fighting their way across her features. Confusion? Fear? I wasn't a girl and yet I wanted to be her nonbinary date-person. Could that work for her? Would it screw with her lesbian identity?

I'd mentally practiced asking Tucker out. I'd thought about kissing her until it was driving me crazy. I tried to work out how to talk to her about me, make it all work, end up with the two of us laughing and holding onto each other like we had over the end of winter break. I hadn't come up with anything.

"I know at least one nonbinary lesbian," I said. "So if you can *be* both, I'm sure you can date like that."

"What do you think, Tucker? Would you get to keep your dykest of the dykes status?" Summer asked.

"Fuck off," Tucker said and stalked out of the room.

"Hit a nerve, huh?" Summer called after her.

I wanted to tell Summer to back off Tucker, because she didn't know all of what had happened to her. She only knew the whitewashed public version: that after Tucker came out as trans, even though she wasn't, she'd been assaulted and harassed and had a horribly bad breakup. For all of her gossip tentacles, Summer didn't know that when they were breaking up, Tucker's ex-girlfriend had raped her.

Only a few people knew and none of us would share that info. Tucker kept trying to play it tough, but this wasn't a thing you could tough through. She'd talked to me about it more than anyone. I listened and hugged her and told her she was going to be okay, but I didn't know how to make her okay, just that she wasn't yet.

"What's your problem?" I asked Summer, loud enough to turn heads in the dining room.

Summer fluffed her curls and chewed her lip, contradictions of confidence and uncertainty. "I'm sorry," she said. "I'm edgy. Everything's changing too fast."

"Yeah," Tesh said and didn't elaborate.

To me Summer added, "And you. I don't know if it's okay to be attracted to you or not. It spins my brain." Her plain-faced honesty made me like her a little more.

"Of course it's okay," I said.

"So you are a girl?"

"No!"

"You're a guy?"

"There aren't only two genders, or two sexes," I was raising my voice. "Shit, for chunks of western history there was one sex, check out early Aristotle. And a lot of cultures have three or more genders. I am never going to fit in your binary."

"Then how do I know if you fit in my bed?"

"You've got to work that out for yourself."

"Yeah but if all the women who have any masculine traits stop being women, what does that do to the feminist movement—if women are opting out of being women instead of changing what it means to be a woman. What does it do to kids looking for role models? To women who like butches?"

From the doorway behind her, on the way back in, Tucker said, "Butch is still a thing," and I wanted to cheer. On Tucker it was more than a thing; butch was amazing.

"But obviously not a thing Tesh wants to be," Summer said. "There is seriously one butch girl at this school right now and it's you. There used to be more but one transferred and one is turning into a guy and I was seriously hoping, Tesh, that when you started wearing guy clothes you were finally coming out as the strapping butch dyke you'd be perfect as."

Summer and Tesh stared at each other with gunfighter showdown intensity. I had missed something big. I had a lot of answers for Summer's questions, mostly about doing away with the binary and seeing people as individuals, but I got the vibe that this was not my fight.

Tesh said, "I'm not. At least not right now. You can't be a role model to anyone if you're pretending your identity. If I have kids, I don't want them growing up in a world where they've got to have a fixed identity all the time."

Summer contemplated her mostly-empty beer bottle, sighed and walked out of the room.

"What is going on with you two?" I asked Tesh.

A deep red blush took over Tesh's pale cheeks. Glancing away, Tesh said, "Her girlfriend left and they broke up and, you know, stuff."

Way more stuff than Tesh was saying, but I didn't push. I had enough of my own stuff.

Tucker was staring in the direction Summer had gone and I couldn't read her face. What would she do when she found out the person she liked and now thought of as a girl—me—wasn't exactly a girl?

CHAPTER FOUR

Tucker

Around midnight, in a house party, thinking about someone else's sex life—that was me. Granted the sex life in question was my adorable roommate Ella's, who by my calculations should have lost her guy-virginity about an hour ago with her boyfriend. But it still made me feel weird. For the first time other people's sex lives were more compelling than mine.

Where mine used to be was blank. I had this fight starting in my head again—like my brain totally wanted to get down with Nico and my body was all "screw you" about it.

It was hard enough being in this house again. I went to get a colder drink from the back porch, to be outside, see if the cool air helped. But standing on the porch made me feel twitchy: that point in a horror movie when the music starts to play and you brace in your seat because you know that despite your best efforts you're going to jump when the killer comes out of nowhere. I got a beer fast and went back into the mass of people in the kitchen, shouldering through them to the dining room and finally the living room.

Summer was back, in the middle of the couch now, with Tesh on one side and Nico on the other. She had one leg pressed up against Nico's and was playing with a curl by Nico's ear. That was a disaster in the making.

Did she think it would make Tesh jealous to see her flirt with Nico? Or was she trying to piss me off? Or, bonus, both at the same time?

"Can I talk to you?" I asked Summer.

"Don't want me flirting with your date?" she asked, brown eyes locked on mine. "I thought you had dibs on Ella pre-boyfriend. You can't call dibs on every eligible…person who shows up."

Her pause before the word "person" was obvious. A glitch in her affected cool. Summer couldn't seem to get over wanting to fit Nico into male or female categories, and some days I wasn't much better at it. Using nonbinary pronouns fluently was harder than I'd expected.

"I'm not—" I started to protest, but that didn't seem right since I very much wanted to call dibs on Nico. I began again with, "I didn't—"

"You called dibs on Ella?" Nico asked, raising sculpted eyebrows. Up close Nico's light brown eyes held hints of green, like flecks of jasper.

"She totally did," Summer told Nico, leaning close, conspiratorial. "She got all Neanderthal when I said I was willing to test out just how bisexual Ella is."

"Maybe because saying you're going to test someone's bisexuality is not cool," Nico suggested.

Summer sighed, flipped her hair and stood up. "Fine, Tucker. What?"

I walked to the front porch, trusting she'd follow me. There were a few people smoking on the steps, but no one in the three-season porch. Cal didn't like people smoking there and it was too cold for hanging out. I liked the cold. And this was the only part of the house I didn't hate at the moment.

Summer followed me to the far corner and folded her arms high on her chest.

"I'm not going to tell anyone what I saw," I told her. "So whatever you think you're doing with Nico, back off."

"You think you get to call the shots? You think you can walk in here as a first year and get whatever you want?"

"Whoa, what are you talking about?" I asked.

"You're the big hero of the campus now after that stunt last fall. I've been working my ass off in Women and Gender Studies and all anyone can talk about is you. Around here." She circled a finger, meaning Cal's house and by extension our student organization. "Nobody moves without asking you or Ella first. Trans is the flavor of the decade and you scammed your way into it. Two years I've been busting my ass to get the good work study, to get considered for research."

She jammed her finger into my shoulder. "You think you know what it's like. You think you saw something today. Me getting shot down. That's not the half of it. What happens when you get picked to do research next year that I should've been doing, that I need for my transcript, and all because you *pretended* to be a trans woman?"

"I'm not trying to take work away from you," I told her.

"Oh good, so you'll turn it down if they offer?"

I didn't think I was going to get offered research work study, but if I did…college cost so much and I didn't make a lot at the hardware store, especially only working weekends and summers. Research work study paid better than my hardware store job and came with credentials for future projects and jobs.

Would I turn that down for Summer? Even before this semester? Even before she started acting like a raging ass?

"I thought so," Summer said while I struggled with the answer. "You've got that presentation in Callander's class when? A month from now? Wait and see what she offers you after that. Then come tell me to back off, moron."

She stalked into the house, slamming the door behind her.

I didn't want to go back into that house. Her jab at my shoulder, the smell of the place, had made me jumpy again. I leaned my forehead against the cool window and watched the smoke rise from the clump of people on the front steps.

Some days I was still foolishly happy I'd even gotten into college. Growing up I wanted all sorts of things, but I figured if I was really lucky I'd eventually run a small contracting company. Summer was planning to go to an ace law school, set herself up for a career in politics, rise as high as she could. She never doubted what she could do professionally, intellectually.

I rubbed the calluses on my fingers. I'd been thinking maybe I did want to be a professor someday. Prof. Callander made that feel doable. But the money for grad school, all those years of study, all that debt…

I didn't get offered help, being big and dykey. People in my town figured I could handle myself, or they didn't want anything to do with me. The best I got was leftovers: my sisters' clothes that never fit right, their marked-up books. If Summer was right about the work study, that would be the first time I got offered something first, something I really needed.

What if I got it, but didn't deserve it?

* * *

When the porch got too cold, I forced myself back into the living room. Nico was talking to Tesh. When Nico saw me, yo pushed off the couch in a single motion that rippled with physical grace.

Holding out a hand, Nico said, "If you have dibs."

Our fingers curled together and yo pulled me down the house's back hall, past the clump of nervously shifting people standing in line for the one bathroom. I was about to protest that I didn't feel right going into Cal's bedroom when Nico opened the door diagonal from Cal's and pulled me through.

The room managed to be Spartan and yet messy. In one corner lay a pile of socks like a nest of snakes, in another was a trash can crammed with old potato chip containers and cereal boxes. The bed wasn't made but someone had thrown a Freytag University wool blanket over it. Lumps and ridges from the underlying bedclothes made it look like a landscape scored by glaciers.

On the foot of the bed was a gray and dark red duffel that said The Ohio State University across the front.

"You're staying here?" I asked.

"For tonight, so I don't have to drive back late. Cal's roommate said it was cool. But hey, this isn't like me inviting you into my bedroom, get it? I want to talk."

"Yeah," I said, but my breath had quickened at the word "bedroom" and caught in my throat.

Around Nico, the jumpy feeling from the porch turned into something much better: warm and buzzing.

"You and Summer, are things okay?" Nico said.

"No. But it's about school. It'll work out."

She couldn't stay mad at me for the whole rest of the semester. And I didn't want to think about Summer anymore.

Standing in front of me, Nico seemed taller than when we'd first met. Still a hair shorter, but barely. Late growth spurt? Yo always struck me as older than Ella but now in the stark overhead light, looked young for mid-eighteen.

Nico took the beer bottle out of my hand and offered me yos half-empty bottle of orange soda. I took a long drink from it. My throat still felt dry after. Nico set the bottle of beer on the desk, far enough toward the back that no one was going to carelessly knock it over.

Since I'd met Nico in the fall, yo had been growing out yos hair. Now it lay in little black curls all over yos head. At the same time, Nico had stepped back the makeup so that yos face appeared plainer, more masculine. Under the orange shirt, I saw the sharp definition of strong shoulders.

Nico said yos gender was nonbinary—what did that mean? I'd seen Nico in the dress in Ella's room looking entirely like a girl and my brain kept going back to that image.

And I didn't want to just talk.

I perched on the bed, near the foot. Nico sat halfway to the headboard, within arm's reach. Yos fingers played along a thick wrinkle in the wool blanket.

"What are we doing?" Nico asked.

The question was legit; we'd been emailing, talking, messaging, video chatting and calling each other since the middle of winter. And there was flirting, but not a lot. Nico was being careful of me. For the first time in my life, I appreciated it.

I shook my head and shrugged. "Having an awkward conversation?"

"It doesn't have to be."

"Do we have to talk?" I asked. I felt like all I'd been doing was talk for the last three months. I wanted to stop talking.

"It's usually a good idea," Nico said, but yo was smiling.

But I thought, "she was smiling" because for a moment Nico seemed very much like a girl, peering up through her eyelashes, flirting with me.

I crawled forward on the bed and kissed her. Nico's lips were soft but agile, like diving into a lake and finding it easy to float. Sensations like water lapping along the surface of my mouth. Her tongue touched my lips gently, harder, pressing against my tongue.

I was off balance, sliding forward, and she pulled me down on top of her on the bed.

Yo, I reminded myself, Nico's pronoun was yo. But wrapped in the kissing, our legs tangling together, my body said "girl" or at least "girl enough." Not that I was thinking that much. It was all mouth and hot and soft and thank God I can do this again, like coming home, Nico smelling of wheat in the sun, peppermint and ginger and salt water.

I brought my lips from yos mouth to yos ear and kissed around its edge, intermittently nuzzling yos neck. Nico laughed, hooked one leg around mine and rolled us over.

Nico shifted yos weight more onto me. I wanted that pressure but it scared me. It was too much like what I'd been trying to forget with Lindy. The world twisted. My hand trailed down from Nico's shoulder to yos arm—touched the solid mass of tricep and that reminded me of my Lindy's ropey muscles. Sickening panic surged through me.

I pushed away: one hand holding Nico back, the other bracing me up. From lying on top of me, Nico flowed into a sitting pose beside my legs.

"Tucker?" yo asked.

"I can't," I said.

I got up so fast I was dizzy and spun around to see if I had a jacket somewhere. No, it was on the porch and I had my boots on. This wasn't the night with Lindy. It wasn't. But spinning was a mistake. I pressed the heels of my hands into my eyes and that made me feel sicker.

"What happened?" Nico asked, yos voice even and soothing.

I had to get out of this house, away from the throbbing, sick feeling.

"I can't do this."

I jerked the door open and shoved my way through the crowded hall. On the front porch, my jacket lay in a heap with others. Snaring it, I kept going down the front steps. I couldn't stop moving until I was a few houses away.

The cold air cleared my head enough that I paused on the sidewalk and looked back at the brightly pink house. I should go back and explain. I owed Nico that much. But I didn't want to walk back into that place, into the people and the memories and the panic.

I put a hand out to the tree next to me to remind myself which way was up. My heart pounded against my breastbone and the bottom of my throat.

Nico hadn't come after me, wasn't anywhere to be seen on the porch or the front steps. Maybe this was better. Without me and my damage, Nico could dance and talk with everyone and have a good party after all.

I walked a few more houses away and glanced back again, hoping I'd see Nico standing out front. Wanting to see anything that gave me a reason to go back. Instead I watched a drunk kid stagger off the porch and puke on the lawn. If that was a sign, it said I should get the hell out of here.

I headed toward the dorms but it was Valentine's Day night and Ella would be in her room with her boyfriend. I didn't want to be anywhere near that. I didn't want to pollute her wonderful night.

I dug my phone out, found my favorites list and hit the third number down.

"Jess?" a sleepy voice grumbled.

As my older sister, Bailey was one of very few people in my life who got away with using my first name. I almost liked it when she used it. Back in high school I'd called her a bunch, to get rides or just hang out and talk. Last semester I didn't. I was in college; I wanted more space from family and the tiny town I'd come from.

"You drunk?" she asked.

"Screw you too, Bay. I'm sober enough but I want to come home. Can you come get me?"

"You buying me pancakes?" my sister asked.

"You know I am."

"Yeah, where are you?"

"I'll be at the gas station on the corner of Tyler and Lawrence."

Bailey muttered an indecipherable affirmative and hung up. My phone said it was one a.m., I owed Bailey more than pancakes. I went into the gas station's 24-hour store, decided on a canned coffee drink for Bailey. I paid and jammed it into the pocket of my oversized coat, went to wait outside.

Bailey's ancient Honda pulled into the gas station, creaking as it came to a stop. I slid into a hot interior that smelled of hair spray and a dozen other sweet and fruity beauty products.

Bailey differentiated herself from her identical twin Brenna by changing her hair color and style every month. Tonight she sported purple braids, starting with indigo near her scalp and going lavender toward the ends that hung down her back.

The color wasn't great for Bailey's skin tone, or maybe it was the effect of the harsh gas station lights on her already cool, white-tan face. She was smaller than me with a rounder build like our mother's, but she carried her weight with an easy confidence and the heavy jewelry in her ears suggested she wasn't someone to mess with.

"You're lucky I'm not on shift until noon," Bailey said.

"Thanks," I told her. I pulled the canned coffee out of my pocket and put it in the worn, cracked blue plastic cup holder.

Bailey nodded at it. "Pancakes first," she said. "Then sleep. Then coffee. You want to go to Mom's or crash on my couch?"

"Whatever's easiest," I said.

Bailey pulled out of the gas station, headed for the all-night pancake place on the outskirts of Freytag.

"You all right, Jess?" she asked.

"Yeah, I'm okay…I wasn't feeling the party anymore and I didn't want to clit-block my roommate."

Bailey howled at that and pounded the steering wheel with one palm. "Clit-block, shit, is that a thing?"

"It sounds better than vag-block. Sounds like a yeast infection treatment."

I kept her laughing as we drove. Maybe I should've called Bailey the night things went so wrong with Lindy. But I hadn't wanted to go home then. Bailey would have known how messed up I'd been. She'd start to see me as damaged and then Mom and Brenna would too. And my presence would have turned her place against me—like Cal's house felt to me now.

I should have gone back. I should have told Nico something.

CHAPTER FIVE

Nico

Jerking the door open, I stared down the hall. No Tucker. If she was triggered and panicking, where would she go? She wasn't the type to lock herself in a bathroom, so maybe she went toward Cal's steadying presence or outside for air. I opened the door to Cal's bedroom in case. Empty.

She wasn't in the living room and neither was Cal. I wove through the crowd to the kitchen. Cal was pulling pop out of the fridge, dropping cans into a cooler.

"Have you seen Tucker?" I called to him over the music pounding up from the basement.

He shook his head. If she'd gone for the back porch, she'd have passed him, so I danced through the press of bodies again to the front of the house. The front steps were full of smokers, the yard empty except for two people: one drunk and trying to sit down on the grass, the other struggling to keep that person from sitting in a pool of puke.

Maybe she had gone past Cal but he hadn't noticed. I went through the house and down to the basement. She wasn't there.

I checked every room again and asked Tesh if they'd seen her. After my third circuit of the house, I admitted to myself that she'd left.

There was no message on my phone from her. Why would she leave without texting me? I knew what had happened to her. We'd talked about it. She could've texted me to let me know she was going.

Unless she was in full panic. But then how could she have gone so quickly? Why wasn't she sitting at the edge of the lawn catching her breath or pacing in the grass? Tucker always paced when she was upset.

Maybe it hadn't gone down like I thought. Maybe she hadn't panicked because of her ex.

When she'd said, "I can't do this," maybe she meant me. Did I feel too non-girl to her?

That would explain why she bolted out of a house filled with friends.

When we were making out, I knew where our legs were. I'd been careful not to let her feel anything from the crotch area. That was a lousy term, wasn't it? Had the word "crotch" ever been sexy in the history of all sex? I doubted it. And since I was being frank, I had to say it to myself: there was no way she could have felt my dick. Not even with how turned on I'd been.

Damn, I was careful. What had I messed up?

Maybe I'd set myself up. Not like I never did that before.

I needed to dance or I'd end up locking myself in the roommate's bedroom and feel like shit for the rest of the night. I went toward the music.

The basement was a big, open, low-ceilinged space with a bunch of workout stuff shoved against the walls. Two speakers pounded out music. It was wall-to-wall sweaty bodies moving, more or less, to the beat.

Since I discovered dance as a kid, I have danced. Every body has its way of moving, I figure. You see a person and you can tell this one was meant for hockey, this one paints, this one was made for soccer, this one for sitting still, and my one self was made to dance.

Ella was made for microscopes and computer screens. You saw that if you watched her up on a stool staring into a lens, chewing on her lip while the corners of her mouth tugged up with joyful intensity. And Tucker's body was for making things. Her hands? Pure making.

I really liked those hands on me. But now the desire was mixed with a dark swirl of shame that I could not abide.

Dance always got me out of a bad headspace. I took classes formally from age five to fourteen. It got to this point where I had to pick if I was going to dance as a boy or a girl and I didn't want to. Plus I was wearing the binder more and it made it hard to dance full out because of the way it compressed around my ribs.

The binder didn't matter for dancing in a crowded, dark basement. I moved to the heavy beat. After a few songs, Summer and Tesh pushed in and joined me.

"Where's Tucker?" Tesh yelled over the music.

"Don't know."

"She still here?" Summer asked.

She danced awkwardly because of the beer she was holding. It was full, the bottle wet with condensation, and she didn't look like she needed another. At least she wasn't driving. But if she kept drinking, I wasn't sure she'd be able to walk back to her room.

"No," I said, wanting this conversation to be over.

"She's an ass," Summer declared.

It didn't have to be true to make me feel better.

"Be back," Tesh yelled and headed away through the crowd.

Summer moved closer, put a hand on my shoulder. I reached for the beer bottle. She didn't need more of that. She pulled it out of my reach. An arc of beer sprayed across my chest.

Laughing and repeating, "Sorry," Summer pushed her hand across my chest, like she was brushing away the beer that had already soaked into my shirt. Except her hand stayed on my chest way too long.

I turned away and went to the basement's sixties-style bar. There were coolers on top. I pulled out two bottles of water.

Summer had followed me and I pressed one bottle into her hand. She leaned against the bar and watched me guzzle half of my water bottle.

"Why are you binding your chest?" she asked.

"How do you know I do?" The question came out hard-edged.

"What?"

"How do you know I'm not wearing a binder so you'll think I have a chest to bind?" I asked her.

"What the hell is your deal?"

"What's *your* deal?" I shot back.

She considered the beer in her hand, set it on the bar and opened the water, took a sip. She said, "You're hot and my now ex-girlfriend is never coming back from her research project so I've been dumped. And tonight…shit. Tonight sucks. But you're cute and alone and I don't even know if you're bangable."

That softened me. Maybe her touching me had been a lame attempt at flirting instead of an assumption that she could have access to my body. So many people thought I was fair game for questions and touches designed to expose me.

"Everyone's bangable if they want to be," I said, leaning against the bar next to her.

She watched the mass of dancers in front of us and said, "I only like girls. Are you a girl?" She curled into my side, put her hand back on my chest. "Because you feel like a girl. What's wrong with being a girl?"

I shoved her hand away. "You don't get to touch me like that."

I saw an opening between groups of dancing people and lunged into it, heading for the stairs.

Summer's voice followed me, ringing triumphant. "Are you afraid of what I'll find?"

I took the stairs two at a time and put distance between myself and Summer. I felt sick, angry, shaky. My tongue was heavy and bitter in my mouth.

In the kitchen, I jerked the fridge open. Miraculously the early partygoers had left most of a pizza. I grabbed two slices, paper towels and another bottle of orange pop. I vacated the kitchen before Summer got herself up from the basement. I didn't think she'd come looking for me but I didn't want the awkwardness of running into her. I felt shit enough already. I didn't know what else I might say to her.

Ducking into the roommate's room, I clicked the lock closed on the doorknob and put the pizza on the desk. Tucker's beer was there, a few lingering drops of condensation gathered on the outside like tears. I rolled the bottle between my palms, thinking about the bottle and me both touching Tucker's mouth—both left behind.

I pivoted and threw it. The bottle smashed on the far wall, foam spilling down the gray surface. I watched the rivulets of beer slip down to join the brown glass shards on the floor.

Picking up a slice of pizza I sat backwards in the desk chair and doggedly chewed the salty, rubbery mass of cold bread, cheese, and meat while staring at the broken glass speckled with bits of white foam. I'd have to clean it up in a few, but for now it made me feel better to stare at the mess. I imagined myself able to throw bottle after bottle like that, to shatter a whole case of bottles, to break everything.

CHAPTER SIX

Nico

I caught a few hours of sleep and woke up having to pee from all the pop. Peering at the clock, I saw in its blocky red numerals that I didn't want to stay here until Cal woke up and asked me about last night and Tucker leaving. It was five-fifty a.m. and I could drive okay. I could make it home for breakfast if I wanted, or go partway to Columbus and crash at a rest stop.

I checked the wall and floor for any hints of staining from the broken beer bottle, but my cleanup job held. There was no trace that anything had happened except for the shards and paper towels in the trash can.

I carried my duffel into the bathroom and washed quickly at the sink. Cal's room abutted the bathroom and I wasn't sure if the sound of the shower would wake him. I put on my "boyfriend" jeans—because it cracked me up that there were guy jeans made for women, like women couldn't just wear men's jeans—and an OSU sweatshirt.

A glance in the mirror showed me that I was skewing toward boy today. I thought about putting on a bright scarf but I didn't care enough. Instead I used my fingertips on my scalp to get my curls to perk up and diffuse a bit, a messier style that also read boyish. Boy felt right: armored, unemotional, brittle.

I set my duffel by the front door. Then I went back into the kitchen to get another slice of pizza for the road and to dig out one of the caffeinated energy drinks I'd seen in the back of the fridge. I wrote Cal a note and left him five bucks with an apology if I took one of his roommate's drinks or his private stash.

My car was parked one house down. Really it was my stepdad Matt's car. I was renting it from him. He'd torn up his leg rescuing a hiker and could still barely put any weight on it, much less drive. Because the car was his choice it was a flat black Dodge Charger that in the right light could be mistaken for a cop car.

I could look like a serious thug in that car, but that's not my style so I put Star Wars family decals in the back window. My mom is Padme Amidala and Matt is Chewbacca; he picked that one himself—it's not me ragging on how hairy he is. My grandmother, Yai, is classic Princess Leia, because Leia is Amidala's mother and because Yai could rock some serious Leia braid-buns if she wanted to.

I picked Yoda for myself because my sister Deena wanted the Ewok and my other sister Hazey wanted R2-D2.

The two people not represented are my dad, Darth Vader, and my big brother Kenan. I'd probably make Kenan take the Luke Skywalker decal because he had that same innocent-guy-caught-up-in-big-crap element to his life. He'd been dragged back and forth across the country as our parents fought about my medical options and divorced. I never knew how much he understood about all that. He focused on school, video games, and girls. Sometimes he seemed more like my younger brother than two years older.

I threw my duffel into the passenger seat. My phone connected to the Bluetooth because the car was fancy, and that reminded me of last night and how Tucker hadn't texted. I studied the phone face. No message from her.

I guess it *was* about me.

Summer's words from last night haunted me. "Are you afraid of what I'll find?"

I flicked through my contacts to Summer and blocked her. I so was *not* in the mood to deal with her.

I stared at my phone a good, long time and then blocked Tucker's number too.

I'd unblock Tucker in a day or two but not until I felt less like breaking things. If Tucker had anything to say, she could email or tell Ella to text me. They did live right next to each other.

Ella would call me dramatic for blocking Tucker. But I blocked and unblocked people on my phone all the time, especially my dad. It kept my headspace clear.

Most of the two hour drive back to Columbus I put the car on cruise control and let the feeling of moving fast calm me down.

Sunday morning at my house was a blend of food, chores, prep, and lying around. Yai slept in the smaller bedroom on the first floor and got up at the crack of dawn to take a really long walk no matter the weather. After that, she listened to her radio shows and chilled.

Mom got up early enough to do her kitchen prep before everyone else was in her face. She was a professor of Astrophysics at OSU, so she did almost all the week's cooking on Sunday and froze it. I helped with the chopping when I was home. She'd picked up cooking as a way to combine her heritage: soul food and Thai cuisine—soul Thai. She said it was the most relaxing thing she did all week. That used to sound made-up to me, but she was always smiling when she was in the kitchen, so I had to admit maybe it was me who didn't like cooking.

I got home around eight a.m., super early for me coming back from a party. They wouldn't expect me until late afternoon.

I opened the front door and paused on the threshold. Mom and Yai were talking in Thai. My Thai sucks, but I heard them saying my dad's name. I dropped my duffel and went into the eating nook. Yai was sitting in her usual spot at the end of the table, facing into the kitchen. Mom stood by the stove.

"What about Dad?" I asked.

Mom set down the spatula and came around the counter to hug me. Putting my arms around her, I felt big. She was very solid but I'd been growing again. Mom was also a lot shorter than I was, but tall next to Yai, who barely broke five feet.

"You're home early," she said. "And you smell like beer."

"You know I don't drink. A friend…someone spilled her beer on me. What's going on?"

A hard sigh was followed by a deep silence, then she said, "Your father is going to be in town for a few months for a project. He wants to talk to you. You can tell him no."

"Oh, I'm going to talk to him," I said, rubbing at the start of a headache behind my eyes. "He has to drop that lawsuit or I'll find a way to countersue his…butt."

Mom shook her head and went back into the kitchen. "Breakfast?"

"Please."

Yai nodded to me as I slipped into the seat beside her. She patted my arm. "How late were you up? You look weak."

"I slept some. It was a party, you know."

She didn't know, but she didn't push it. She went back to reading movie reviews in the newspaper.

Mom slid a plate of eggs, rice, and sausage in front of me. I shoveled food into my mouth, more starving than I thought. It was great as usual. Mom has one of those palates where she can eat a dish in a restaurant and know how to make it at home.

"You do smell terrible, Noknoi," Yai said.

I said, "Oh thanks," and swallowed another mouthful of egg and sausage. I knew Yai saw me smiling down at my plate.

Nehal was my given name and Nico my nickname, but Noknoi was my Thai nickname. It meant "Little bird." Everyone in Thailand has one or more nicknames, so it's the same in my house. My mother, whose given name is Arinyah, got the name Fah, which means "sky," because as a baby she'd fall asleep staring up at the night sky.

Thai nicknames are usually words that mean something, or have a cool sound, or are a shortening of your full name. Matt is

Mat and for some reason Hazey counts as both an American and Thai nickname, short for "Hazel." But Deena is "Dear," which is a Thai nickname that uses the American word, to make it extra confusing. At least none of us got the super weird nicknames like "Pepsi."

My brother Kenan didn't get a nickname. He hadn't liked it when Yai moved in with us. He felt that as an eleven-year-old man, he didn't need two women looking after him. But he was on his way out by that time anyway. He went to live with Dad in California. Dad didn't have a nickname either. Well, I had a few nicknames for Dad, but I couldn't say them in front of Yai.

I hadn't seen either of them in over a year. Not since Dad started this ridiculous lawsuit.

Dad wanted me to be his son. He had this idea, since I'd lived as a boy my first ten years, that I *was* a boy. He thought Mom and the doctors were trying to turn me into a girl or worse.

It's not like I didn't enjoy being a boy sometimes, but not all the time. And not his son—you have to hear that with this deep, ominous inflection—bum, bum, bah, HIS SON. Like if instead of "Luke, I am your father" Darth Vader said, "Luke, you are my son."

I'm not his son. I'm his kid.

He got weird enough when he saw me as a girl but then when I went openly nonbinary he couldn't deal. There were threats and bullshit and a custody battle that he totally lost because I was almost sixteen and told the judge what I wanted. Next step? Sue my mother for child abuse because she let me be myself.

He wasn't going to win that one either, but that wasn't the point. Lawsuits were majorly expensive. He thought the pressure of that would get me to make a choice, pick a gender.

Mom said he was trying to get back at her for taking me away in the first place. She didn't say it to me—wouldn't say something like that to me. But I heard her talking with Matt when they thought I wasn't home. She doesn't talk to me about what happened unless we're meeting with a therapist. Doesn't talk about why we left California and Dad when I was four. Why she divorced him and moved us halfway across the U.S.

I remember it in broken pieces like a box of photos thrown down a flight of stairs. My body holds the memory of screaming. Trying to stop the people who were hurting me. Needing to run and not being able to move. A person looming over me, touching me like I wasn't real. Hurting my dick and not stopping even when I screamed and cried. Not telling me what was happening or even looking at me like I mattered.

I told Dad I never wanted to go back there. He said I had to be brave, to be a man. He said they were going to fix me. He made me go back. Mom had been over in Thailand with Yai. I knew at four that I shouldn't be going to doctors without Mom. She was the one who kept me safe.

I'd felt like those animals in the tar pits, sucked down into sticky death, inescapable. Not being able to breathe, panic, dying.

Before the pain, I had an earlier memory of Dad telling me there was something wrong with how I peed and that the doctor had to fix it. I remember him talking to a doctor about me like I was a broken machine. It had never been a big deal that I sat down to pee. Mom said it was nothing to worry about, some boys were like that, and told my brother to correct the other boys if they teased me.

But dad and this doctor said standing to pee was an important part of being a man. They joked about peeing in snow. I didn't understand why it was funny. The doctor said it was easy to fix, routine surgery, he did this all the time.

I must have told Dad no, to wait for Mom, but he didn't. He'd planned this for when she was gone. Nothing was functionally wrong with how I peed, I just couldn't do it standing up like the "normal" boy he wanted me to be.

I was knocked out for the surgery but afterward the pain was unbelievable. They'd cut into my dick, made stitches there. They gave me drugs and I slipped in and out of a fractured nightmare world. Strangers came into my room and examined my genitals, touching me. They talked about me and I didn't understand what they were saying. But I knew it meant I was wrong inside.

Dad stayed with me the whole time. He kept saying not to cry, be a man, that I'd be happier now.

I don't remember if we stayed in the hospital for more than a day, but I know we had to go back for the doctor to check on my progress and every time it hurt my body and my self.

I didn't have words as a spindly four year old to say how disgusting I felt inside from those dismissive touches. The doctor made me into nothing. He was allowed to touch me any way he wanted, anywhere he wanted, even after I'd said no. And Dad told me I was wrong to say no.

I was overwhelmed by a burning, shivering fear. Because to be a non-person was to never be safe.

Mom had told me that I wasn't like other boys but that it was okay to be different. But now I saw she must've been wrong; I was wrong. I stopped playing with the neighborhood kids. I'd learned how precarious my world was. In my kid logic, I thought the doctor had told them I was a bad person. That it would be obvious to everyone.

When Mom came home from Thailand, I wanted to be around her all the time. She was the lighthouse of safety. I clung to her.

Until the day she put on a blue shirt. Then I ran away. Blue was the color of the people who'd hurt me and I was terrified that she'd become one of them.

She found me in the back corner of my bedroom.

"Nehal, what's wrong?"

I was shaking and pointing at her shirt. It took a few questions and pantomimes for her to figure out what I meant. She changed shirts and came back to me.

"Did something scare you?" she asked.

"I'm not supposed to say."

"Who told you not to say?"

"Dad."

"It's okay to tell me," she said.

She sat down next to me and I climbed into her lap. She put her arms around me and rocked me.

"You can tell me anything and I won't be angry at you," she said.

"Dad took me to a doctor who hurt me in my bad parts and then they made me fall asleep and it hurt more. I didn't want to go back but he made me. He said I was made wrong and they had to fix me."

She was quiet for a long time and then said, "Nehal, my beautiful child, you don't have any bad parts. You're wonderful the way you are and I love you very much."

I held onto her until I fell asleep in her lap. She carried me up to my bed.

When she could bring herself to leave me sleeping there, Mom's first call was to Grandpa Bolden. Then she called the doctor to find out what had been done to me.

Grandpa Bolden arrived the next morning. I hugged his legs and he gave me a toy ship he'd brought. While I was upstairs playing with it, a locksmith came and changed all the locks on the house. Mom told Dad to get a hotel room. She told him that he wasn't welcome in the house anymore. At least that was the cleaned up version she told me.

Grandpa Bolden sat out on the front porch that evening and wouldn't let me stay out there with him. He was a tall, lean man, fit as an athlete, who kept a buzz cut long after his military service ended. He didn't need to do more than sit out there with a book in his lap to send a very clear message that my dad had no chance at getting in the house.

There was a divorce and a bunch of adult stuff I didn't understand. What I knew was that Mom made the world safe again.

She took to me a different doctor who talked to me in ways I could understand, let me know what he had to check to make sure the surgery went okay. I ended up needing another surgery to fix problems the first one had created. But I was lucky; some kids needed surgeries for the rest of their lives. They got a few surgeries trying to "fix" their genitals and then needed more and more to fix the fixes as problems mounted and scar tissue built up. Some people had twenty or more after their first hypospadias surgery and still had to sit down to pee because the doctors could make pee come out of the tip of the penis, but couldn't make it not spray everywhere.

In addition to the new doctor, I saw a trauma specialist who had me do cool stuff with art, play, movement, and breathing. That's when I got into dance. I learned that being in my body protected me from the fear taking over. I learned how to be a person again, how to feel safe.

Mom got a position at OSU and we moved cross-country without Dad. I missed him. I still did sometimes, irrationally and deeply. He was my dad.

For a while, I think he was ashamed of what he'd done—or at least the way he tried to do it. When he came to visit, he brought a ton of presents and we did fun stuff. I almost forgot what he'd done, though my body always remembered.

We had some great dad/son times before I was eleven. Then I decided to be girl for a while and he started being weird. Living nonbinary was the final straw.

The last time we'd talked, he seemed to be lightening up about things, sounded like he'd drop the lawsuit. It made me sort of want to see him again. But not so much that I wanted him living in the same town as me.

I did not want my dad in the same town as Mom and the family and all my queer, trans, genderfluid friends—and for sure not my friends with intersex traits. I didn't trust him with that part of my life.

CHAPTER SEVEN

Tucker

My sister Bailey woke me before noon as she was getting ready to go to work at the beauty salon. Of my two sisters, I was closer to Bailey. She kept a spare pillow and blanket in the ottoman so I could crash on her couch when I wanted.

I went to the salon with her and let her play with my hair. She put a crazy braid into my Mohawk and neatened up the shaved sides, all the while chatting about some guy she'd met at a concert. Bailey had a thing for music guys.

I wanted to say, "Hey, I think I messed something up and I don't know what to do." But then I'd have to explain too much to her, not only about Nico but about me.

I hadn't told her about Lindy. Not everything. Only that the breakup was hard. I didn't say, "She raped me." I never wanted to say that and I hadn't told any of the family. It would seem too strange to them. It would get all caught up with the fact of me going to college. And anyway I was used to being the tough one; I didn't want to give that up.

When Bailey got bored with my hair, I gave her a hug and walked up the street to Shipley's Hardware. I'd worked there on and off since I was thirteen. My job wasn't official back then, but by sixteen Ship paid me on the books and started teaching me. I could paint anything and fix simple around-the-house damage. This last year, he'd begun showing me how to cut and lay tile, even the fancy patterns in shower surrounds. If I couldn't get a cool job, like being a professor, I could always do home remodeling.

I waved at the guy behind the counter and kept going. Ship was in the back contemplating a lawn mower motor. He'd squatted down on the concrete floor, lean body bent over the guts of the machine.

He tipped his weathered face up. "Tucker, you home all weekend?" To Ship "home" meant here in Bluffton where I'd grown up, population four thousand, not at the university.

"Came in last night with Bailey," I told him. "Probably won't stay. You find a mower that stumped you?"

"Nah, trying to figure out how it got this nasty. You here to chat or keep busy?"

"Busy," I said.

"Go clean the windows aisle and see what's sitting in storage. Let me know what we're going to need for the spring rush."

"Sure thing, Boss."

It was a busywork job that no one in the store liked, but it fit my mood. Ship had good intuition. I went from the windows aisle to the back storeroom about a hundred times, cross-checked lists that no one had looked at since last spring, and scoured the ordering books for new items. Plus I fixed a few screens that had come in for repair and had been sitting in the back for months. Customers hadn't complained because it was too cold to use them anyway.

While I worked, I played over last night in my mind. What had set me off? Was it a memory of Lindy? Those still freaked me out. Was it the way Nico's body felt in my hands? The combined soft curves and hard angles?

That wasn't fair to Nico. We'd been talking since Thanksgiving, more and more, mostly online, text and chat.

Nico sent hilarious videos. Yo was the most playful, funny person I knew. Every time I got a note or a pic or a video, it made me happy. Wasn't that how you were supposed to fall for someone?

Hell if I knew. My first "girlfriend," we'd gone to school together and she was the one who'd started things, but she always dated guys too and she never wanted to be seen with me. I wouldn't say that I loved her, but when she called it off for good, it sure hurt.

In the middle of my senior year of high school, I started hanging out at Freytag University to be around other queer people. I met Lindy right off. The first few times, she didn't pay much attention to me and then suddenly she was inviting me to all sorts of events. We made out afterward in the front seat of her car, like I thought regular dating should be.

I fucking loved her. How stupid was that?

It was hard for me to remember being in bed with her. I mean sex. I didn't even want to say that to myself. Sex. Fucking. Fuck sex.

I stopped in the back of the hardware store, in the storage section where it was cold, beyond where Ship worked on the lawn mower. I scrubbed my sleeve across my face. Fresh tears started in the wake of the rough fabric. For a while I stood over the rack of broken window frames and let the tears slip down my face. One fell onto a raw wooden edge and soaked into the grain like a drop of rain.

I'd loved Lindy. As much as I hated her for what she'd done, I also hated myself for having loved her like that.

She'd raped me. It was immensely hard to say, even in my head. It was hard to believe. But now I couldn't stand to remember any of the times we'd had sex or even the times we cuddled and were close. I never wanted to remember her touching me or kissing me.

That didn't stop me from seeing the edges of those moments, over and over, and making myself turn away from them. Screw Lindy. If her girlfriend before me, who I'd learned had been beaten up by Lindy, could pull it together enough to have a cheerful relationship, then I could handle dating too.

I rubbed my sleeve across my face until the tears were gone and then pulled out another frame that needed to be re-screened. The work calmed me, except when I messed up cutting the edges of the new screen and had to start over.

I thought about the time Nico came up to visit Ella and we all drove out to Shipley's so yo could sort through the boxes of old junk for cosplay props. I'd never heard of cosplay before—dressing up like fictional characters for conventions and other events—but apparently Nico did a lot of it.

I could use some costuming about now. Be nice to be anyone but me.

Nico had been searching for props for a science fiction show, *Torchwood*. We'd watched a few episodes together but I didn't get the appeal other than the British accents. The guy Nico liked to cosplay had a cool wrist device, mostly leather encasing metal with a few buttons, lights, and a speaker. I'd been meaning to see if I could make one for Nico.

There were bins of busted electronics in the back. Ship said he never knew when he'd find a button or dial or bit of wiring that he could use. I searched for a picture of the device on my phone and went back and forth between that and the bins, pulling out anything I thought could go into a "vortex manipulator."

Nico had one yo'd bought online, but it was junk. I wanted to make one with lights and sound. I grabbed a small box from receiving and filled it with bulbs, buttons, bits of metal, a few tiny speakers. I'd have to pick up leather pieces and borrow a rivet gun. Was there a craft club on campus? Someone had to have one. Holding the box, having a project to work on, I felt better.

At six, when Ship told me to get lost and have some dinner, I was sweaty and tired from the walking and carrying, but less knotted up inside. I tucked the box of parts under my arm and walked the few blocks back to Bailey's salon.

* * *

Eating dinner with Bailey, reheated too-bland burritos from her fridge, I kept thinking about how fast the fear came over me at Cal's. I liked Nico so much and in a heartbeat that was all gone, replaced with terror. If my reaction to Nico was panic from Lindy, I needed to figure that out and let Nico know. No idea how to do that.

After Lindy raped me—still so hard to think that word—I went to the campus health center for a medical exam. I was trying to say what had happened and the nurse gave me this vacant, alarmed expression like: *um…what?*

She did the exam but she kept peering at me like I was a puzzle missing a bunch of pieces. Like, how does that even happen? How does one woman rape another? How does the person you've loved, the person who said "I love you" a hundred times, how do they wipe you out like that? Blot you out of existence like you're nothing?

Yeah okay, maybe I was more messed up from it than I thought. But I couldn't face the "um…what?" again. I couldn't have answered that nurse any better now than I could have months ago.

It felt gross and stupid and lame to have to talk to someone. I didn't want to talk. If I never talked about it again, fine by me.

But I had to. If this kept screwing with my life, I'd have to ask someone what to do. So start somewhere, right? If I couldn't tell my sister what had happened, how could I tell a stranger?

I waited until after dinner when I was on the couch, holding the TV remote but not turning it on. I leaned forward, arms between my knees, trying to take a deep breath and failing. "Bay, a bad thing happened. Not now, a while ago."

Bailey dropped into the armchair by the side of the couch. She set her mug on the scarred wooden table with a dull thunk.

"With my…" I stopped because I didn't want to say "girlfriend" and I didn't want to say Lindy's name out loud. "That relationship I was in last fall. When it ended."

"You said, bad breakup, it messed you up."

"I didn't tell you all of it. When we were breaking up, she said she wanted to talk at her place. I didn't want to, but she… the sex…I didn't consent. She made me…"

"She raped you?" Bailey's voice rose as she leapt up from the chair. She stalked across the room and back. "She fucking raped you? Is that it? Say it. Say it!"

I shook my head. Not to negate what she was saying, but because I couldn't talk with her yelling at me. I couldn't get the words out of my mouth. I was trying to agree but I couldn't stand to hear myself say it. I turned the headshake into a kind of nod.

"I'll fucking kill her," Bailey said. "Where is she?"

"Bay, no. She's gone. Left school. Expelled."

"I will fucking kill her." Each word spat out separate, falling like acid to the floor.

"Um, thanks?" I pressed back against the couch cushions, trying to stop shaking.

Bailey paced and paused, paced again, saying, "I will hire a goddamned hit man and end her. How are you doing? Are you okay?"

"No," I said. I felt the pressure of tears behind my face, but I couldn't cry in front of Bailey.

I saw the flash of fear in her eyes, that feeling of: *Um…what?* And of: *oh shit, what do I do?*

She sat close to me on the couch and threw her arms around me, pulling me against her. Her hand patted the back of my shoulder. "You'll be okay," she said. "You're going to be okay."

I hugged back, not too tight because she was already smothering me and I wanted to get away.

"Yeah, thanks," I said. "Don't tell Mom, okay?"

She nodded.

I disentangled myself and took my glass into her kitchen. When I got back into the living room, she was in the same spot on the couch. I sat halfway between her and the end of the couch.

"You want to talk about it?" she asked.

I shook my head. "It feels gross to talk about. I wanted you to know so if I seem different or whatever you know."

"You want me to tell Bren?"

Our other sister, Brenna, didn't need to know. She and I weren't close like me and Bailey.

"Nah. I want to forget about it. I just can't seem to."

"I get that. Same with my ex, when he hit me, took a while to stop thinking about it all the time."

I reached for the TV remote. "Can we watch something mindless?"

"Pick it," she said. "I'll make popcorn."

Now I had two things I didn't want to think about: Lindy, and Bailey getting hit. Just great.

CHAPTER EIGHT

Nico

Tuesday I had the day off classes because it was time to see my doctor again. I could've rescheduled it. Medical trauma was a really good excuse. With Dad in town the memories of being four and powerless and operated on and erased felt closer than usual. But I wanted to dance through the fear, show myself how far I'd come, face it down.

I went to the doctor twice a year for ultrasounds to make sure nothing was going weird with my non-average setup. The medical name for my setup is "ovotesticular disorder of sexual development (DSD)." I preferred "difference of sexual development." Anyway, along with that came a higher risk for cancer in my gonads. I'd been getting ultrasounds since before I could remember.

My clinic was associated with the university. It was this huge metal and glass building in a ring of metal and glass buildings: extra modern, like I was on the *Star Trek* future Earth. All my stuff was in the same building, with ultrasound down on a lower floor and the clinic two floors up.

I joked with the receptionist and waited for them to call me. Then it was the usual: weight, blood pressure, go into this room and lie down on a table like a pregnant lady. At least I got to keep my clothes on.

The technician was a heavyset guy whose nametag said Mark Ribera. He had receding hair but made up for it with a cool, short beard trimmed so it was only sideburns, and on his chin and lower jaw.

As I settled back on the bed, he asked, "You comfy?"

"Yeah."

I pulled up my shirt and he spread the gel across my abs.

"Tell me if anything hurts." He moved the wand around on me. The wand was like a heavyset white plastic spatula. He pressed it down and moved it pretty smoothly across my abdomen. I studied his beard and wondered if I could make myself one with spirit gum and prop beard pieces. Because it looked great.

He had his other hand up by the screen he was reading, pointing things out to himself, like he was puzzling out a map of an unfamiliar territory. After a while he said, "Huh."

"If you're looking at the lower gonad, it's both," I told him. "It's my ovotestis, it's part testicle and part ovary. The squiggly side is the ovary side."

He shook his head, staring at the screen and said, "I know, it's in your records," in this distracted tone.

"You're scaring me."

"Can you shift a little to the left? Rotate about fifteen degrees, I want to see if I can get a better angle."

I moved, watching him. He nodded and pressed the wand low into my right side.

He said, "I'm not sure what I'm seeing here. Could be a lot of things. Can you stick around? I'd like the radiologist to look at this."

"Yeah, of course," I said, though I wanted to get up and run.

He gave me a towel to wipe off the goo. "You can sit in the waiting room."

In the waiting room, my bones started feeling like shaky Jell-O. "I'm not sure what I'm seeing" was not what I expected to hear during ultrasound. Usually the technicians said "Cool" or even "Wow."

I sat and jiggled my legs. Got up and went over to the coffee pots and poured myself a cup with a bunch of powdery creamer and sugar. Sat back down and jiggled worse.

After we'd moved to Ohio, Mom did everything she could to make medical visits okay for me. I got scared when I saw doctors, even from a distance, but worse were the feelings of despair, being trapped and doomed, humiliated. I'd shut down and hunch into my chair, not lifting my head, not talking.

In addition to the breathing and movement I was learning to help me stay in my body and weather the panic, Mom got me all these story puzzle games. She'd only let me play when we went to a medical office. They were hard so I had to concentrate, but also fun. She'd start to tell me about the story puzzle the day before and I'd get excited about it. She'd say: "Tomorrow we're going to play a story where there are five kids with five kinds of candy, but all the candy gets mixed up so you have to figure out how to get each kid their favorite candy." I'd go to bed thinking about candy and about my friends and wondering what the kids in the story liked, not thinking about cold metal instruments and strange people poking me.

While the doctors scared me outright, the other people in the waiting room made me nervous in a different way. They stared at us when we came in, or when they came in and we were already there.

Mom was darker than me. She looked mostly black but with eyes and a nose that were pure Thai if you knew how to recognize that. I'm ambiguously brown with a splash of green in my eyes that comes from my father's side. People would keep staring at us while we played like they were trying to read a secret code. I got the feeling that if I could read that code, I wouldn't like what it said.

When the nurse called "Nehal Bolden," Mom always let me tuck the puzzle book under my arm and carry it with me down the hall. The whole time in the exam room with the doctor, I held onto that book and Mom would tell me how good I was being. She'd say "Nehal, my beautiful child, my gift from the gods."

She still said that to me sometimes. I still loved hearing it.

In her world, the sacred walked with the mundane. The great mystery and all the answers sat down to tea together in the afternoon and talked about the mischief that ignorant mortals got up to. She learned Buddhism and animism from her mother, a loving God from her father, and everything else from the night sky.

The only fear she had was fear for me—fear that if I grew up unable to talk to doctors, unable to talk about my body, then bad things could happen again. She showed me photos of the stars and of diverse people's bodies. She named the parts of my genitals the same way that she named the stars in the night sky. I grew up knowing I was part of nature.

I wanted to hear her voice now, so I called, not sure if she had a class or not. It went into voicemail. I left a short message because not leaving one would freak her out. "Hey Mom, I'm at the doctor's. I got a new guy, he's checking some stuff. Love you."

I hoped that sounded casual enough.

My friend Sharani would understand this nervous agitation. She also had intersex traits. Different from mine, but she'd get why I was jumping out of my skin about a medical tech saying, "Huh."

I texted her: *New ultrasound guy, doesn't know what he's seeing. Tripping me out.*

Is your doctor there? she wrote back. Sharani knew that I liked my regular doctor.

Upstairs, I said. Because I wanted to think about anything else, I added: *Did you ask that guy out?*

You're impossible, she texted back.

I think you mean that I'm improbable.

Hahaha. Come by later?

Maybe. Have to stop at home first.

Ok. I'm here if you need, she texted.
Thx.

I held the phone with both hands, read her words a few more times and waited.

* * *

The meeting with the radiologist was short and confusing. He called the mass "unusual." He also described it as the size of a peanut, which got me thinking about an evil peanut lodged somewhere up in my business. That almost made me smile.

He wanted to talk to my doc and then I'd talk to my doc, so I went up to the next waiting room. This one was brighter because the endocrinologists for adults and kids shared the same space. I sat at the edge of the play section with all the big, colorful blocks.

My phone buzzed and it was Mom.

"Nico," she said. "What's going on?"

"They found a mass or something. The radiologist said it was like a peanut and he thinks it's in my ovotestis, but he doesn't know what it is. He's talking to Dr. Peace."

"I'll come down," she said. Her office was three blocks away.

"No, Mom, wait. Let me talk to Dr. Peace, okay? I want to do this on my own. I'm okay. I'll walk over when we're done and tell you what she said."

"Nehal, my baby."

"I know," I said quickly because if she said anything else I was going to cry. "I'll come over as soon as we're done."

She let me hang up. I flipped through the games on my phone until I found one I could stand to play. It was hard to stay seated. After another quarter-hour, I had to go into the bathroom and jump up and down for a while until I could manage being in a chair again.

I'd been back in my seat for a few minutes when the nurse called my name. She took my blood pressure and weight again, as if this was a regular visit. Maybe it was so much a habit she couldn't help it. Or they wanted to see how much my blood pressure went up in the last hour.

In the exam room, I waited in front of a weirdly cheerful poster about low blood sugar and bounced up and down on the balls of my feet. I might have left the floor a few times. I didn't want to be leaping around when Dr. Peace came in, so I started stretching my quads and hamstrings.

Dr. Peace was awesome, not merely because of her name, but because it fit her. She was this skinny little woman, not that much shorter than me but she seemed like it because she was petite. She had a bunch of messy blond hair that was always wisping out of a knot or bun. My favorite thing was that every time she opened the exam room door and saw me, she got a big surprised smile on her face, like we were running into each other in a restaurant.

Even today she looked delighted to see me, but there were worry lines above her blue eyes. She sat in her desk chair and rolled around to face me, not even expecting that I'd sit down. I guess she knew me by now; she'd been my doctor for the last eight years.

"Nico, how are you?"

"Scared," I admitted.

"Let's get to it. The radiologist says he told you the basics. This mass could be anything."

"Like a real peanut?" I asked, hoping to make her laugh.

She did, but lightly, passing right back to serious. "It's doubtful that it's a real peanut. There are a lot of kinds of benign growths that can happen in there, atypical cell development that isn't cancerous, but there's also a five percent chance that it is cancerous. Even if it is, it's quite likely that it's contained in the ovotestis. That means once we get it out, you're fine. No chemo, no radiation. Do you want to sit down?"

I must have looked as bad as I felt. I put a hand out to the exam table and steadied myself toward the chair, dropping into it hard.

"Five percent or more is bad," I said.

"Nico, hear what I'm saying, it's not five percent malignant. It's much lower than that. But it has to come out and we need to run tests. We can take out the whole ovotestis and run tests or we can biopsy it first."

"Hang on." I took out my phone. "Can you say that again and can I voice memo it? Mom's going to want to know everything and I'm not sure I'm going to remember all this."

"Go ahead," she said and let me turn on the recording app. "Hi Professor Bolden," she said toward the phone, "This is Dr. Peace. I'm here with Nico and we're talking about the options." She repeated everything she'd said and added, "My preference would be to do the biopsy within a week and then we'll know what the surgical options are."

I was trying to get it all into my brain. I had one hand over my abdomen, as if I could feel what was going on in there.

"Nico, take a deep breath," Dr. Peace said. "We knew this could happen."

"Yeah."

She'd been after me the last couple of years to have my ovotestis removed because of the increased risk of cancer. I'd been thinking about it. Problem was, once it came out, my body wouldn't naturally produce testosterone. I'd have to decide if I wanted to take T so that I could stay more balanced male/female or if I was willing to run on female hormones from the remaining ovary.

Plus, I might be good at coming to the doctor now, but anything that involved surgery shot me through with terror.

She stayed quiet for a minute and I tried to breathe more deeply. My heart raced and my head wanted to lift off my body and float away. As I breathed, my head felt more solid. I still wanted to jump out of my skin, or to be accurate I wanted to jump with my skin into some other place that wasn't here.

"How do you feel?" she asked. It helped that she held my gaze, showed me that despite all this medical stuff I was a real person to her.

"Less bad." I tried to smile. It wasn't her fault. To show that I'd heard what she said, I added, "Okay so I get the biopsy and then you tell me how bad the peanut is?"

"Yes. We test the peanut. We can do the biopsy in the next few days. Monday at the latest, okay? Usually we get results in a day or two, but I want to make sure we know what we're dealing with, so I'll probably send it out to a specialist and that could take an extra week."

I nodded. Dismally.

She said, "There's a good chance I'm going to ask you to have the surgery to remove all of your gonadal tissue: the ovotestis and the ovary. That would prevent this from happening again and it drops your cancer risk a lot. It's your choice, but I think it's a good idea. We'll know for sure how good an idea when we have the biopsy results."

"If we do that, I can never have kids, can I? Unless I freeze my eggs. So we'd have to do that first, right?"

I couldn't carry a kid in my body, I was used to that knowledge. But this was heavy. That amount of planning and thinking and poking into my body when I wasn't sure if I'd want biological kids or not someday.

She nodded slowly. "I know it's a lot to think about at eighteen," she said. "I'm sorry. Also…" she sighed. "If we take the ovary too, you're going to have to go on hormone replacement therapy."

"Yeah, I figured. What would you do?" I asked. "I mean, which hormones would you take?"

"I can't answer that for you. I have fifty-three years of experience feeling like a woman inside and out that would inform what I'd pick."

"You'd become a woman," I said.

I switched off the voice recorder on my phone. I didn't want Mom to hear me talking about this part. I knew she supported me no matter what I chose, even if it was both, but I had the feeling that she expected I'd pick before now—that when she said I could be whatever I wanted, she thought I'd do boy for a bit, girl for a bit, and then settle into one.

I asked, "What if…if I did want to be one or the other, what's best?"

"What's best is the one you want," Dr. Peace said.

"I'm all of them. It doesn't matter. In a physical binary, I could be either one. They're both okay and they're both not right. What's the best outcome?"

She studied my records for a while. Then said, "I'd want to talk to a surgeon who specializes in this, but on the surface I'd say woman is easier. You would keep your breasts, expand your vaginal opening. In terms of sexual activity—"

I waved my hand to stop her. There was only so much I could handle.

"If I want testosterone shots, would you prescribe them for me?" I asked.

"Yes, it's what your body is used to. If it doesn't feel right without it, I'll prescribe you the shots."

"Thanks," I said.

"We'll get you in for the biopsy and I'll see you back here as soon as we have results. Think about what you want for surgery and we'll talk about it more then, okay?"

"Yeah. Thanks, doc."

She smiled and patted my shoulder in a combined "I'm sorry" and "there-there" gesture. Then she was out the door. Probably had a ton of other patients to see. I sat for a minute but worried some nurse was going to stick her head in and wonder what I was doing there, so I went out to reception and scheduled the biopsy.

I walked halfway to Mom's office, stopped, and dropped onto a bench.

I'd known that I might not be able to have kids, certainly not in the carry-them-yourself way, because my uterus wasn't big enough. But if I couldn't produce my own hormones anymore, what was I? For the past few hours I couldn't sit still and now I didn't know how to get up and move.

Maybe it was time to pick a gender.

CHAPTER NINE

Tucker

I left a lame message for Nico. I didn't know what to say. And after talking to Bailey I really did not want to talk about anything intense. It didn't surprise me that Nico didn't call back right away.

I had plenty to think about. In a month, I was giving a presentation to Prof. Callander's class about the harassment I'd experienced last semester when I came out as trans to protect Ella. I'd never given a presentation before. The last time I was on a stage was in fifth grade and I was a tree.

Ella thought I'd really enjoy doing it, but she was so googly-eyed over dating Shen that she seemed wildly optimistic about everything. Their Valentine's Day night went a thousand times better than mine had.

Mid-week I needed a break from homework and presentation prep and Ella going on about Shen. I volunteered to help with the sandwich run. A sandwich shop across town sold discounted bulk sandwiches to student organizations for fundraising. Once or twice a month, our group got boxes of sandwiches, marked up the prices, and sold them during lunch. They had cool flavors like herbed tuna salad with capers, Korean BBQ with kimchi, and a club with fancy cheese and thick bacon.

I signed up for the early shift: getting the sandwiches, setting up, not selling. When I got to the Union, the empty sandwich table on the mezzanine had two people sitting behind it: Summer and a tall, handsome woman with deep brown skin and black hair pulled into a short ponytail. I'd seen her before and I think she'd been in a close-fitting athletic shirt then too, but I couldn't remember her name.

"Tucker, Quin," Summer said. "Quin's an organizer for the Black Student Union. We're talking about joining in on their dance on March first."

"Cool," I said. I was trying to figure out too many things at the same time. Summer was wearing an oversized red flannel that was so not her style, why? New girlfriend?

And I thought Quin was queer, because she'd come to a meeting of ours, but if she was only working to bridge our two student groups, I'd have to re-think that. Too bad because she was an inch or two taller than me and I always wanted more tall girls around, made me feel like I stood out less.

Quin led the way out of the Union to a moderately beat up Ford Fiesta. It wasn't quite the junk heap that Bailey's car was, but only because nothing was held on by duct tape.

"It's Katee's," Quin said.

"Tell her thanks from us," Summer replied and slid into the front passenger seat.

I crawled into a narrow backseat littered with candy wrappers. Not sure how we'd fit sandwich boxes in here with three people. Probably end up with some in my lap.

As we pulled out of the parking lot, I couldn't resist telling Summer, "Nice flannel. You going to help represent the butches?"

"Quin loaned it to me. I thought today was going to be warm."

That explained the style and the size. It would look so much better on Quin.

Normally one woman wearing another woman's clothing was a clear sign they were together, but the way each one sat distinctly in their seats, the way they hadn't turned toward each other in the Union while talking, didn't add up. I wanted to ask but wasn't going to risk Summer blowing up at me.

Summer rambled on about how rough her life was between school and the upcoming LSAT until Quin asked, "You sure you have time to help us with the dance?"

"Oh, of course." Summer turned half around in her seat and said to me, "The Black Student Union lost some of their leadership this spring and it turned out their finances are, well, not as good as anyone hoped. I told them we'd help out, co-host the dance, help raise money."

"Yeah, great," I said.

"I don't know how to explain it to Cal."

On paper, Cal was the leader of our LGBTQIA+ student group, but in practice most of the organizational decisions were made by the whole core group. Summer and Tesh were always in on decisions and now they'd taken to including Ella as our one out trans person.

"Just like you explained it to me?" I suggested.

"We should donate some of our funding."

"Oh."

That was going to be a hard sell. Cal was only ever serious about fiscal responsibility. When it came to money, he was one step away from being a gay Republican. Also this explained why she was being semi-nice to me. She wanted me to help her persuade Cal.

"Maybe see how this sale goes and start by suggesting BSU gets all the profits?" I offered.

"That'd be awesome," Quin said.

We pulled up at the sandwich shop. I paid extra attention to how Summer and Quin moved around each other. Best I could tell, Summer was flirting lightly to see if Quin was interested and Quin enjoyed the attention but wasn't flirting back. When Summer touched her arm, she didn't pull away but she didn't get closer either. She didn't make excuses to touch Summer.

Maybe she didn't know how to flirt with a woman. Or she had someone else in mind. Or she wasn't into Summer.

As the treasurer for our group, Summer paid for the sandwiches. Quin grabbed two of the flat boxes so I grabbed two. Heavy but not ridiculous. Summer ran ahead, took too long fishing the keys out of Quin's jacket pocket, and got the back of the Fiesta open.

It was clear the boxes weren't going to fit.

"Put the seat down," I said. "The big one on the left."

Summer went around and tried, but couldn't find the catch, so Quin had to put her boxes on the roof of the car and help. I shifted my boxes to rest against my hips, weight in my heels and waited. When they got the seat down, Quin came over to me and took the boxes out of my hands, fingers brushing mine. Bolt of warm, fuzzy electricity.

She slid them into the car, got hers off the top and put those on the pile. "Can you watch the car?" she asked Summer. "We only need one more trip."

Summer nodded, leaving me and Quin to head back into the restaurant.

Quin said, "You know, you can help with the planning too if you want."

I hefted boxes and grinned. "I've impressed you with my lifting and carrying skills?"

Her laugh was full and loud, made me smile, but also made me miss Nico. If Nico were here, we'd never have gone this long without everyone laughing.

"Let me know when the meetings are and I'll try to show up," I told her. "But I've got this presentation due soon that I'm freaking out about, so I don't have a ton of time right now."

Back to the car, boxes in. I crammed myself into the small backseat next to the stack of boxes.

Quin backed out of the parking space and asked, "What presentation?"

That was hard to explain, but I gave it a shot. "Last fall a bunch of students were being assholes about there being a trans girl in the dorms, so I said I was the trans girl they were talking about—to shut them up and keep her safe. And then I got harassed and beat up because of it. But I pepper-sprayed the shitheads who attacked me and they got kicked out of school, so that was sweet. Anyway, Professor Callander asked me to come talk to her class about it."

"Damn, girl, that's incredible."

Summer sighed and stared out the window. She fluffed her hair in the pissed-off way, abrupt rather than flirty.

"It's just one class," she said.

"Yeah but that's some heroism," Quin replied.

"It's not any more heroic than anyone who stands up for what they believe in," Summer said. "Last fall, that protest for Trayvon Martin, standing up to people who called him a thug and acted like that meant a kid deserved to be executed in the street. You were there, Quin. I saw you. I didn't see Tucker. And I'm not *pretending* to be brown. I can't hide who I am."

"Like I'm ever not obviously a big-ass dyke," I shot back. "We all get harassed."

"Yeah, but I'm at all the queer events. When are you planning on showing up for Black Lives Matter?"

I shut my mouth and stared out the window. We drove the rest of the way back to school in heavy silence.

Quin and I carried the sandwiches in while Summer set up the table. On the level below us, Cal and his boyfriend were joking with Tesh. The boyfriend was showing Tesh a dance move, Tesh repeating it, and the three of them collapsing into laughter every time Tesh's angular body flubbed the steps.

Summer had stopped setting out sandwiches and watched avidly, smiling, eyes soft. Summer was seriously pretty when she wasn't being a jerk. At my elbow, Quin pointed toward Summer, then Tesh, and asked, "She likes her?"

"Them," I corrected automatically.

"Huh?"

"Tesh's pronoun is 'they/them.'"

"But Summer likes them, right?"

"Yeah. I wonder, if Summer is actually *more* attracted to Tesh as nonbinary. That would mess her up."

"Why?" Quin asked. She took over setting out the sandwiches and I went to the stack of boxes to hand her more so it would go faster.

"The answer to that is long and convoluted and includes words like heternormative," I told her.

She finished a row of club sandwiches and raised an eyebrow at me. "Are you going to say hegemony?"

I laughed. "Probably."

"That's where I draw the line," Quin said. She picked up two empty boxes and set them behind a pillar. "See you at the dance?"

"Sure."

Confusing. I had to talk to Ella soon about all of this. I got the impression that Quin was a lot more eager to see me at the dance than she was to see Summer.

CHAPTER TEN

Nico

In Mom's office I played her the recording. She hugged me a lot and said, "You'll be okay." The whole ride home was about how great the OSU doctors were and how this would turn out to be a little bump in the road, nothing major.

She was trying to convince herself along with me. It didn't work. As soon as Yai saw us, she asked, "What's wrong?"

"Nico needs surgery," Mom said and explained it all while I went to put my backpack in my room. I didn't want to hear it again.

Mom and Yai were at the kitchen table when I came back downstairs, both with mugs in their hands, serious-talk style. Like when Ella and I broke up the second time and they ganged up on me about how depression is really serious. As if I hadn't known.

Yai watched me walk into the kitchen to get my own mug of tea. "Okay, so you get the bad thing out and you put good in," she said.

I smiled. "Yeah, just like that."

"You're afraid. It will be okay," she said to me while she patted Mom's hand. She was way better at the convincing thing. I couldn't even tell if she was bullshitting. She sounded completely certain.

I put my mug on the table and hugged her. She patted my back. "Okay, okay," she said, sounding mildly impatient. "These things happen all the time. Your pops had two tumors out and in the end what was it? His heart."

Pops was Grandpa Bolden and she had a point. I let go of her and sat down. I didn't want to leave Yai's side. I wanted her to keep telling me and Mom it was no big thing. But I didn't want to stay too long or I'd blurt out the gender situation and I wasn't ready to discuss that.

"When did you schedule the biopsy?" Mom asked.

"Monday."

"That far out?"

"It's six days. It's not that far. I have to go see Dad for dinner on Thursday and I don't want those both at once. Plus I might be sore and I want to dance this weekend."

"You don't have to see him," she said. "Especially not now."

"Might as well get it over with."

The door from the garage opened and Matt thunked into the hallway, one leg heavy in its brace. Mom must've texted him because he yelled, "How bad is it?"

I glanced from Yai to Mom, "Can I skip this part?"

Mom nodded. She'd explain it to Matt. And if she was going to freak out, she could do that in front of Yai and Matt and not me. I needed to be the only person freaking out around me.

I went up to my room and watched *Torchwood* on my tablet until dinner. Deena and Hazey hugged me a bunch and kept watching me like I was going to fall over. But then life got normal again: eating and doing dishes, Mom asking how my classes were going, Yai talking about taking the girls to the children's theater.

For the next two days, I went to class and did my usual homework, all the time thinking about gonads and hormones and impossible choices.

I had to talk to someone who'd get this. Not Ella, because she always knew what gender she was. I wanted to talk to Tucker. Every time my phone buzzed, I expected to see her name pop up and it wasn't her.

I kept flopping back and forth in my head about her. I'd persuade myself that she'd panicked and was embarrassed and I should text her and tell her it was okay. And then doubt would creep in. Maybe she wasn't getting in touch because she didn't know how to tell me it wasn't going to work.

I felt like I was forgetting something important about Tucker texting me. Maybe I shouldn't contact her until I remembered what that was.

And even if she wasn't texting because of the panic/ embarrassed thing, what if after all this I decided I wanted to be a guy?

The desire to talk warred against the part of me that wanted to wait until I had all the info from the biopsy. Why scare more people if it was no big thing? Why panic if they could snip out my badly-behaved ovotestis with robots and call it a day?

To add sucking to injury, before the ultrasound I'd texted Dad with a super casual: *You're in town? Dinner?*

I would love to see you. What night is good for you? he wrote back, formal for a text, but that's how he was.

So two days after finding out I had an evil mass up in my business, I went to go see him. We met at a steak place. He was a steak and beer guy, not steak and wine. I liked that about him. I was mad as hell at him, but I liked him, if that made any sense. Or at least I liked him except for anything related to gender or the legal system or medical decisions. It was mad complicated.

I arrived a few minutes late. He'd gotten us a corner booth and was reading his tablet. He was a long person. In addition to the height I inherited from him, he had a long nose and a long face. Short hair, though, and a short beard, very black, that made his skin seem paler than it was.

I got his cheekbones and chin, Mom's eyes and nose. Great combo, no complaints. My brother Kenan resembled him more closely. Kenan had the most don't-screw-with-me Turkish nose possible combined with a Cro-Magnon forehead.

"Nico." Dad got up to hug me. He held me away from him, looked me up and down and gave me a big, eye-crinkly grin.

"Hey Dad, you're in town for a while?"

"Three, four months, to kick off this project," he said as we settled into our seats. Dad was an engineer, bridges and stuff. "Your brother will come out for spring break and when school's done. You two can spend some time."

"Sure," I said, making an effort not to sound too indifferent about Kenan showing up. He and I had nothing in common. But I guess it would be good to see him.

"Good weather so far this spring?" he asked.

"Seriously? We're talking about the weather now?"

"School?"

"It's fine. I don't have a clue what I want to major in, but the classes are interesting. I've been a little distracted, though, by the fact that my father is *still suing my mother*."

"I have to do what I believe is right," he said. Hands flat on the table, facing me evenly, not giving an inch.

I kind of appreciated how straight up he was about it. Everybody wanted me to be something. Lots of people thought they could decide for me. They'd say, "I know you're really a boy" or "I know you're really a girl" when they didn't know jack. Lots of them didn't even say what they were deciding for me. At least my dad said it so I could fight it out with him.

"I'm eighteen, I'm the one who gets to say what's right for me," I told him.

"Your mother took you away and made many choices without me—choices that shape who you are now."

"I made those choices," I said. "You're the one who wants to make decisions *for* me, not Mom."

"Some decisions should not be made by a child."

"Oh, like the shape of my own body?"

"Nico, I don't want to fight with you."

I slumped back in my chair and picked up the menu. We ordered and talked about school and work and dance.

I'd decided while I was driving over that I should tell him about the whole surgery thing. Sooner or later, Kenan would hear the news from someone in the family. We had a lot of chatty cousins. The minute he heard, he'd tell Dad. And if Dad heard it from Kenan and not me it would wreck all the bridge-building, don't-sue-my-mom work I was doing.

I waited until we were done eating.

"I want to tell you something and have you not flip out or get obnoxious," I said.

His bushy brows went up. "All right."

"I'm going to have surgery this summer for a mass on my ovotestis. It's probably nothing. I'm getting a biopsy soon. I'll let you know what it says."

He reached across the table and covered my hand with his. "Nico, I'm sorry. Tell me about it."

I wanted to hug him for that Dadness of that. His big hand was warm and comforting on mine. He did the protective thing really well. I held myself back. In two minutes we'd be fighting again.

"We don't know that much yet," I said. "I mean, this is why I've been getting the ultrasounds, so it's not like it's advanced or anything. Could be a random growth or pre-cancerous, not dangerous."

"The doctors said this could happen."

"Yeah."

I didn't mention that every year Dr. Peace wanted me to have my ovotestis taken out and every year I said no. It was part of me and I didn't want my parts taken away. But probably also because the idea of surgery terrified me beyond words.

"When you have this surgery, will they normalize you?" he asked.

There was the side of him I wouldn't hug.

"Um…" I had to stall. I was pissed off enough to blurt out something nasty. That wouldn't help change his mind or stop the lawsuit. I said, "I don't understand your question."

"Will they make you into a man?"

So many replies ground against each other in my brain. Depends on how you define man. You can make men surgically? When did that happen? I'm already a man whenever I want to be, why would I want to be that all the time?

I asked, "You think surgery makes men?"

"You're being difficult. You know what I mean."

"Yeah, you're asking if I'm going to let them chop off my breasts and sew my vagina shut and then try to meet some Hollywood standard for dick length."

"Why are you being so rude?"

"Because you are. You're being horribly rude to me and you don't know it and that makes it worse. What would've happened if you let them do all the surgeries to me when I was a kid and it turned out I felt like a girl inside? I saw this video of a woman with intersex traits, like me, who was being raised as a boy and when she started growing breasts the doctors lied to her and said that happened to some boys and did surgery on her. Years later she realizes she'd felt like a woman all along, but now someone had chopped her up, telling her it was for her own good. They took her breasts, Dad, for no reason."

Dad leaned back and steepled his fingers. "What is it you hate about being a man?"

Surprised, I thought about it. Did I hate qualities associated with the cultural idea of being a man? Not the way I defined it. But I hated the way everyone assumed they knew what it meant and that they could dictate how I could and could not be.

I didn't know how to explain that to Dad. His idea of "man" was so rigid that a dinnertime conversation would never budge it.

I said, "It doesn't feel like me."

"You feel like a woman?" He couldn't keep the edge of a sneer off his mouth as he asked it. He hid it most of the time, but in his mind men were always better.

"Don't you get it? I don't feel like either. I feel like both. All the time."

I didn't add that I felt like I was so much girl and so much guy that they barely both fit in this one body. And I loved all of it: being a girl, being a guy, being able to choose from day to day, sometimes from moment to moment. Being able to add in features outside of girl or boy, play with, recombine, redefine what all these categories meant.

I didn't think my nonbinary gender was from having intersex traits, unless I got the deluxe package. Most people with intersex traits did feel like they were one gender or the other. I was the lucky intersection between a nonbinary brain and an intersex body. And maybe if we didn't live in a world that was so messed up about gender, maybe most of us would be everything all the time.

He sat back, glaring up at the ceiling. "If only we had chosen for you."

"I would be miserable," I said.

"You don't know that."

"I've heard from enough people who had other people pick for them. The ones who didn't kill themselves. The ones who don't understand why so much of their lives feel wrong until they discover that doctors took away their dicks or their breasts, cut off core parts of themselves. You really want that for me?"

"No," he said. He spread his big hands on the table and stared at them. "I want you to prosper. I want you to live. I want you to grow up strong and brilliant and find a girl who takes your breath away and marry her and have children who are so beautiful you don't even care when they break your heart. That's what I want for you. Not to spend so much of your time and energy trying to be this in-between person, so much that you don't live your life."

Being strong, wanting me to thrive and have the kind of life he thought was great—I thought it was great too. I did want to be with someone amazing—and of course right now that person looked uncomfortably like Tucker—and have a family.

Not that I was going to give in to him.

He said, "The things that happened when you were a child, I think you're spending your whole life now proving me wrong."

"That's not how medical trauma works. It's not conscious like that."

He waved a hand. "Trauma, such a serious word. You were a child and afraid. Now you're becoming an adult. Can't you leave that behind and choose?"

"If I consider it seriously, will you drop the lawsuit?"

His dark green eyes narrowed, watching me. "What does it mean to you to consider it? Haven't you already?"

I had this half-baked idea I'd been mulling since the ultrasound, so I voiced it. "I haven't spent a big block of time as a girl or a guy for a few years. I thought I'd spend time as each and see how I feel."

"This is a good step."

"Drop the suit."

"Do your consideration first and let me know how it goes," he said. He added, "You understand that surgery I took you in for was warranted."

We'd had versions of this fight before, but each time we had it, I came to it with more information.

"No. I got access to my medical records. There was nothing wrong with how I peed except that I had to sit down to do it."

"Hypospadias is a recognized birth defect."

"By an establishment that has a vested interest in 'normalizing' children assigned male at birth. Do you know how often that surgery goes wrong? Some kids, some babies, are given twenty surgeries or more trying to give them a 'real man's' standing up to pee dick. And at the end of it most of them still have to sit to pee because the scar tissues, the surgery, the infections have messed them up for life."

Not to mention the people assigned female at birth who got surgeries to make their labia more "pretty," or who had clitoral reduction surgeries. Those surgeries had no real medical reason either and could leave people with damaged nerves, painful scar tissue, and without the ability to have an orgasm.

People acted like genital mutilation was a thing that happened in third-world countries, but our country was one of the worst. And Dad had completely bought in to the system that cut people up for nothing.

I stood, put my folded napkin on the table.

"Mom's not the parent who fucked things up. Think about that the next time you have your attorney send some asshole letter to our house."

CHAPTER ELEVEN

Tucker

Days later, I still hadn't heard from Nico. I jumped every time my phone buzzed, but it was always Bailey or Cal or Ella. I'd texted and called, left messages, but I didn't want to be pushy. Was yo so mad at me for leaving the party that yo had blocked my number? Or was it not that serious to Nico?

Maybe I was too messed up for this to work? I didn't want to work on my damage, could I blame Nico if yo didn't want to either?

I read through the messages Nico had sent me over the last few months: pics, jokes, thoughtful stories. I contemplated reading the long emails we'd exchanged in winter when I was spinning and raw from everything with Lindy, but I couldn't.

Maybe there was something about me that screwed up relationships.

I caught up with Ella over at the Union. Most of us got together for Thursday dinners. Fridays and Saturdays it was too hard to get everyone's schedules synced up. She had her books spread out on the table, but was chatting with Cal. He hadn't bothered with the pretense of books.

"Have you heard from Nico?" I asked.

"Not for days, which is strange." She pulled out her phone, typed a few words, sent them.

After a minute, she read the reply and said, "Yeah, Nico's being weird. We'll chat later and I'll find out what's up. Unless you know?"

"Why would I know?"

"Because both of you have been seriously odd since the night of Cal's party." She tucked a strand of hair behind her ear and stared at me until I backed away a step.

"Uh. I should eat," I said.

I went to get garlic cheese bread. Waited around the end of the food counter for a few minutes until my plate was ready. Cal and Ella were still sitting at the table waiting for me to come back and tell some kind of story. If I couldn't wait them out, I might as well get it over with. And I did want Ella's insider information about Nico's long silence.

I sat across from Ella. "Me and Nico kissed at the party, sort of made out," I admitted.

"No you didn't," Ella said.

"What?"

"You didn't *just* kiss," she insisted. "Nico didn't call me to tell me that you'd kissed. It's been almost two weeks and Nico hasn't said a thing about it. That means yo didn't want to talk about you two kissing. And that means you hurt Nico."

"Dang," Cal said. "That was a deductive chain of some awesomeness."

"We dated," Ella explained. "I know what Nico's like when yos feelings are hurt."

I contemplated the browned spots on top of the cheese, the little craters where a burnt bit had broken open, the lake of oil that pooled in the middle. It made sense: I'd run out without saying anything, hadn't even texted to tell Nico what was going on. I'd be mad at me too.

"I don't want to talk about it," I said. "But I'm sorry. If you talk to Nico…I tried to call…I'm sorry."

"Tucker, you couldn't have done anything that bad," Ella said.

I shrugged and looked at Cal.

"Fine." He and threw up his hands. "You two have your girl talk, I'll be back in a few."

When he was far enough away, I said, "I kind of panicked," more to the cheese bread than to Ella.

"That's normal," she told me.

She brushed my arm with her fingers and I moved it an inch toward her. She rested her hand on my wrist.

"For what you went through, that's totally normal," she repeated.

"But what if it's not that? What if it's Nico? What if it doesn't work, me being lesbian and yo being nonbinary?"

"Well, that would suck in a profound way."

"I have to figure it out without messing up things with Nico any worse," I told her.

"Are you going to the counseling center?"

I'd thought about it, but every time I did, I saw the disbelieving face of the woman who'd done the exam on me. That had been the final layer of wrong on top of a huge pile of wrong. What if I showed up to talk to someone and they gave me that same look?

"No," I said. "Not here. I need more time."

"Tucker, you need to do something. You're not you."

"Yeah, I know," I said. It was weird to hear Ella say it.

I mean, sure, I'd never felt panicky making out with anyone before. I used to feel on top of the world. I wasn't me and I didn't know what to do with this person I'd become.

I didn't like her very much. I didn't want to hang out with her.

I wanted to roll back to who I'd been, but I couldn't figure out how.

I watched my garlic cheese bread get rubbery.

"Summer said you were flirting with Quin."

Ella's words shocked me and without thinking I spat out, "Since when do you gossip with Summer?" I jerked my arm away from her.

"Tucker, she's hurting. Everyone's hurting after last semester. If we don't talk to each other…And for Nico's sake, if you're not that into Nico…Are you into Quin?"

"I just met her."

"I think Summer's interested in her and…Summer's a mess. She was a drunken jerk to Nico at Cal's party and came to talk to me about—"

"What?!"

"She spilled her drink on Nico and sort of groped Nico," Ella said, wincing at the idea. "I think she was trying to be flirty, but she crossed a line for sure. She feels bad about it."

"She was trying to flirt with Nico at that party after I left? I have a fucking panic attack and she decides to go flirt with Nico? Forget this shit. Tell Nico I'm sorry."

I grabbed my bag and the half-eaten garlic bread. I hadn't considered Nico not calling because yo liked someone else. But Summer, no way. Still, why hadn't Nico called me back? Or even texted?

I was on my own like always. Maybe I should just get through this semester and spend the summer forgetting everything. I tossed the garlic bread into the trash on the way out of the Union and ignored Ella calling after me.

CHAPTER TWELVE

Nico

I'd gone in for the biopsy on Monday and ended up in bed for a day from gut cramps. Mid-week, when I was mobile again, I headed for the people who understood me—my friends at the Noodle. It was this cool performance space full of geeks and cosplayers and all flavors of queer and trans. There was a big sign out front that read: "Jim's Glorious Noodle."

There was no Jim. The sign was a typo. It was supposed to read "Jin's Glorious Noodle," which was the original name of the Chinese restaurant that lived in this space for about twenty years. It moved downtown, went fusion, and changed its name.

Five years ago when the performers bought the place and were trying to think of what to name their theater, someone found the discarded typo version of the sign in the basement. From then on it was Jim's Glorious Noodle. The sign even had a squiggle on it to artfully represent noodles; someone drew a head around it to create a giant cranium full of noodle.

The Noodle was in a three-story house long ago zoned into the business part of town. The whole place still smelled like fried egg rolls. I'm not really an egg roll person, but after a few years hanging out there, I found the smell comforting.

On the first floor there was a big performance space with a stage, bathrooms and a side room where you could buy drinks and snacks. The second floor had classrooms for dance and acting, and costume rooms. The basement was a hangout space and had more costumes in process. And the top floor was where Sharani lived—she managed the troupe of performers and kept the space going. She was how I'd found out about this place and I'd never be able to repay her for that.

Sharani was this amazing Romani woman who rode motorcycles way too fast and could kick ass a gazillion different ways. She was the only person like me that I saw on a regular basis. That wasn't a completely fair thing to say. I knew a lot of people like me in the performance sense. Most theater people were like me. What I meant was that she also had intersex traits. She had a totally different intersex situation than I did, but we had a lot in common when it came to people and medical experiences.

Usually I went down via the side door to the basement to check on the costume work. That's where the cosplay projects were. The second floor was for official theater costumes. Sharani figured out she could rent a corner of the basement cheaply to the local geeks and have tons of kids available to fill in as extras and help with work around the place.

This time I went in the front door because I wanted to see her. I poked my head into the snack bar and got a wave from Kaj, the only full-time employee at the Noodle. Kaj ran the bar, organized shows, and kept everyone sane.

"Hot, Captain Jack," Kaj said.

I grinned. "Love that hat. Where's Sharani?"

Kaj pointed in the direction of the theater space. "Watching rehearsal."

I slipped through the entrance that opened at the back of the audience, and spotted her right away. This wasn't hard because she always sat in the back and she was six-foot-two.

Seriously, if all the Romani women looked like her, no one would ever have dared mess with them. She had raven-black, coarse hair to below her shoulders and one of those strong, beautiful noses that people called hawk-like but I think are super regal, probably because my nose is so flat. Her face had a stark, structural beauty like Cher, but her eyes weren't sleepy and she was way bustier.

I could hardly fathom the abuse she went through as a kid. Of the different kinds of intersex traits—some happened naturally and some folks ended up that way because of modern medicine. Sharani's mother was given drugs to keep her from miscarrying and it turned out those drugs also masculinized girl fetuses. So she had XX genes and she felt female in her mind, but in the womb the drugs made her body more male-appearing than it would've been.

And to add to the bullshit, it turned out the drugs her mother took didn't prevent miscarriages anyway.

At that time in the sixties, doctors thought you could raise a kid any old way. They suggested raising her male, which her father was totally into. You can see how we'd connect, right? Except her father was a lot worse than mine. He beat her for acting like a girl until she hit puberty and grew breasts and got a period.

I thank the universe all the time that she found this performance group and people who loved her as she is so she could stop trying to kill herself and learn how to enjoy life.

I watched the rehearsal with her for a few minutes. When the actors took a break to talk about the script, she turned to me.

"Doctor Who?" she asked because I was wearing a button-down shirt and military jacket. She wasn't into a lot of the sci-fi shows but had a rough sense of the costumes I liked.

"Captain Jack Harkness—he started in *Doctor Who* but he's mostly in *Torchwood*."

"How's your day going, Captain Jack?"

"For shit," I said with a laugh. "The whole week. How's yours?"

"I like this new production. What's going on?"

I sighed and stared up at the dark ceiling, not knowing where to start. Worst news first? If so, which news was worse?

I went chronologically and said, "My dad's keeping the stupid lawsuit going. *And* he's in town for the summer."

"I'm sorry. Are you going to see him?"

"I already did. Asked him to drop the suit. He's thinking about it. We fought about all the usual stuff. If he doesn't drop it, maybe I can countersue for mental anguish."

Nodding, she said quietly, with a hint of humor, "Do you want me to teach you some Krav Maga?"

"Is that the martial art that's like seventy-three different strikes to the balls?"

She chuckled.

The actors got their next scene going. We watched until one flubbed their lines and everyone cracked up.

"I have to get surgery," I told Sharani. "There's a mass on my ovotestis."

I was surprised by the weight of relief at saying that out loud to someone outside my family who got it. She wasn't all, "Your what?"

"How bad is it?" she asked.

I told her everything, turned half toward her in the theater seating. I reassured her that it probably wasn't any kind of malignant cancer, feeling so much better getting to say that with more confidence than I felt.

"You want me to come to the surgery?" she asked.

She knew about my medical trauma. For sure nobody would dare mess with my body with a six-foot-plus black belt around.

"Maybe, yeah. But it's not just having surgery and the cancer thing. It's the hormones and everything. I feel like everyone's going to make me pick now. They've been waiting for years for me to grow up and settle down, pick a gender, and maybe this is it. I mean, I'm even starting to think I should."

"Do you want to?"

"How would I know that with all the noise of everyone's expectations? Dad wants me to be his son. Kenan can't stand to be around me if I'm not one or the other. I know he wants me to be his brother again. I'm sure Tucker wants me to be a girl. I think Ella likes it better when I'm a boy; at least she did when we were dating. Yai thinks of me as a kathoey—Thailand's third gender. Matt tries to be good, but he treats me like a guy. Mom and the girls and you are the only people who don't keep trying to gender me one way or the other. So how would I know?"

"Try some and feel if they fit?"

"Yeah I've been thinking about doing that. I stopped being a girl about four years ago."

"Eighteen is very different from fourteen. Nico, you get whatever you want, okay? Surgery's not bad. Having a gender's not bad. It's having someone else decide it for you, that's what screws you up. Choose anything you want, but make sure it's you choosing."

She made it sound doable.

I kissed her cheek and she swatted at me. Slipping out of the theater, I crossed the hall to the snack area. I got a sandwich and a ginger tea and settled down to discuss the upcoming cabaret lineup with Kaj, who was emceeing.

While she was getting coffee for some of the actors, I pulled out my phone and stared at it. Nothing from Tucker. I wanted to talk to her about this but she'd been the one to walk away, to leave without saying anything.

I still felt like I was forgetting something about Tucker, something important, but what? Had I said I'd call her? No. I hadn't had a chance to say anything when she bolted.

How cheap would it be to use my medical situation as an excuse to intrude on her? I had to give her more time. And if this was her way of telling me no…I'd have to live with it.

CHAPTER THIRTEEN

Tucker

Saturday night, the Black Student Union party, Quin—I could not figure out what to wear or even if I should go. I was afraid of running into Summer there. What was she even up to? She still watched Tesh like they were the only person in the world, but she'd flirted with both Nico and Quin. And she remained pissed at me for seeing her kiss Tesh, seeing her cry. Plus that wild idea that I was taking her place in the Women and Gender Studies department. Like there was only room for one of us.

I wanted to walk away from it all, or run. But everyone else from our student group was going to this party and I did want to support the BSU. I threw on jeans and a T-shirt with a heavier long-sleeved over it. I'd show up long enough to be supportive, then bail.

I was going to walk over by myself. Maybe flirt with Quin after all. Every time I thought about Summer touching Nico, my chest burned. Maybe if I fought back more, she'd back off.

Ella knocked on our adjoining bathroom door and popped through when I said, "Yeah?"

She was in a fitted blue and pink flannel that made her look like a pixie lumberjack. Impossible not to smile at her.

"Walk over together?" she asked.

"Sure," I said. It wasn't her fault everyone was so screwed up. "You hear from Nico?"

"Nico hasn't called you?"

"Nope."

She shook her head. "That makes no sense. Yos dad is in town, which is really freaking yo out, but I know Nico's been thinking about you. And there's nothing going on with Summer, other than Nico being royally pissed at her. Yo thinks the flirting, groping thing was just Summer trying to fix a gender for Nico."

A wash of relief that Nico wasn't interested in Summer. But that got swamped under a wave of anger at Summer.

I snatched my jacket off the back of my chair and kicked the chair so it rolled into the desk with a bang. "Let's go."

Ella followed me into the hall. "I don't get it," she said. "Of everyone, you and Nico should be talking the most. Don't you see?"

"I called and texted and nothing. I don't know what else to do," I told her.

"I'll talk to Nico."

I slowed my strides as we hit the quad. Walking fast I'd outpace Ella easily. The anger settled into a slow burn and I blew out my breath. None of it made sense. Except Summer being an ass. I'd come to expect that.

"Don't," I said. "Not yet. I need more time."

"What about getting support, like therapy or an online group, anything?" Ella asked.

"I don't want help. I want it never to have happened." My voice broke. I turned away from her, head down, standing on the night-dark grass of the quad.

Ella put her hand on my back. First her fingertips and when I didn't pull away, her whole palm. I leaned into the pressure and yanked the fraying parts of myself back together.

"Can we just go dance?" I asked.

"Yep, let's get Shen."

We walked in silence to the Math & Science dorm. On my side, it was an angry, confused silence, but not a weird silence. Ella did quiet in a grounding way that I needed. Shen was also a pretty quiet guy, except when it came to gaming. He met us at the front door full of excitement about some challenge he and his cousin had finally surmounted.

Ella knew enough about it to ask questions. I let the patter of their voices wash over me, settling me back into my skin.

The party was in the lower level of the arts building. We went through the two-story lobby with its tall glass windows, student art lining the walls, flying sculptures hung from the ceiling. Down a broad flight of stairs was a huge open room, filled with people and vibrating with music.

With my bleached Mohawk and Ella's porcelain skin, we looked like blinding bright lighthouses in a sea of attractive brown faces. I considered hiding under a table. But I made myself dance with Ella and Shen because they were sweet enough to include me. We did the rhythmic shuffling from one foot to the other that passed for dancing in crowded spaces until I got thirsty.

When the next song started, I turned away from them and ambled around the edge of the room. I found a table with a guy pouring cups of a bright orange punch. Cup in hand, I leaned against the wall to drink it.

The punch was sweeter than I thought possible and my teeth ached as I sipped. Quin leaned against the wall next to me, a cup of punch in her hand. Her hair was loose, falling past her chin, and her mouth turned up, already amused.

Maybe I did like her.

"You dance?" she asked.

"I suck at dancing," I said. "But I can shuffle to the beat if needed."

She chuckled. "Not my thing either. You play anything?"

"Like guitar?"

Her laugh was a rolling "hehehe" sound that I wanted to hear more often. She asked, "Basketball? Soccer? Track?"

"No," I said, but that didn't seem like enough of an answer, so I added, "I work in a hardware store."

She narrowed her eyes at me like I was from another planet. Tonight I might be. The music throbbed, too loud and insistent. Her body was close enough to radiate warmth on my arm.

I liked that she didn't know my history. Maybe better to hang out with people distant from all that.

"You want to go for a walk?" I asked.

She threw back the rest of the liquid in her cup and tossed it into a trash can. I did the same, minus the drinking, and followed her out of the cavernous room, up the stairs onto the small quad. The night sky's low clouds looked gray in the lights set around the walking paths.

Quin's legs were longer than mine, which rarely happens, and I had to lengthen my stride to keep up with her.

"How about food?" she asked.

"Sure."

"I hate March volleyball practice," she said as we walked. "It's cold and we're working hard. I'm hungry all the time."

"I get that. I have a harder time running this time of year. Though, I run inside."

"No track?" she asked.

"I'm not into the organized competitive stuff, I run because I like it."

She grinned. "That's cool."

From the edge of campus, she took us down Taylor Ave, away from the school. I usually went north off campus. I wasn't as familiar with this side of town. We'd gone by the sports fields and the stadium. Now there were some businesses, but not the kind students would use: a seamstress, a tax office, a vet. We passed those, our breath showing silvery and then ghostly gray as we went from the well-lit street by the school to darker streets.

We turned another corner and she stopped in front of a diner-style restaurant with wood paneling and plate glass windows. The sign said: Mill's Vittles. Inside about half the tables were full.

I followed Quin in. It was a seat-yourself place and she picked a small booth near the back. I pulled off my coat as I sat down and stuffed my scarf into the sleeve. She shrugged out of her jacket and I admired the size of her shoulders and her chest. Good thing she wasn't one of those skinny-muscle jocks. Lindy had put me off skinny forever.

God, I had to stop thinking about Lindy.

"This okay?" Quin asked.

"It's great. I didn't know this was here."

She pulled two menus out from the napkin holder and held one out to me. This was a breakfast-all-day place. I could always eat breakfast.

She talked easily about how she was from North Carolina and came here on a volleyball scholarship. She found Ohio cold and gray, but the team was great to hang out with. She didn't miss home as much as she'd expected.

I told her about growing up in a town of four thousand people and she expressed deep sympathy.

She got a monster omelet: four or five eggs with a half-dozen kinds of veggies plus ham and cheese. I got pancakes to remind me what sweet was supposed to taste like and chase away the lingering orange syrup flavor in my mouth. And strong, black decaf so I could pretend to be more awake than I was.

After a minute of us seriously eating, she asked, "Tesh said you had a bad breakup?"

"Yeah, basically."

"Dumped?"

I shrugged and pushed a piece of pancake through a line of syrup. "It got…too bad to keep going. You?"

"She left me for one of the basketball players—who used to be a friend of mine."

"Oh, shit."

"It was real messed up. She started seeing the other girl and didn't tell me and two-timed both of us for a few weeks. And that girl on the basketball team didn't even dump her for that. She was like 'sorry, man.'" Quin sighed and stared across the restaurant, jaw tight.

"Is it tough being lesbian on the volleyball team? Or bi, or queer?"

That got a smile. "Queer," she said. "I like girls mostly but not exclusively, so I don't know if I should say bi because that makes most guys think they've got too much of a shot. You?"

"Lesbian," I said. "I think guys are gross. I mean, sexually, not as people."

"Some of them are nice. But girls are better. Volleyball's okay. You don't get shit for it, but you're expected to not talk about it much. Basketball's worse, they're all in the closet with fake boyfriends. I hear Soccer used to be like that too, but now it's one of the more open teams."

"I've seen some of the players at our parties."

"Does Katee go?" she asked. "She's the left forward."

"I don't know what that is," I admitted.

Quin laughed. "She's the stocky, mixed girl with the short red-brown hair and calves like this," she held her hands in a big circle.

"I've seen her around. You like her?"

Quin glanced away, tapped a finger fast on the table top. "She's in my civics class. She's cool."

"Why don't you ask her out?"

She ate a few more bites of her omelet and said, "I don't even know if she's single."

"Ask Tesh, they can find that out for you," I told her and forked more pancake into my mouth.

"Seriously? What's up with Tesh and Summer anyway?"

A quick swallow so I could turn the topic away from her question. "I wish Summer would get her shit together. At the last house party she was flirting with my friend Nico, who was kind of my date. And then apparently she crossed a line, but I don't know the details because yos not talking to me now. Nico is nonbinary, isn't a boy or a girl. If you ask, Nico says yos both."

"Yo?"

"Nico uses gender neutral pronouns, that's the current one."

Quin shrugged. "Huh, cool."

I blinked at her. I thought with all the stuff about sports and not being all the way out, she'd be a lot more thrown by the gender stuff. I guess that showed me for thinking I knew jocks.

"Someone talked to Summer, right?" Quin asked. "I mean, she's all politics, she should get coalition building."

I said, "If we keep talking about Summer, I'm going to say 'intersectionality' a whole bunch. I'm just warning you."

"I love me some intersectionality, as much as the next queer, brown girl, but it's late. And anyway, what about Nico, why aren't you making a move?"

I didn't want to talk about *that* either.

The wild idea that had been nagging my brain for the last hour surfaced. Maybe if I made out with Quin, I could see if I freaked out or not. I could recreate the experience with Nico, but with someone else. Then I'd know if the problem was just me, like I thought it was.

And maybe I could push the last dregs of Lindy out of my brain. Maybe I could forget everything for a while and be the way I used to be.

I held her gaze in a way that I hoped was meaningful and not creepy and said, "I thought maybe I should get my rebound out of the way first."

"Oh," she said. "Ohhh. You want to walk some more?"

I nodded, but my brief flash of confidence drained away as we paid the bill and walked out of the restaurant. This was a stupid idea.

The wind had picked up and was chasing snowflakes in the light of the streetlamps. There wasn't any accumulation, but the sight of snow and bare tree branches made everything feel wintery.

We walked the first few blocks in silence, reaching the edge of campus. Empty fields stretched in front of us, painted with lines, lit by a fraction of the lights they'd use for game nights. I couldn't think of anything to say. I didn't know what I was doing.

As we crossed the practice fields, she talked about the volleyball season last year: who was good and who wasn't, which games they should've won that they lost. She kept on like that across the big quad. When we got to the alley between the buildings that led to the north quad, she stopped walking and turned to me.

"I picked the restaurant," she said. "You pick where we're going next."

"Um, we could go to my room, but that sounds weird when I say it out loud. It's, you know, warm there, and I don't have a roommate. We could talk or whatever."

"Works for me," she said.

We crossed the north quad to my dorm. In the elevator I couldn't look at her. Electricity buzzed under my skin. Did I want this? I couldn't tell.

I unlocked the door and flicked on my desk lamp. We considered each other in the dim blue-white light of a single bulb turned toward the wall.

She dropped her coat over my desk chair and faced me. Her fingers reached for the front of my coat, slowly, her face questioning. I nodded and she pulled my coat off, folded it in half and draped it over hers.

I moved closer to her. I'd forgotten how to kiss. She came the rest of the way toward me, her lips heavy on mine. Her tongue was salty and it cut through the lingering maple syrup flavor in my mouth. My hands closed around her shirt behind her shoulders. She circled my back with her arms, setting us both off balance. We moved a step and her shoulders and my hands pushed against the wall, steadying us.

Her kisses were big and open, not controlled and tight like Lindy's. Thank God not like Lindy. And not like Nico's agile, playful kisses. I wanted Nico so badly my knees wavered and Quin had to brace against the wall and hold me up.

I pulled away, thought about stopping. But there'd been a few moments when we kissed where I hadn't thought about anything but Quin's mouth and her body, so I kissed her again.

We made out standing up for a long time and then sat on the bed and kissed more. Shoes got kicked off. Hands up under shirts and then shirts off, bras off. She sprawled back on the bed looking so amazing I had to follow.

Quin fumbled with my belt and got it open, worked the button loose and pushed my zipper down while I was on top of her playing with her breasts. When I stood up to kick my jeans all the way off, she undid her pants and shimmied out of them.

I knew how to do this. I had this. I could be the old Tucker again, the Tucker I liked being. I could rebound from everything.

I returned to the bed, crawled on top of her and kissed her. She rolled us to the side. One hand made its way to the top of my boxers, fingers sliding under the elastic.

Fear shot down my spine. All at once I felt the chill of the wall against my back and the vulnerability of my body nearly bare.

I jerked away and hit the back of my head on the wall.

"Ow, shit."

"Ticklish?" she asked.

I rubbed the back of my head. "Yeah," I lied.

Her body was too close to me, the heat of her skin oppressive on mine. I sat up and couldn't stop myself from crawling down to the end of the bed. I climbed out to stand at the foot, shivering cold in my boxers.

Dizzy, coming loose from myself. She rolled onto her back, rising on her elbows, watching me. Her chest rose and fell fast, eyes narrowed: confusion, insecurity or anger?

I put a hand over my mouth and coughed. Said the word, "Water," roughly and, "Back in a sec." I dove into the bathroom between Ella's room and mine like a soldier going for cover.

I splashed cold water against the closed lids of my burning eyes. I put my mouth under the faucet and ran the water between my lips, swallowing and letting water rush through my mouth and out again. Spitting.

My skin was clammy from sweat. I felt covered in a layer of grime and filth that I couldn't see. I soaped a washcloth and washed quickly, went over my skin with another washcloth, went over it again with the towel. I wanted to scrub hard, take off the top layer of cells and the layer under that. I couldn't scrub hard enough to get the filth off me.

I twisted the towel in my fists until my knuckles were almost as white as the worn cloth. There was a hot girl in my bed in her panties and I'd mostly proven to myself that what happened with me and Nico had nothing to do with gender and everything to do with how messed up I was.

If I went back to bed with Quin, would I freak out again? How would that make her feel? And if I backed away now, what did it mean about me? Could I never have sex again?

"Fucking get it together," I mouthed to my reflection. The wide eyes hardened as I watched. We glared at each other.

Tonight should be a banner night.

It was going to be a fucking banner night. Screw Lindy. She was nothing. I'd show her how fucking nothing she was.

I threw the towel into the corner and pushed through the bathroom door to see Quin putting on her pants.

"Hey, don't," I said.

She reached for her shirt.

"I mean, you don't have to," I told her.

"Could've fooled me."

"It's not you—" I started and realized how bad that sounded. "It's been a while and, you know, it got kind of fast there and I… shit, I got scared, okay?"

Not saying why or about what. Not thinking about it. I kept my eyes on Quin's face, on her body, filling my brain with her, holding onto her like a lifeline.

The edge of her mouth turned up in a half smile. "You don't seem like a girl who gets scared."

"Yeah, usually I'm not."

I didn't know what else to say and I needed to be closer to her now. So close that she was all I saw. I kissed her. Her lips started out tense and careful. I kept kissing until she relaxed.

I pushed her back onto the bed, determined, and she let me take the lead in getting her pants off again. Her hands roamed over my back and shoulders, but when she tried to touch lower, I pulled off her panties and moved down her body.

I kissed my way down her belly. She laughed.

"Tickles," she said.

I turned my face up, raised my eyebrows at her and kissed lower. "How about here?"

"Oh, no. I mean, doesn't tickle, but yes, yes."

She said yes a lot more after that and I worried that Ella could hear us through the walls, but it wasn't enough to stop me. I needed to stay in this world filled with Quin's body. I needed to not think.

In the morning I woke curled along Quin's back and snuck out of bed to use the bathroom. When I stepped into my room, she was awake, lying on her back with her arms folded behind her head. I crawled over her and snuggled in beside her.

"You want anything?" she asked, gesturing in a general way down my body.

I shook my head. "I'm okay."

"You sure?"

I was deeply not sure. Pretty convinced I was so far from okay I couldn't even see the signposts pointing back toward okay, but that wasn't what she'd been asking.

"Yeah, I had fun, I'm good."

"The offer stands."

"Thanks," I said.

She kissed me but when it started to heat up, she pulled away. "I've got to head out. Give me your cell if you want my number."

The fact that I'd had sex with a girl whose number wasn't even in my phone made me feel worse than almost anything else about the night. I fished in my coat pockets for my cell while she put her clothes on. No call or text from Nico. That sucked. And the feeling that I'd been stupid was back.

Quin typed herself into my contacts.

"I'll text you, so you've got mine," I said.

I didn't know if I was supposed to kiss her goodbye or what, but she hugged me and gave me a quick kiss before breezing out the door. I sat down on the side of my bed, still in my boxers, feeling the chill of the room, and studied the phone in my hands.

Now I knew my panic had nothing to do with Nico. If nothing else, I owed it to Nico to tell yo that.

I texted Nico: *Call me?*

And then: *I'm sorry, I can explain, please call me.*

CHAPTER FOURTEEN

Nico

The night before the appointment to go over the biopsy results with Dr. Peace, I had a hard time getting to sleep. When I finally did, I had terrible nightmares. People in white coats dragged me down a long institutional hallway as I screamed and fought. When they got me into the surgical suite, they were going to carve up my dick like a garnish flower made from a carrot. Make it pretty and useless and numb.

I woke myself up yelling, curled in a ball with my hands between my legs. The door to my room flew open and Hazey threw herself into my bed. She wrapped her skinny arms around me. I hugged her close.

Mom came in too. She got into the other side of my bed and put an arm around both of us.

"I'll be with you tomorrow," she said. "I'll be with you for all of it."

I leaned into her. "I know. Thanks. Would you tell me a story?"

"Fable or science?" she asked.

"You have a good science story?"

"I think it's good, but you can tell me." She leaned around me and touched the tip of Hazey's nose. "Did you know that our galaxy is still making stars?"

"Cool," Hazey said.

"And the places that make stars are inside of nebulas. They're called stellar nurseries. Some people have been studying these stellar nurseries in the Snake Nebula. They're looking at cosmic seeds: glowing areas in the nebula where stars are created."

Hazey made a drowsy "mmhm" sound. Curled into my pillow, tucked under my arm, she was half-asleep. I grinned at Mom.

Mom said, "We used to think that high-mass stars formed from extremely massive cores. You'd have a very big core and it would collect the star material around itself." She held up one fist and circled it with a finger. "But now we're learning that stars don't form alone. Stars are born in groups. One of the study's authors called them villages or families."

"Big stars are made in families?" Hazey asked blearily. "Like us."

"Yes, like us. Eventually the Snake Nebula will have all these clusters of stars that formed in these families. The stars will all grow up together."

"That's good," Hazey said.

I kissed the top of Hazey's head. "Go to bed," I told her. "I'm okay."

She grumbled, a sound I'm sure she learned from Yai, and went back to her room. I bunched up my pillow and put my head on it. Mom brushed her fingertips across my temple and stayed until I fell asleep.

* * *

Ella texted every day, a bunch. She was onto me. I told her I was doing family stuff and I'd talk to her after the weekend. I said enough about Dad being in town and fighting with him at the steak place to get her to give me some space. I figured I'd call her when the biopsy results came back and I could tell her it wasn't serious.

But the results came back and it was serious. Not malignant, not quite cancer, but pre-cancerous. Dr. Peace wanted both the ovotestis and the ovary out. As soon as I was back home, alone in my room, I called Ella.

When she answered, I couldn't talk.

"Nico, what's wrong? Are you hurt?"

"I'm okay," I managed around the lump in my throat. I hopped up from my desk chair and circled the middle of the room to loosen my words.

"What's going on?" Ella asked. "Tucker says she's called you a bunch and texted you and you're ignoring her. What happened?"

I pulled my phone away from my ear and stared at it.

I hadn't gotten any calls or texts from Tucker.

Then I remembered and my gut dropped with horror: after I'd blocked Summer, I had also blocked Tucker. That's what I'd forgotten.

I'd meant to unblock her right away, a day or two at most, give me a little space not to be angry, not to react. But with my dad in town, the lawsuit and then the evil peanut...

That had been weeks ago. She'd been blocked all this time. She'd been calling and texting while I thought she was ignoring me.

"Are you mad at her?" Ella asked while I worked to uncurdle my brain.

Matt's favorite non-swear words, like "numbskull" and "nincompoop," circled in my head. Tucker must think—I had no idea what she thought.

That I was an ass?

That I wasn't into her? Oh hell, what if she thought I didn't want her? What if she thought I was punishing her for panicking? That would be beyond awful.

I'd avoided calling her because I thought she wasn't calling me. Tried to give her space.

"Why would I be mad at Tucker?" I asked as my fingers flew through the steps of unblocking her number.

"I don't know, neither of you are telling me anything. What *IS* going on with you?"

"Ella," I drew out her name to buy myself another few seconds. "Babydoll."

Steel came into her words. "Tell me."

I flopped back onto my bed, put a hand behind my head, tried to sound light. "I've got to get some surgery."

"What?" Her voice dropped into the quiet-mad-worried range.

"The radiologist found a…something like an evil peanut."

"What!"

"There's a mass in my ovotestis, they have to take it out," I said, staring at the blankness of the ceiling and trying not to cry.

"Nico!"

"And the ovary too," I said. "They have to take it all."

Her voice was high, tight with worry, "No! Are you okay? How are you doing?"

"So-so."

"Will that change your hormones?"

"I'll have to go with shots and pills," I said.

"The pills aren't bad."

She would say that. It was how she got her hormones. But I was glad to hear it.

I told her, "I have to decide what hormones I want and, um, while they're in there they could change some other stuff. Make my junk more generically picture perfect. And my dad's pushing for that. He's still on his 'be a man' thing."

"Oh, Nico."

"Dr. Peace says female would be easier, but I don't know. You knew me as a girl for a bit, what do you think?"

"I can't," she said. "You have to decide that. I can come down this weekend and we could talk about it."

I wanted that. Wanted to see her and hang out and talk it all through. But it would be tough on her, the parts about me freezing eggs so I could have kids someday when she never had that option.

Plus she'd always been so sure about herself, she didn't seem like the right person for a conversation about picking a gender. She'd say things like 'you just know' and other unhelpfulness.

I asked, "Aren't you and Shen going camping for spring break?"

"I'll cancel it."

"Don't. Come down for the surgery but go have your trip with him. He's going to be gone all summer, right? Back to China to hang with his family? You should get your romance on. Besides I cannot wait to hear the Princess Ella Goes Camping stories. Shen does not know what he's in for."

"Nico..."

"There's time."

"Can I tell Tucker?" she asked. "I mean that you've got a surgical thing going on, not the part about ovotestis."

I grinned thinking about Ella talking to Tucker about my ovotestis.

"Is that like the initiation for advanced trans and intersex conversations—the graduate level course? You have to have a detailed and polite conversation with friend B about friend A's junk?"

She was laughing, but softly with this edge of worry in her voice. "You talk about your own junk, but I know she'd want to know that something's up with you. She's been asking about you. A lot."

My heart thumped its approval of that. Asking was good. Not giving up on me because I was the dolt who'd blocked her and forgotten, very good.

"Yeah, go ahead."

After a pause she said, "Nico, I love you."

"Love you too, baby."

We hung up and I immediately listened to all the messages Tucker had left and read all the texts. The first were close together. Then they trailed off like she was trying to give me space and not bug me.

Yeah, I'd been pissed off, but way more about Summer than about Tucker. With Tucker it had been that old echo of shame, like she ran away from me because of me. Summer's words "you're afraid of what I'll find" had hit so deep in me, so close to my fears about Tucker's reaction, that it all got mashed up together. I'd wanted to block out the fear, not Tucker herself.

I decided to wait a few minutes so Ella could go over and talk to Tucker first, and then I'd call her.

CHAPTER FIFTEEN

Tucker

Ella pounded on my door. She never pounded but maybe this was how we were now. I threw it open, half mad in case she was going to lecture me about Quin. After the sex of last weekend, I'd been out to dinner with Quin twice more but hadn't invited her back to my room. Did she think we were dating or just rebounding? I was afraid to ask.

I glared at Ella through the open doorway. I didn't need her giving me grief about Quin on top of the dump truck of guilt I felt.

"What?" I clipped out the word and stared at her.

Ella was not a girl you could stare down. Her cool green eyes were thunderstorm dark. She cocked her head and waited. I took a step back, letting her into my room, because I got that I was being a jerk.

"Nico hasn't called you because yo had a medical situation and is scheduled to have surgery in a few months," she said.

"Oh, hell. What for?"

"There's a mass; it's complicated. Nico says it's not a big deal, but I know yo's scared."

"No shit."

I paced across the room and back a few times. I was the world's biggest jerk. I'd hooked up with Quin, all the while thinking Nico was blowing me off. Lately, I'd been pissed at Nico for not calling. But this turned it all around.

"Should I call?" I asked. "I should call, right? I mean, we're friends and Nico was…when I needed…I should call."

"Yes," Ella said and almost managed not rolling her eyes at me. "Nico said I could tell you, so yo expects you'll call."

"What do I say?"

"Maybe listen?" Ella tipped her head to the left, gazing up at me like she was trying to puzzle out how big of a dope I was. She added, "I offered to drive down for spring break but Nico told me to go ahead with the camping trip. I think yo's going to need someone to talk to."

"I don't get it. Is it like cancer or a tumor? What does it mean to find a mass? How does that even happen?"

Ella's eyes focused on me and then clouded over. She shook her head. "It's not for me to say."

I'd paced to the far side of the room and spun fast to face her. "What the hell?"

She fired the words at me, crisp and hard-edged, "It is not. For me. To say." She had to be as scared as I was, maybe more. She'd known Nico so much longer.

"All right, all right I'll call," I said.

"Finally," Ella huffed and went back into her room.

I got out my phone but the first call I made wasn't to Nico. It was to my sister Bailey.

"Bay, what are you doing?"

"Laundry," she said with a snort. "You need another ride?"

"I want to borrow your car."

A barking laugh, loud and harsh, followed by, "Forget it."

"Twenty bucks in cash and I bring it back full tomorrow."

"Jess, what are you doing?" she asked.

"A friend of mine got some seriously scary medical news. I want to drive down to Columbus and, you know, be a good surprise."

"Well shit, yank on my heartstrings. Give me the twenty up front."

"Of course," I told her. "Pick me up in fifteen?"

"Deal."

I'd borrowed Bailey's car a few times my senior year of high school but hadn't had a reason to while at college. Our hometown was so small you could walk across it in less than twenty minutes, outskirts included. She lived maybe ten minutes walk from the salon. She could live without a car for a day.

I was throwing things into my bag, trying to think of what to say to Nico, when yo called.

"Hey," yo said. "I'm sorry about not calling you sooner. I would've. I wanted to."

I pressed the phone hard to my ear, wishing I was so much closer to Nico. "Ella told me. Medical stuff. It's okay about not calling. I'm sorry about…a lot of stuff."

"You don't have that much to be sorry for. I'm sorry too." Nico sounded like yo was going to say more, but the words trailed into silence.

Oh yeah I do, I thought. *Hooking up with someone else while you're scared and dealing with surgery shit.*

"Feels like it," I said. "Do you want to talk about what's going on with you?"

"We're about to sit down to dinner. But I wanted to just call and hear your voice. Can I call you in a bit?"

"Give me about two hours?" I asked. "I have to do a thing. But I want to talk."

"Sure. Call me when you're done."

"Perfect."

I had a few minutes before heading down to meet Bailey. I searched for coffee houses in Columbus. I knew where Ella's house was. I figured Nico had to live within a few neighborhoods of her since they went to the same high school. And Nico's mom was a professor at OSU, like Ella's, so I went halfway between Ella's house and the campus. When I saw the place named Chocolate Cafe it was no contest.

My hometown was twenty minutes southwest of Freytag, nearly on the way to Columbus. When I dropped Bailey back at her place, the GPS on my phone said it was an hour and forty minutes to the cafe. I made it in an hour thirty-five because I was determined but not stupid.

I called Nico from the parking lot.

"Hey, you get your stuff done?" Nico asked.

"Sure did," I said. "You want to come meet me for coffee and maybe chocolate fondue?"

Nico chuckled. "It's pretty late to drive up."

"How far do you live from Chocolate Cafe on Northwest Boulevard?"

"Tucker, where are you?"

"I'm in the parking lot."

"Ten minutes," Nico said and hung up.

I grinned at the phone. Okay, Nico definitely wasn't mad at me.

I didn't like waiting alone in strange restaurants, so I sat in the car until I saw Nico pull up in the badass black Charger. Yo moved toward the front door, but I called across the parking lot.

Nico ran at me. I caught yo in a hug and felt yos muscles tighten, holding me close. Shivering. No, shaking. Nico's whole body was trembling against me, crying. I held tighter and leaned back against the car, bracing to stand like that forever if I had to.

Yo was crying hard. I knew what that felt like, though I didn't know Nico's mix of pain, fear and desperation. I pressed my cheek to the side of Nico's head and tried to remember what yo used to say to me in the winter when I was torn apart about Lindy.

"I got you," I said.

Nico sobbed harder for a minute and then started to settle and catch yos breath. Yo pulled back enough to dig a tissue out of a coat pocket and blow yos nose.

"You want to sit in the car for a minute?" I asked. I wouldn't want to go into a restaurant after crying like that.

Nico nodded and peered around me at the car. "That made it down from Freytag?"

"Hey, it's my sister's. She's not big on bodywork, but it runs fine."

"Come sit in mine," Nico said.

Nico's car was a hundred times nicer and it didn't smell like hairspray. It smelled like leather and men's cologne. I coughed.

"It's my stepdad's," Nico said. "I drove him to physical therapy. I keep telling him he's overdoing it."

In the glow from the front windows of the cafe and the parking lot lights, Nico's face looked more gray than brown. Nico wasn't wearing any makeup or jewelry. And yo still looked male and female: strong lines, soft edges, eyes like a geode broken open, a sparkling array of crystal and shadow.

Nico got a box of tissues from the back, blew yos nose again and said, "Sorry."

"For what? I've cried on you plenty."

"Yeah." Nico smiled. "Thanks."

"Ella said it's complicated. Do you want to talk?"

"Kind of. But I was promised fondue. Do I look like I've been crying?"

"More like you smoked a pound of weed," I said.

"That works. Let's go in."

I walked ahead of Nico and got us a table, watched Nico take off yos long, blue, military style wool coat and settle across from me.

"Nice coat."

Nico smiled. "It's my Captain Jack Harkness coat."

"Who?"

"He's a sci-fi character. I cosplay him at conventions sometimes."

I raised my eyebrows.

"You wouldn't believe how much flirting I get in costume," yo said with a wicked glint in yos eyes.

"Seriously?"

"Girls love the captains. Any of them. Some guys too. It's probably my most effective, since I'm not into slave Leia. Kidding about that last. I mean that it would ever be a consideration."

We paused to read the menus and order our chocolate fondue. When the server was gone, I asked, "So you dress in costumes and flirt with people?"

"Basically. You should come with me sometime. I'll bet I could scare up a *Battlestar Galactica* flight suit if you want to be Starbuck. You'd look hot. I mean, not that you don't now."

Nico glanced down and peeked up out of the corner of yos eyes, the gesture perfect flirty girl. I laughed, but the comment and the gesture reminded me of kissing Nico and that reminded me of the party at Cal's.

"I'm sorry about the party," I said. "Leaving like that. It wasn't anything to do with you."

"Are you sure?"

"Yeah. I am."

Nico sat back in the booth and sighed, a grin returning to yos face. "We have a lot of stuff to talk about," yo said.

"You want to start with what's up with you?" I asked.

"I think you got the gist of it in the parking lot."

"You're scared as fuck? And kind of pissed off and freaking out and you don't want to tell the people around you how messed up you feel? You don't want them to worry any more than they do?"

Nico's eyes were bright. "Just that. I figured you'd get it."

"I haven't told my mom or my one sister about what happened. I don't know how to explain it to them. And I don't want to stop being the tough one."

"I don't want to stop being the playful one," Nico said. "And Mom has gone through enough with me already."

"How bad is it?"

Nico shrugged. "It's pre-cancerous which is medium bad. It means they've got to take out more stuff than they would otherwise. I should have let Doc Peace take it out years ago, but it's part of me, you know."

"Um, no, you lost me. What part are we talking about?"

The fondue showed up and Nico waved my question away. We dug in. I'd had cheese fondue once, but never chocolate. I made a serious mess of my side of the pot and table. Nico was a lot more deft, even though yo kept glancing at me.

Finally yo said, "I forgot how hard this talk is."

"Hey," I waved my fondue fork in a little circle. "I'm your friend who's mostly not a douche. You can tell me stuff."

Nico ate another fondued bread piece, chewed it slowly, stared at the top of the table. Then yo said, all in a rush, "It's not just that my gender is nonbinary, I also have intersex traits."

"Hang on while I Google that." I pulled out my phone because I wasn't sure I was remembering correctly what that meant. Plus I had to cover anything stupid my face was doing.

Nico reached across the table and pushed down the phone I was holding up between us.

"I have physical characteristics that we'd culturally describe as both male and female," Nico said. "Naturally. I produce all the hormones in decent amounts. In a binary system, I really am both."

I put a big piece of chocolate-dipped bread in my mouth and mumbled an affirmative so I'd have time to think. I'd figured Nico was some form of trans that didn't go neatly into male or female categories. I'd wondered if Nico took hormones to stay in a nonbinary space physically. But it hadn't occurred to me that Nico's body could produce that situation naturally.

In my whole life I'd probably read one paragraph about intersex people. Yes, it was in our group acronym: LGBTQIA+ in which the "I" stood for "intersex" but it wasn't like anybody knew a real intersex person. Except we did. We had for a while.

Nico dipped another piece of bread in the chocolate but paused, holding it over the fondue pit, dripping.

"Not all people with intersex traits are nonbinary or genderqueer, you get that, right?" Nico asked. "Most identify as female or male. So don't think you know things about people with intersex traits that you don't."

"Like Ella?" I asked.

Nico's eyebrows went up because we both knew Ella was trans, which was a whole different situation.

I explained, "The way that people were more willing to believe that I was a trans woman because I'm closer to the stereotype than she is. People don't get how many trans women there are who aren't out, who are living their lives. You're saying that being intersex, or, I mean, having intersex traits is like that, most people are men or women and you'd never know."

Nodding, Nico said, "Yeah, and sometimes people don't know they've got intersex traits until they try to have kids or they're being raised as a guy and suddenly get a period. And most nonbinary people don't have intersex traits."

"Okay, sure. Like Tesh."

"Well, we don't know about Tesh because we'd have to know all their inner and outer business, and we're not about to ask. But yes, the most important thing is that a person doesn't have to have anything going on with their bodies to be nonbinary, to not fit into the cultural gender molds."

I nodded and swirled a piece of banana in chocolate.

Nico went on talking. "And heck, I may change my gender presentation again, I don't know. I was a boy for a while, and then a girl, and then neither seemed to fit, or rather both did. I don't like having to be one thing all the time."

"I think I get that," I said.

Nico waved yos fork at me. "I wasn't kidding about the cosplay. Come with me sometime."

"Okay."

"What are you doing tomorrow?"

"Taking the car back."

"There's a little con down in Cincinnati, we could drop off the car and go. I like science fiction more than fantasy, but I'm open to both—you like either?" Nico asked.

The topic switch felt abrupt. I wanted to get back to talking about Nico and about what intersex traits meant, but I couldn't think of a smooth way to do that. And maybe Nico needed this change, the space of it.

I said, "I watched *Firefly* and most of *Battlestar Galactica*."

"You're one of us already." Nico beamed at me. "Did you like *Battlestar* okay? There are some flight suits in the basement of the Noodle, we could pull off Starbuck and Athena pretty easily."

"Um, yes? Noodle? What?"

"Can you pull your Mohawk into a ponytail?" Nico asked.

"Yeah."

"Starbuck and Athena it is. Where are you staying?"

"I didn't think that through," I admitted.

"You heard what was up with me, borrowed a car and drove down without a plan? Tucker!" Nico laughed and didn't wait for me to answer. "Want to crash at my place?"

"I didn't mean to invite myself over like that," I said.

"Whatever. I think Hazey has a sleepover, you can sleep in her room so, no pressure."

"Thanks. I mean about the place to crash. Well, and everything."

We talked about shows and costumes and a bunch of the theater productions Nico had been in. As Nico talked I started to see it all come together: acting, costumes, using artifice to project yourself for others, cosplay. And then I did want to get into a flight suit, even though I was going to feel like a huge dork, and walk around some convention so I could see what Nico was like in that setting.

When the fondue place kicked us out, I paused in the parking lot between our cars and asked, "What if I have more questions?"

"About my intersex traits, right? Because it's completely natural to have questions about *Battlestar Galactica*."

"Uh, yeah."

Nico bounced on the balls of yos feet and gazed off into the darkness. "I'm sorry, it makes me antsy talking to you about this, you know. Let's go somewhere."

"I'll follow you," I said, because I would. Anywhere.

CHAPTER SIXTEEN

Nico

Tucker got in her sister's junker and followed me through the dark streets to a small playground. It was in the middle of the winding park system by my house. I'd never seen kids there, but I usually went in the middle of the night.

Tucker leaned against a post of the wooden monkey bar structure. I kicked around in the wood shavings spread across the playground.

"So questions, go," I said.

She'd driven down here at the drop of a hat for me, I could put up with the usual curiosity and feeling like an alien.

"What makes people have intersex traits?" Tucker asked.

"I'll take genes, hormones and science for two hundred," I said. "But if you ask Mom she'll tell you it's all nature doing its diversity thing because that's how nature rolls."

"You have a cool mom."

"Yeah. She took me away from my dad because he forced surgery on me." Having said that, I had to go on. "My dad's all about how men are better, though he knows not to say that outright. He was sure I should be a boy. They raised me like that for a while but Mom wouldn't let anyone do surgery on me until I was old enough to say what I wanted. That's the right thing, the current standard of care. Not all the docs know that, though. Dad had no trouble finding one who'd do a surgery that I didn't need medically but that would make me more 'normalized' as a boy."

"How old were you?"

"Four."

"Jesus…" The word whispered out of Tucker's lips low and sad.

"That's when we moved here. My brother Kenan too, but he went back to live with Dad after a few years."

"So it's you and your mom and…you have sisters too, right?" she asked.

I'd sent her pics of me goofing around with my sisters, but we hadn't talked much about family. "Oh, I should prepare you. There's my step-dad Matt and my sisters Hazey and Deena, and Yai, my grandmom. You'll meet them tomorrow."

"Whoa," she said. "That's a lot."

"They'll like you. They love Ella and you stood up for her. You're already a hero to them."

I went hand over hand along the bars, knees bent up. The strength and pull in my arms felt good. At the end I turned without putting my feet down and swung hand over hand back. Tucker hopped up to sit on a platform, her feet dangling. When I dropped from the bars, I sat next to her.

"Hazey's the one who started calling me Nico instead of Nehal, because when they moved in, she was young enough to have trouble with her Ls. She called me 'Neho' but that had the word 'ho' in it—not cool when I was eleven—so we settled on Nico."

I was babbling from nervous energy, knowing the next part of the story I wanted to tell Tucker, but scared of her reaction.

"I lived as a boy until I was ten. And then I switched to girl until I was almost fifteen. Since then I've just been Nico. But there's an M on my birth certificate, if that's going to freak you out."

"But you're not a guy," she said.

"I'm me."

"I liked kissing you. Before I…I got scared. It wasn't you. You know what it was. I'm sorry I left, but I had to. Um, and there's another thing I should tell you."

I nodded, because how bad could it be?

"I hooked up with someone else last week," she said. "You know, to see if I was okay. And I thought maybe I should rebound."

The idea of Tucker having sex with someone else made me way more mad than I wanted to be in the middle of the night alone with her. Mad and sickeningly jealous, when what I wanted to feel was the soft closeness we'd had a minute before.

After a lot of silence, Tucker said, real quietly, "I wasn't okay. Last week, in bed, I could hardly stay there. I got all shaky inside. But that also made me happy—messed up as that is—because I knew at the house with you, it was all me. And that house. That night, with Lindy, she came up to me on the back porch. That's where she talked to me about going to her place. It started in that house. If I hadn't gone with Lindy, she couldn't have done what she did to me. The house reminds me of her and of how stupid I was."

I should've thought of that. Should've suggested we go somewhere else the night of Cal's party. No wonder she left so fast if the house was triggering her.

"You weren't stupid," I said.

She waved away my comment. "If we kiss again or whatever, I might freak out."

"It's okay to be scared."

I moved my hand toward her and she laced her fingers with mine. What was the right way to talk to her about panic and trauma and what it did to your brain? I knew how to explain it in theory, but not in a way that would feel okay to her.

She said, "Anyway, that's enough about that. What happened after you all moved out here?"

"You can talk about it," I said, squeezing her hand.

"Do I have to?"

"Of course not."

"I don't want to," she said, not looking at me, a slumped shadow in the dark.

"Hey okay, back to me," I told her. "After we moved here, I got into dance and school plays. Yai moved in with us. I got to spend summers in Thailand with her. Most of her family's still there. Over there, people aren't weird about appearance like here. Yai's sisters would say, 'Hi, you got fat' and it wasn't an insult. People in the family had birthmarks and scars and it was never a big thing. Over there things like that make you who you are. It's okay to be different. It was good for me to see that as a kid.

"Plus there were kathoey people all over. Thailand has a third gender. I remember hearing one of my mother's cousins saying to Mom once when she was over for part of the summer: 'You're lucky if Nehal grows up to be a ladyboy. They're the most fun. I wish I had a ladyboy child.'"

"Ladyboy?"

"That's how some people translate kathoey in English. It's not my pick. And it's not the same as trans."

"Why'd you switch from boy to girl?"

"I wanted to try it," I told her.

I didn't mention that I'd started growing breasts at eleven. I liked that we weren't talking about my body. I'd had too many conversations that went, "I have intersex traits,"…"Oh, what kind of junk did you get?" Coming out as a person with intersex traits—not a reason to ask me about my genitals. But Tucker got that. She hadn't asked.

I played with her index finger, rubbing it between my finger and thumb as I talked. She had a callus on the outer edge. I liked the contrast of the soft side of her finger and the hard thickness of the callus.

"The boy pressure started to get scary," I said. "We fought when we were little, the boys in the neighborhood, and we talked about fighting all the time: endlessly rehashing whether our group could take some other group of kids. A new guy would come along and we'd spend days talking about who could kick whose ass. Or which superhero could beat another, which sports team kicked another team's ass, you get the idea. And all the rest of the time was about girls. I liked girls, but I didn't want to spend all that time talking about them. I'd rather talk to them and I figured maybe I'd rather be one.

"Mom put me in a junior high away from my elementary school and I went as a girl. I did slightly better as a girl than as a boy. I'm better at seeing the emotional stuff people are trying to pull than acting tough. I got in with a decent clique of smart girls and had a pretty good time in junior high. But first year of high school sucked. I had to dress girly and do makeup and all that because with my shoulders, and the muscles in my legs from dancing, and the way my cheekbones look in harsh light, if I'm not careful I don't get read as a girl."

"Yeah, you do," Tucker said. "I mean, if you want to, you can totally look like a girl."

"Not a heteronormative clique girl."

"Me either," she said with a snort. "You know I was about this size by the time I was twelve. I got called dyke before I knew what it meant."

"That sucks."

"Yeah, but it got me to look up 'dyke' and that was a pretty sweet discovery in the long run."

"I like your size," I said. "And this." I ran my fingertips along the shaved side of her head under her Mohawk. "And this." I tugged at the collar of the men's shirt she was wearing under her jacket.

"My dykiness?" she asked.

"Yes."

I was grinning at her and she started to grin back. The heaviness that had been on her before lifted away. If we kept sitting here like this, just grinning at each other, I was going to kiss her.

"Can I ask another stupid question?" Tucker asked.

I nodded.

"You said genes and hormones, but, I mean, how do you actually end up with both male and female characteristics? How is that physically possible?"

I'd been watching her lips move, still thinking about kissing. It took me a second to digest the question.

"Tucker, you know everyone's junk is made from the same stuff, right?"

She stared at me blankly, shook her head.

"Everyone's biology starts out from the same place."

"Well yeah, we all start as a glob of cells," she said.

"No, after that part. When you're starting to form organs and everything. The exact same tissue makes up your genitals and reproductive kit, no matter what. There's a bunch of cells that can turn into a penis or a clitoris or some combination, a cletis. And another bunch of cells turns into labia or a scrotum or a mix of the two. It's all the same material for the first couple months you're in the womb. Hormones make some parts go one way or the other or both."

"For real? How does that work? Penises are way bigger than clits," she said and then blushed.

She clearly hadn't had nearly as many conversations about genitals as I had. I said, "Actually clits are really big. They extend way back into the body, they're much bigger than they look."

I got out my phone and found a drawing of the whole thing. I held it out to her. "That's what a clitoris actually looks like."

"For real? It's that whole alien-looking thing? That's awesome. I should have more swagger."

"You should."

She contemplated the image on my phone. I pondered how weird this was, sitting on playground equipment with a girl I wanted to kiss, talking about genitals. At least, for once, we were talking about her genitals instead of mine.

How much of my life was going to be like this? If I got the whole surgery, picked a gender and got the business to match culturally, maybe I'd never have this conversation again. Of course I might be missing out because Tucker was very cute blushing and staring at my phone.

Tucker said, "So it's sort of like clothing."

"What?" I asked. I was almost used to her broadly leaping analogies.

"You know how everyone has a waist and shoulders and some kind of chest, but clothing styles make it so that 'women's' shirts emphasize the chest and waist and 'men's' emphasize the shoulders. So walking around it seems like most men have way bigger shoulders and women have narrow waists. It erases the women who don't have waists, like me, and guys who have narrow shoulders. And then we feel bad about how we're different. The pictures of people's parts are like that—they only show this perfect ideal, not all the different variations."

"Right!" I said. "Like there were debates about how small a guy's dick could be before it constituted a medical emergency. Or how big a girl's clit can be before doctors freak out and think they should cut it off. If you've got a small dick or a big clit or labia, you think there's something wrong with you instead of getting that nature is unbelievably diverse."

She peered down at my phone screen and dragged the image larger. "It's all made out of the same stuff," she said. "People stuff. It's all the same parts in different places."

I put my fingers on her cheek, the barest suggestion of pressure, asking that she turn toward me. She did, eyes bright. I leaned toward her, watching her eyes until it got awkward, watching for signs of fear. She met me partway, lips dizzyingly warm. Her fingers curled around the fabric of my jacket, pulling at me.

The kiss went on. My phone fell into the playground mulch. Tucker tried to get both arms around me while I was trying the same, sitting side by side on the bumpy logs. I pulled away when I was in danger of falling into the mulch next to my phone.

I hopped down and picked it up, brushed off the surface and shoved it in my jacket pocket. Tucker stood up too. I wanted to kiss her again, but that front-to-front contact I wasn't ready for yet. She seemed cool with everything and I wanted it to stay that way.

"Follow me home," I said. "I'll set you up in Hazey's room."

CHAPTER SEVENTEEN

Nico

I couldn't sleep with Tucker down the hall. I wanted to crawl in bed with her. Or get her to crawl into mine. Not for anything intense, just to be close to each other. But I was scared.

Flirting I could do. Kissing I really liked. Relationships were so much harder. Not that I'd had a lot of them—only three. The one in junior high was for show. And another one almost didn't count because I was in costume the whole time. I'd met her in costume and wore that same costume every time we got together.

Ella was the only relationship I'd had with someone who knew all about me. It was the easiest one and the hardest.

I'd met Ella during my first year of high school. Our moms met at a therapy center info session for parents of trans kids. Mom was there because there wasn't a group for parents of kids with intersex traits. And I'd gone from presenting male to presenting female, so that was close enough.

Mom and Ella's mom decided we should meet, but getting us together was dicey. How do you go to your trans daughter and say "I want you to meet this intersex kid whose mom is cool" without sounding like a giant meddler?

Mom took me to one of the big parties Ella's mom was always having. With all the people around, Ella and I could hide from each other if we wanted. I went to the party plain-faced and butched up clothing-wise, wearing one of my brother's old, ratty jeans jackets, cargo pants and boots.

At thirteen Ella was a tiny slip of a person. She had short hair and liked to wear layers: a T-shirt over a long-sleeved shirt with another shirt to go over that if she got chilly. She was hiding the fact that she didn't have breasts. She looked like a sad elf who'd fallen out of her tree and gathered up a bunch of human clothes for security.

Before we got there, I wasn't sure how I'd feel about meeting her. But the minute I saw her, I was taken with her broken little elf look.

"Hey, I'm Nehal but most people call me Nico," I said and she introduced herself with her boy name, which I won't repeat here because it's not relevant to who she was or is.

We got awkward for two or three hours while we tried to figure out if we had anything to talk about other than gender. She liked reading books, hiking, historical dramas—boring stuff. I danced, I moved, I watched cartoons, I went to conventions in costumes, and when I wasn't miserable, I collected friends like metal to a magnet.

We tried to talk and gave up. Tried again and failed.

I ended up in the basement rec room watching *Doctor Who* with a couple of the grad students from Ella's mom's department. Ella came down and sat with us.

"What is this even about?" she asked after a while, about the TV show.

"It's about Rose," I said. "She's the blonde—the Doctor's companion. She started out as just a nineteen year old shopgirl from London. She's super awesome."

"She's pretty," Ella said.

When the grad students wandered off—one to the bathroom and one to get snacks—I told her, "That's what you're going to look like."

She faced me, grinned and managed the grin into a compact smile.

"Not really," she said, but she went on smiling. "That actress looks pretty Anglo-Saxon. I've got a good dose of Swedish somewhere on my dad's side. See how my nose and face are narrower." A pause and she added, "I'm really into genetics."

I stared back at her because I'd never heard a white person distinguish themselves that much from another white person.

"You're still going to be pretty," I said. "I mean, you already are." And then because I was embarrassed about that, I added, "I'm Thai, and black, and Turkish-American."

It was the first time I'd volunteered that to anyone.

She cocked her head to one side and studied me. I thought she was going to say something about all that, but instead she offered, "Mom says you hate your school. Do you want to come with me to mine some day and see if you like it better? It's cool."

"Yeah, that'd be awesome."

Her school went well beyond "cool." They had two hundred students in this old building that used to be a kindergarten. Every room had the walls painted in a theme like jungle or sunrise or starry night. All the kids watched out for each other. And they had the same teachers every year, so there were a lot of in jokes between the teachers and students.

I came home after one day at that school and said I wanted to go for my sophomore year. And I wanted to go nonbinary. Mom seemed a little exasperated about that, but we talked to the administration and teachers and they said it was fine. They already had some nonbinary and genderfluid kids, plus a few in transition. It was no big deal. I loved that place.

And I loved Ella. She stuck to me the whole first semester. I thought she wanted to make sure I did okay there, but then I caught on that she felt safer around me. My big flamboyant nonbinary presentation drew attention away from her. Next to me, she could dress more feminine and it worked, even when she was living in boymode.

The summer after our sophomore year, she was starting to get breasts from the hormones. Of course we had to compare.

After we had our shirts back on, I realized that I wanted to kiss her.

I'd kissed another girl that year, but it was weird. We couldn't work out who was supposed to move the action forward. We'd kiss and stop and get all awkward and talk about a lot of nothing. She'd play me a song, we'd kiss, end up back at awkward. After a couple of hours it was too much trouble to keep coming up with excuses to kiss her.

I didn't think it could get awkward with Ella. I was scared because I liked her so much. I didn't want to mess up our friendship. But I didn't want to keep hanging out not kissing her.

We'd always been super straightforward with each other so I asked, "Do you want to try kissing?"

"What?"

"In the fall you get to go to school as Ella and people might ask you out and, you know, you could practice."

I got up from the chair next to hers by the computer and moved across the room because my face was way hot and we were too close. Her hair was starting to grow out past her ears in this messy pixie bob that was adorable. She watched me with her big green confused innocent elf eyes. I took a step toward the door, ready to bolt.

"It's cool," I said.

"How were you thinking this would work?" she asked. Because she was practical like that.

"Um, I hadn't worked that far ahead yet," I said because I was not practical in the least.

"Go sit on the bed," she told me.

I did and she turned in her chair and stared at me for a minute before getting up and sitting next to me.

"You have to tell me if I'm bad at this," she said. "Or if I don't kiss like a girl."

"I only kissed one other girl and it wasn't that good," I admitted.

"At least the bar's low," she joked.

I put my hand on the side of her face and tried to go in slow and romantic like they do in movies. I hadn't counted on the fact that she'd also be moving forward. We bumped our teeth together behind our lips and it hurt. I pulled away and came back softer. Hers lips were thin with tension.

I pressed my lips against hers harder, but that didn't feel any better, so I tried touching them with the tip of my tongue. She opened her mouth enough to touch her tongue to mine. That made her lips relax. The kiss was starting to feel good when she pulled away.

"That's kind of strange," she said. "Not you, just kissing in general. Am I supposed to keep my eyes closed?"

I shrugged. "If you open them and I look stupid, close them again." I wanted to kiss more, not to talk about it.

She laughed. I scooted closer on the bed and leaned in, kissing the side of her jaw and her neck. I kissed up to her ear but when I got there I wasn't sure what to do. I knew not jam my tongue in her ear because my junior high pseudo-boyfriend had done that and it was nasty.

I kissed her on the lips again. More of the tension was gone so I ran my tongue across the inner edges of her lips. She opened her mouth. I touched her tongue and circled it. We were both breathing fast. I felt puffs of air from her nose on my cheek. This made me worry that I was snorting on her, so I sat back to catch my breath.

She grabbed one of the throw pillows from her bed and put it over her lap. I took that as a good sign. I was starting to get hard too.

"It's okay," I told her.

She shook her head. "I don't like how it feels."

"Kissing?"

"No, you know what I mean." She gestured at the pillow in her lap and what it hid.

Back then she still had her "boy parts," which is what she called it when she ran out of girlie euphemisms like "my bits." I had no trouble saying penis or dick—though never about Ella's because she'd glare at me. I'd talked about my penis to enough doctors in my life.

I preferred dick or junk or clit or cletis. Even Ella, with all her knowledge about trans stuff, did a double-take if I said dick and clit in the same conversation. But it was the same for me. Same for everyone really when you got down to it.

I didn't know how to tell Ella how great she was even with the parts she didn't like. Back then, I didn't know how to explain that it was all the same. Probably wouldn't have made a difference. It wasn't the same to her. Not at all.

"Do you want to kiss more?" I asked, bracing a hand on the bed to show that I had no intention of messing with her lap-pillow boundary.

"Not today."

"Should I go?" I asked because of how uncomfortable she seemed.

"Yes," she said.

My heart did a dying-fish flop into my belly. But she'd said "not today" instead of "never again" and I hung on to that.

She texted me later: *I'm sorry.*

We okay? I replied.

Always, she said.

Then don't be sorry.

We didn't talk about it and went back to our usual patterns of hanging out. She sat a little further away from me for the next few weeks. Then she started sitting closer.

"Can we try kissing again?" she asked one night in her room. School had started, but we were searching for cute clothes online, not doing homework.

"Yeah, totally."

With her serious expression on, she climbed onto her bed, grabbed a pillow and set it in her lap. She patted the space next to her. I levitated across the room because she was so much cute all in the same place.

From then on, we made out every time we were alone together at one of our houses. We started junior year with her as my girlfriend in an unstated way. I even butched up so we could walk around together like a picture-perfect hetero teen couple. It made her feel safer. She thought people were less likely to read her as trans if she was out with a boy.

I tried to tell her no one would read her anyway, but that first year she was super paranoid. And I got it, I'd gone from boy to girl too and you had to be highly vigilant at the start. If people saw something too boyish or too trans in how you did girl, you could get hurt.

We went to movies and I put my arm around her. We parked by the river and made out in her dad's truck once she got her license. That's where I broached the idea of taking us further. At either of our houses, it felt more dicey because someone could walk in. Ella's house was safer; her sister was at college and her parents knocked first. So did my mother, but not my sisters.

But the safest place of all was in her dad's truck when she could borrow it. There was a big armrest/cupholder thing in the middle that was about a mile wide, and by "mile" I mean at least eighteen inches. We'd start out each in our seat, but then Ella would keep scooting forward until she was sitting half on top of the armrest.

So one night I said, "Turn around, put your feet in the driver's seat."

I wrapped my arms around her waist and pulled her into my lap. She giggled and pressed against my chest. We both squirmed around until we were fairly comfortable. She'd taken off her mid-weight winter coat because the truck was plenty warm, and bunched it in her lap in place of the pillow.

I pushed up her shirt and her bra and kissed all over her breasts. She leaned back, trapping my other arm between her back and the door. She was breathing fast and making happy murmurs. Kissing down the center of her chest, I tucked the fingers of my free hand under the edge of the jacket and moved slowly up her leg.

"Nico, what are you doing?" she asked. With her head higher than mine, her lips tickled my forehead.

"I want to touch you," I said. It had been eight months since we first kissed and it seemed like forever. "It's okay. It's not weird. I'm like you."

"No," she said. "We're not the same. I'm a girl."

"I know you are. I get it, what you've got under your pants doesn't matter. I want to touch you."

"Girls don't have dicks." Her words came out short and bitter. She was talking about herself, but it felt like she was talking about me too.

"Some do," I said.

"Not me." Her voice was rising. "I don't want you to see me like that."

"But I don't care. I like you how you are."

"That's not me!"

Her fingers fumbled on the catch of the door, opening it behind her. She swung around in my lap and hopped down, out of the truck.

I was shaking. I got out and stood, bracing myself against the truck with one hand. You would think we'd be the best couple in the world. I couldn't tell if I was more sad or scared about losing her or mad at myself or frustrated about all of it.

She went around and got in the driver's side and sat. After a while I grabbed my coat from the passenger side floor where it had fallen and put it on.

"I'll walk," I said.

"It's too far and it's the middle of the night."

I shook my head. "It's fine. I look like a guy from a distance."

"Nico," she started. I closed the truck door, barely short of slamming it, and walked away down the sidewalk.

She didn't try to follow me and when I looked back she was slumped down in the truck, probably crying. I felt like an asshole, but too mad to go back to her. I jammed my hands in my pockets and kept walking.

"Some girls do have dicks," I muttered. Maybe that was me, maybe it wasn't. But it was someone. It was plenty of people with intersex traits. And it wasn't freakish or weird, it was nature. And Ella, of all people, should not make me feel so wrong about myself.

That was the thing tonight in the playground with Tucker. She might like making out with me. She might really like me, the way I liked her. But when it came down to my body, was she, as a lesbian, going to have a bad reaction? Would it be like Ella all over again—only different in the details of *why* my body was wrong? How many times could I go through that and not hate myself?

CHAPTER EIGHTEEN

Tucker

Women's voices woke me, speaking cheerfully in a language with long vowels and sudden stops. I didn't want to wander into a strange family setting. I snuck down the hall to the bathroom and back to the bedroom where I sat and read on my phone. The doorknob turned softly and clicked open. Nico peered in and grinned when yo saw me up.

"Hey, didn't want to wake you. Ready for breakfast?"

Nico's curls were uneven from sleep, tight against one side of yos head and tousled on the other side and top. I beamed back at yo and ran my hand through my hair.

"Sure."

I followed Nico down the stairs into the kitchen nook. A stout woman with light oak skin, crinkly, smiling eyes, and a mass of white hair piled on and behind her head, sat at the table. She had a bowl of porridge in front of her and a book propped up. I caught part of the title, *Broadway*, before she set it down.

Another woman moved in the kitchen, her walnut skin less wrinkled, her smile more compact and internal, like she was smiling at herself. She was in loose pants and a sweatshirt with a white apron that said in scrawling red script, *When this apron is on, I'm the boss. Any questions?*

She had the same eyes and broad, flat nose as the woman at the table. The same nose that I saw resemblance to in Nico. That had to be Nico's mom in the kitchen and grandmom, Yai, at the table.

"This is Tucker from up at Freytag," Nico said. "Where Ella goes to school." That last was directed at Yai, who nodded.

"Eggs?" Nico's mom offered, holding up her spatula.

"That would be great," Nico answered for both of us. "Thanks."

"What brings you to Columbus?" Nico's mom asked me.

"Um, I heard that stuff was going on with Nico and I wanted to come down and be supportive and stuff." That was too many "stuffs" for one sentence, but her smile widened.

"Ella's coming down for the surgery but I told her to go camping for spring break with Shen like she planned," Nico said. "Tucker, coffee with cream?"

"Yes, thanks, and sugar."

Yo went into the kitchen. The kitchen wasn't any bigger than the one at my mom's house, but it was in much better shape. Everything gleamed, even the handles on the cupboards. The kitchen was open to this dining area, where I was, which was open to the living room. The TV played cartoons and a young girl sat in the middle of the couch, enthralled. She had very black hair but light, birch-toned skin.

Nico took the chair next to Yai and set the coffee by the empty chair to yos right so I sat there.

"What do you want with the eggs?" Nico's mom asked.

"Can we have some of the sausage you put in Yai's jok?" Nico asked. "Would you fry us some?"

"You want the McDonald's special?" she asked, shaking her head.

"Oh are you making McGriddles too?" Nico replied.

She rolled her eyes at Nico and went back to the stove, smiling to herself.

I liked this side of Nico. Not outrageous and flamboyant, like when yo came up to the parties at Freytag, but joking, laughing, playful in a soft way.

"What are you two doing today?" Yai asked.

"I'm going to take Tucker over to the Noodle to get some costumes. Then I want to run down to Cincinnati for that little convention I told you about last week." Nico called into the kitchen, "Mom, can we stay the night there?"

"Text me when you get there," she replied. "And at bedtime so I know you're safe."

"Of course," Nico said. "I want to show Tucker what cosplay is like. We're going as Athena and Starbuck from *Battlestar Galactica*. She's Starbuck."

Yai pulled her reading glasses further down her nose and gave me a good once-over. "All right."

"You watched *Battlestar*?" I asked.

"It would be better live," she said and tapped the back cover of the *Broadway* book.

"Oh, I would so go to that," Nico said.

"Noknoi, you're always welcome to come with me," Yai said. "Even if it's not *Battlestar*."

Nico's mom asked me, "What are you studying?"

"Women's and Gender Studies," I said, feeling like that was a goofball thing to say in front of Nico. As if I was studying Nico.

"She's the one who came out as trans for Ella," Nico said. Nico's mom paused at the counter where she was picking up plates and gave me a long, appreciative look.

"That was quite something," she said.

"Thanks."

Yai had finished her porridge and took the bowl to the sink to rinse it. I couldn't think of anything intelligent to say, so I asked Nico, "What does 'Noknoi' mean?"

"That's my Thai nickname. It means 'little bird.' Everybody gets one. Mom is Fah, 'Sky.' And Yai is 'Daeng,' but it's not respectful for us to call her that because we're too young." Nico paused and then grinned, "Ella's nickname is 'Baby'."

"I thought that was an endearment."

"Nope, even Yai calls her that. You can borrow English words. I hear there's even a poor guy over in Thailand whose nickname is 'Airbus.' Yai named Ella 'Baby' because she's always been so small. It sounds different when Yai says it, though. I wonder what she'd call you."

Nico turned toward the kitchen, "Yai, what's Tucker's nickname?"

Yai finished washing out her bowl and set it on a dishtowel folded on the counter. She leaned against the sink, contemplating me.

Nico's mom stirred the contents of a frying pan and pulled it off the heat. She slid eggs onto two plates and from another pan small patties of fried sausage. Nico got up and carried the plates from the stove into the eating nook, putting one in front of me. The eggs were cooked so that their whites swirled and scrambled around intact golden yolks, thickened by the heat.

Coming back to the table, Yai said, "Dtao."

Nico laughed. "Perfect."

"That's my nickname? Dtao? Like in the Tao te Ching?"

"No, in Thai it means 'star.' She's making a play on Starbuck." Nico turned to Yai. "So I can go on calling her Starbuck?"

She said, "Dtao is better."

"I like it a lot," I told her. "Thank you."

After breakfast Nico hopped in the shower and then I did. I got a clean pair of jeans, sweatshirt and T-shirt from the duffle. I hadn't thought through where I was going to stay, but it was always a good idea to carry around a change of clothes or two, even if you ended up sleeping in the car. Nico met me in the hall.

"Hey, I need to do my Athena makeup before we go, so you have to promise no teasing," yo said.

"I can't promise that. No evil teasing, sure, but not no teasing at all."

"Fair enough." Nico grinned and disappeared into yos room.

I could see over the railing that Nico's stepdad, Matt, was in front of the TV now too. He sat on the couch next to the black-haired girl who had to be Deena since Hazey hadn't come home yet. He had the same thick hair and light skin, a broad face balanced by heavy brows. His right leg wore a thick brace and he'd propped it up on an ottoman covered by a pillow. I went down and sat in one of the two armchairs that flanked the couch.

"Are you Nico's girlfriend?" Deena asked.

"Um, not…yet?"

"But you want to be?

I nodded.

"That's good. I think girlfriends are better than boyfriends. Boyfriends have sweaty hands."

"Hey, I was a boyfriend once," Matt said.

"That is so gross, Dad."

"I did have sweaty hands, I'll grant you that."

Deena made a gagging scream and shot off the couch. She nearly collided with Nico who was coming down the stairs.

I blinked and stared and, even though it didn't help, shook my head trying to clear it. Long, straight black hair, thin brows, makeup that de-emphasized the breadth of Nico's nose and emphasized the graceful shape of yos eyes.

"Oh, wow."

Nico winked. "I'll do your makeup when we get to the con. You're easy. This wig takes forever to get on. Come on, let's run by the Noodle and get our flight suits."

"Uh, yeah," I said, trying to get over how pretty Nico was.

How big a problem was it going to be if I did like Nico better as a girl?

* * *

The Noodle turned out to be a big, old three-story house with a sign that said Jim's Glorious Noodle out front but nothing restaurant-like inside. Nico unlocked the side door and took us down a flight of stairs to a large, finished basement.

"Nobody's here yet," Nico said. "Too early. But by afternoon this place will be packed with folks working on costumes. Hey,

I'm in a genderfluid cabaret here in two weeks, you should come."

"Definitely."

Garment racks lined the far wall of the basement. Nico pulled one forward and stepped behind it.

"What are you, like a size twelve?" Nico asked.

"Fourteen," I said.

"Gotcha."

A minute later Nico was back holding two full *Battlestar Galactica* flight suits on hangers. Yo held one out to me.

"A lot of the costumes down here are from theater productions they did upstairs. But then as more and more geeks came down here to work on stuff, people created a lending library of popular costumes," Nico explained.

Yo hung the other costume on the end of a rack and pulled off yos shirt to reveal a genuine *Battlestar Galactica* gray and white tank top. Under the tank top was the rise of breasts. I couldn't even not stare. I'd seen the hint of breasts when Nico was in the tennis dress the night of the party. But when we'd been making out, Nico felt flat-chested so I thought maybe I was wrong.

Nico stepped out of yos pants, revealing a pair of dark gray boxer briefs edged with white, and pulled on the smaller fight suit. Zipping it up, yo noticed me staring.

"You own a *Battlestar Galactica* tank top," I said lamely, trying to come up with anything better than: omg, boobs.

"Yep."

"Um, can I ask? At Cal's party, you were binding?"

"Yeah," Nico said. "Close your mouth, you look like I invented breasts."

"That wasn't you?"

Nico laughed. "Suit up, Starbuck."

I stripped down to T-shirt and boxers and got into the other flight suit. I saw the wisdom of taking off outer layers. The fake leather of the suit was hot and not breathable for long stretches of it along the legs, arms and torso.

Afterward, we drove up north separately so I could drop the car off at Bailey's. Nico waited in yos car while I gave Bailey her keys back. She raised her eyebrows at my flight suit but didn't ask. Probably thought it was some kind of hardware store coverall. But she had to peek out the front window at Nico.

"She's pretty," she said. "That your new girlfriend?"

I wanted the answer to be yes, but her question was a lot more complicated than it sounded. Was "girlfriend" the right way to describe what I wanted Nico to be? Plus there was Quin, who'd been texting me steadily since yesterday to see if we were going to do anything this weekend. I hadn't responded to any of her texts; I was on the verge of being an asshole.

I got out my phone and quickly texted Quin: *Out of town, catch up with you Monday.*

That gave me two days to figure things out. Bailey was giving me her what-did-you-do-now look.

"It's complicated," I told Bailey.

She shook her head. "Sweet car, at least."

"It's Nico's stepdad's," I said, feeling worse for using Nico's name to avoid using a pronoun.

"Well don't get her pregnant or anything," Bailey said.

"Uh. Yeah, okay. See ya."

I went out to Nico's car shaking my head and wondering if Nico could get pregnant—then kicking myself for getting caught up in the plumbing and wiring. Being around someone where I couldn't make assumptions made me realize all the times I was on autopilot.

CHAPTER NINETEEN

Nico

The convention was at a Best Western on the outskirts of Cincinnati, but all the rooms were booked. I got us a room across the street at the overflow hotel and we went in to drop off our bags. The room was humid and smelled like sweaty dogs. At least it was big, with two queen beds, a couch and two chairs.

It had taken two hours to drive up and return the car to Bailey. Then we got lunch and had to drive two and a half to get down to Cincinnati. We'd talked our way through all our classes, everything we knew about Ella and Shen, about Cal and his boyfriend, what I had been watching, what Tucker was reading.

She spilled some amazing drama about Summer and Tesh that made the whole Summer-groping-me situation less awful. No wonder that girl was messed up. She was way in love with her best friend, maybe more so now that Tesh was rocking the nonbinary, and she'd been shut down hard. That had to hurt in a deep, bitter way.

Tucker also updated me about the Quin situation—how they'd only hooked up once and called it a rebound thing from the start. The fact that Tucker drove down on a moment's notice to be with me when she'd heard about the evil peanut, and our kiss last night, made it a lot easier to hear. I wondered what Quin thought about all this, what she was going to think when Tucker got back to campus. But I figured that was for Tucker to deal with.

All the best stuff at the convention happened at night, so I told Tucker we had time to chill in the room. We both used the bathroom and settled our stuff where we wanted it. For Tucker, that meant dropping her bag on the bed near the door and flipping through the TV's movie channels.

I unpacked my makeup kit and touched up. Then I hung my extra shirt in the closet so it wouldn't be a mass of wrinkles by morning. Tucker watched me with raised eyebrows. Did that mean she was anti-closet or did this read as super girly to her? Like dapper guys couldn't use closets.

I was worrying about the "binding" moment at the Noodle. Not that I didn't want her to know, I totally did, but she'd looked so surprised and delighted. She hadn't been like, "Dude, how weird is it that you have boobs?" which I'm actually used to, but more like, "Oh wow, presents!" On the one hand, awesome. On the other hand, what would the reaction be when she saw the rest of me?

I couldn't deal right now if that freaked her out. Not on top of the evil peanut news, and Dad, and her hooking up with Quin. Way too much. I needed to disconnect and get some distance. Then I could come at it again, maybe find answers in there.

Thinking of Dad, this was the perfect way to do my experiment with being a girl again. Not any girl—a badass cylon girl from a science fiction future, my favorite kind to be. With the long hair of my wig brushing my shoulders, I could settle in and see how much I really liked this.

We went to the Best Western restaurant to get burgers, lucking out with a corner booth. The décor was forest green and brown and even the wallpaper smelled of old grease. But the table top was clean and the menus non-sticky, so overall a comforting "we've been here for decades" vibe.

Since I was trying out this gendered thing, I asked Tucker, "While we're here, could you use female pronouns for me?"

"Um, sure." Her jaw was tight, lips compressed.

I asked, "How are you doing?"

"Sweaty. I feel like everyone's staring at us."

"They're not," I reassured her. "The Klingons were probably in here earlier. After them, few other costumes stand out."

"How'd you start doing cosplay?"

"A ton of kids at the Noodle were into it. They'd throw parties every few months and I started going." I held the menu up, read it for a bit. I wanted the conversation to go deeper, but not too deep. I said, "It's, um, actually how I got laid the first time."

Tucker's jaw had relaxed while I was talking and now she laughed. "You are going to tell me the whole story, right?"

Her blue eyes had copper in them, close around the pupil. Like Tucker herself, bright and metal, solid. I wanted her to keep looking at me so I settled into my side of the booth and tried to pick the right place to start the story.

"You know I dated Ella for a while, kind of a long while, but we broke up in the middle."

"Why?"

I did not say: because I was a lot more comfortable having a dick than she ever was. I said, "I wanted things to go faster than she did. And we had a fight and…" I circled my hand to indicate complexity.

She nodded at me, smiling, so I continued.

"There was this girl at the Noodle, Sian, pretty high up in the general pecking order. She organized a party blending all the vampire, werewolf, and zombie shows. Her invitation line was, 'Blood, brains, or carnage?' I picked carnage because I was in a crap mood that day. She told me to dress up as Alcide from *True Blood*."

"He's the tall, cut one who's also in that male stripper movie, right?" Tucker asked. "Ella dragged me to that."

"Yeah."

"So, this girl…" Tucker prompted.

"Five and a half feet and curvy—one of those girls who has boobs, a belly and a butt and carries it all like 'screw you, I'm cute.' A ton of copper red hair that she put into cool updos. And she had freckles. She seemed way older than me at the time, but she couldn't have been because she was in high school too."

I sipped my water and continued the story, "I put together a pretty solid Alcide. It seemed to me the defining characteristics of the *True Blood* werewolves were facial hair and a strong desire to take off their shirts. I did fingernail claws and a spirit-gum short beard. Plus two thick, ribbed white tank tops over my binder and one of those red checked flannel plaid shirts. Thick-soled boots and my shoulders got me close enough to tall, hunky guy."

"Yeah, that sounds pretty hot," Tucker said.

I grinned back at her, because if she thought that was hot, we were so going to be okay.

"Sian was playing Jessica, the young, red-headed vampire character. She had her hair long and wavy—realistic-looking fangs with a trail of blood running down one side of her mouth. Grey cardigan sweater with a red push-up bra under it so you could see bright red lace framing her cleavage. On the bottom she had a short black skirt and fishnet stockings with garters. She looked amazing. I was completely scared to talk to her."

"Did you?"

"No. She came and found me."

"And…?" Tucker asked.

"We ended up in one of the upstairs studios. The door was locked but Sian had the key ring because she'd done the setup. She said we were going to talk. We did talk for a while, but then she was like 'Are you going to kiss me?'"

"You did, right?"

"Oh, yeah."

Our food arrived and it dawned on me that if I kept this much detail in the story, I was going to end up telling Tucker everything about my anatomy. I ate my burger steadily for a few minutes.

Tucker asked, "Was she out before that or were you surprised?"

"Oh, I was surprised. I don't know what her orientation was, she never said. She liked me, for sure, but I always wondered how much of that was the Alcide costume. She'd seen me before, but she seemed to get really interested after I showed up as a werewolf guy."

"Was that weird?"

"It was fun. I was less self-conscious. She invited me to come over and watch movies. She lived in the basement at her parents' and I could slip in the side door at night. We hooked up a few more times."

"Was it different out of costume?" Tucker asked.

"I don't know."

Her eyebrows went way up. "You kept having sex as Alcide?"

"Yeah, it worked."

I hadn't told this story to anyone start-to-finish like this and hearing myself, it sounded different than it did inside my head. Cool but with a hint of pathetic.

I said, "I was seventeen. I liked that I didn't have to have 'the conversation,' that I could simply be a hot werewolf guy hooking up with a hotter vampire girl."

I'd only had sex with two people and, thinking back, I'd always been in costume.

In a sense, I was always in costume anyway. Did I know what the real me looked like? Felt like?

The real me was the person who'd been with Ella in her bedroom. But that person, that me, wasn't right for Ella. Was I right for anyone?

"What about you?" I asked.

"I've never had sex in costume."

"You should try it." The words came out automatic, fast, as a defense. Then I realized how that sounded considering she was in a costume right now. Blushed a bunch and went back to my burger.

Also…Tucker had had sex with Ella and I hadn't. How unfair was that? I'd been smitten with Ella for years and she wouldn't have sex with me, but she did with Tucker after knowing her for how many months?

"What's that look on your face?" Tucker asked.

I swallowed the bite of burger that had gone dry in my mouth, gulped some water.

"Ella and I dated on and off for two years and never had sex," I said.

Emotions flashed across Tucker's face. Eyes widening then narrowing, brow creasing. She shook her head.

"You get why she had sex with me, though, right?" she asked.

"No."

"She could afford to lose me. She can't afford to lose you. If you'd hooked up and it got super weird, so weird you couldn't be friends—you two just can't do that. She can't take that loss. With me if it went sideways, at the end of the year she could bail on me."

"She'd never do that."

"When you love someone, there's a lot more pressure for the sex part to work out," she said. Her face closed like a shutter slammed over a window.

I had a flash of fear that she meant me. But the way her face went empty, she had to be thinking about her ex. Thinking about how messed up ideas of love and sex got when someone took away your right to your own body, your self.

"That wasn't your fault," I told her.

"Don't." She picked up the cloth napkin and wrung it around her finger. She said, "I don't want to talk about it. Go back to you and Ella, why did you split up the second time?"

"On the surface, because I cheated on her, sort of," I said. "There was this guy I knew from conventions. We made out a few times. I met him when he was dressed as the tenth Doctor and I was Jack Harkness, and we were both about sixteen, and it all made sense. But that was before Ella and I were together, before Sian. I stopped seeing Sian after Ella and I were okay again. We started going on dates, but we never talked about if we were dating officially."

I thought about it for a second and added, "No, that's not fair to Ella. We were going on dates and she wanted this perfect hetero couple date situation. The longer it went on, the less it worked for me. I was so into her and it felt like not having sex was a criticism. Like my body wasn't right. I ended up in this shitty place in my mind. The next time I was at a con and that guy, the tenth Doctor, asked if I wanted to go up to his room, I did."

"I get that," Tucker said.

"But that led to a huge fight with Ella and she broke up with me. I think the cheating was the excuse. She was going to get her surgery soon and she wanted to be with a guy. She wanted the dream relationship, the hetero romance movie thing. I'm never going to be that."

"It's never real anyway," Tucker said. "Dream relationships suck ass." She plastered a grin on her face, barely covering the sadness. I loved the attempt. I grinned back and stuck a fry up my nose.

What I didn't tell Tucker was how bad our fighting had been. Ella and I had started yelling at each other in her driveway. Days later we were still fighting. In her bedroom, I'd perched tensely on the edge of her bed while she sat rigid in her desk chair.

"I'm never seeing him again," I told her. "And I'm really sorry."

"I know," she said in the sad Ella voice that was highly worse than the angry Ella voice. "But we're never going to work."

"Of course we are, we're perfect. Baby, listen, I can do what you want. I can be that."

"Even if we never have sex?" she asked.

"What, like never?" I got up and bounced on my toes to work out the nervous, angry energy. "Why never?" I paused and stared at her. "Is it me? Are you not okay with…with *me*?"

She shook her head and I bounced harder. I knew she hated that she still had "boy parts," that she wanted to block that out and never think about it. I understood that.

But what if my body was the real issue? We'd seen each other naked in quick flashes, changing in her room back before we'd started the kissing phase of our relationship. She knew what I looked like. Why had I never thought this through?

"What, like my dick isn't good enough for you?" I asked, full on furious. "You need to have a 'real' one to prove you're a 'real' girl? It's not going to be right until you have some hetero cisgender guy's dick up in you?"

For the record, that *is* the worst thing I've ever said.

Ever.

She started crying and I slammed out of her room and out of her house. I went home and did a lot of crying of my own, but at least she couldn't see me doing it.

And then I shut off everything. I shut off boy and I shut off girl and I shut off both. I made myself into neither and nothing for a while. I did school and I cleaned the house so I'd have a reason to get up on weekends. I watched every season of every science fiction show I'd ever liked even a little.

Ella wrote me a letter and emailed it to me a few days before she went for surgery. It was scary, like she was worried that the surgery could go wrong and she'd never wake up, never get a chance to say this stuff to me. And it was super sad. She said that she was sorry for everything and that there wasn't a thing wrong with me. She said she'd always love me, but that my body—how I looked when I was naked—reminded her of a part of her life she never wanted to think about again.

And I got it.

I felt like such an asshat. I could rock what nature gave me, but I did look similar to Ella's mid-transition phase. She shouldn't have to be reminded of that all the time.

As soon as she was home I went over with flowers and a teddy bear and we were friends again. But that was it, that was all we were ever going to be. I didn't want to love somebody else like that and get turned inside out ever again.

CHAPTER TWENTY

Tucker

After dinner, Nico led me into the dealer's room. I imagined poker, but it turned out to be a ballroom filled with tables of people selling books, comic books, action figures, toys, games, props and costume pieces.

We were hardly the only people in costumes, which made me super relieved. There were so many Klingons—I'd seen enough *Star Trek* to pick them out. I saw Batman, Superman, Spiderman and a lot of super heroes I didn't recognize; more *Star Trek* uniforms; a pack of zombies; and a gaggle of girls about whom Nico simply said, "Manga" as if that explained the pigtails, makeup and schoolgirl uniforms.

Halfway around the room someone called out, "Excuse me, Starbuck," and I realized they meant me. Turning around, I spotted a guy with a blond kid about ten.

"Boomer," she said excitedly when Nico stepped up next to me.

"Can my daughter get a picture with you?" the guy asked. "She's a huge fan."

"Of course," Nico said. Yo turned sideways—I corrected myself mentally because Nico had asked me to use female pronouns while we were in costume—*she* turned sideways. She stuck her thumbs in the belt of her flight suit, making a tough serious face.

The girl gave an excited hop and ran to stand between us. I stuck out my chin, jammed one thumb in my belt and put my other hand on the girl's shoulder. She glanced up and grinned. I tried to muster a tough but approving look. The phone clicked as the dad took photos.

When he was done, I knelt down level with the girl. "What's your name?"

"Joanna," she said.

"You want to be a pilot when you grow up?" I asked.

"Yeah, I want to fly a Viper like you."

"That's right. You get good grades, okay? And you keep in good shape. You've got to be top notch to fly in my crew."

"Yes sir," she said and saluted.

I saluted back and stood up. Her dad pulled her away as she chatted excitedly about Vipers and Raptors and Battlestars.

Nico's mouth was half-open, grinning. "Frakkin-A, Starbuck, that was adorable."

"Zip it, Lieutenant, I don't want any lip from you," I said and managed to hold a straight face for about three seconds. We both burst out laughing.

Nico threw an arm around my shoulders. "See, you're good at this."

I wasn't so sure. On my own I'd never do this, but following in Nico's wake, watching her joke and play with random strangers, made it all easier.

After circumnavigating the dealer's room and the art room, we ended up back in the hotel restaurant eating fries while Nico argued playfully with half of the Klingon delegation. It reminded me of going to a convention in Wisconsin with Lindy, but not in a bad way. It made me miss my Minnesota friends, Claire and Emily. I'd met them at that convention—the only other one I'd ever attended. They'd been great friends to me and they were the reason I knew anything at all about trans people.

They knew I'd been spending time with Nico. Claire got over her disappointment that I wasn't dating Ella and had started cheering for this pairing. She'd be thrilled when she heard about tonight.

"Hey, can we get a picture of us?" I asked Nico. She asked one of the Klingons to take photos with her phone. She texted me the best one and I forwarded it on to Claire with a note to also show Emily.

While the Klingon debate wrapped up, I studied the photo on my phone. I couldn't get over how girly Nico looked.

"How you holding up?" she asked when we were alone again.

"This fake leather is hot as hell," I said. "And those Klingons smelled like wet cat, but otherwise I'm great."

"You want to hit the parties? There's also a costume competition, but no way we beat some of the ensembles I've seen, so I was going to skip it."

"Works for me."

Fliers advertising room parties covered the hotel walls next to the elevators. Nico picked one. When we got to the second floor, I realized all the parties were clumped together so it didn't matter where we started. Each room had its door propped open and you could peek in and see the themes from the halls.

We went into the *Doctor Who* party first. The door was made up like the entryway to the Tardis. That one wasn't very active yet, so we wandered across the hall to the Hogwarts party. They had a ton of snacks and huge bowls of jelly beans. We got plates and nibbled.

Back in the hall, as we considered the next set of doors, someone shouted at us, "Hey, Toaster!"

It was an insult from inside the *Battlestar Galactica* world.

Nico spun around. "Frak you."

I turned too. There were three guys in space cowboy outfits, like *Firefly* but with tacked on random *Star Wars* bits. The one who'd said the insult was a badger-faced white guy.

"Which one are you, Boomer or Athena?" he asked Nico.

"Athena, I always liked her better," she said.

"Then what are you doing with Starbuck? Those two would never hang out together."

"They do all the time in the Starbuck/Athena slash fic," Nico said. She spun around, grabbed my lapels and kissed me.

Or was it Athena kissing Starbuck? And what the heck was slash fic? I tried to remember the show but my brain was scrambled. Either way I figured this should be a good kiss. I put my hands on Nico's hips and kissed back. Someone cheered and another person took a photo. Nico pulled away, laughing and flipped her hair over her shoulder.

"Come on," she said and pulled me away from the now speechless space cowboy. She drew us into the women's bathroom and leaned against the sink. "Was that okay?"

"Uh, more than. But what was that even about?"

"I think he was trying to hit on us. Badly. Challenging my cosplay, indeed." Nico leaned in toward the mirror, checking her makeup.

"Seriously?"

"Guys don't try to hit on you much, do they?" Nico asked.

"Pretty much never. It's the Mohawk. And the boots."

It was driving me crazy watching her redo her mascara. It was hot in a way my brain didn't have categories for. And I still worried that I was more attracted to her as a girl than as plain Nico. If there was a plain Nico. Was there?

Was it the Nico who met me in the parking lot of the Chocolate Cafe and cried into my shoulder? If so, I really really liked that Nico too. But was I as attracted? Or was this not fair because Nico was crying then and now she'd kissed me?

Frak, my brain was going to explode.

Out in the hall again, Nico led me down to the end where the Klingons had set up in a big suite. The whole two rooms were covered on every wall with fake stone, like being in a cave, and the AC was cranked up to freezing. I didn't know if the Klingon home world was full of ice caves or if this was from some movie I'd missed. I didn't care because at last my flight suit was the right temperature.

Spacey techno beats pulsed through the room and most of the Klingons were dancing, despite their heavy, armor-plated costumes. Someone came by with a tray of glowing blue drinks in plastic glasses. I took one.

"Be careful with that," Nico said. "I hear Klingon drinks are strong."

I sipped it and tried not to cough. It had twice as much alcohol as I expected.

"You want to dance?" Nico asked.

"No, I kind of suck," I said.

"All right, I'll dance, you stay here." From anyone else that might have sounded pouty, but Nico said it with a smile. She moved into the dance area amid the partying Klingons like she belonged. And then I was glad I hadn't said yes because I would have looked even worse than usual next to Nico.

"Is that your girlfriend?" a middle-aged Klingon woman asked from the wall next to me.

"Maybe," I said. "I mean, I hope so."

She laughed. "Ah, young love. Glad I'm done with that."

I didn't know what to say to that. I asked, "How did you become a Klingon?"

Her story was cool: mother of three, bookkeeper, met some of the other Klingons when she took a Russian Kettlebell class at the local gym and realized it was way more fun to try to get in shape as part of an interstellar warrior culture.

I finished my drink. Nico was still dancing. I wanted to be closer to her. Maybe it didn't matter if I looked like a malfunctioning robot on the dance floor. She grinned at me when I stepped out there and danced around me.

When the music slowed, she stepped in and put her arms around my neck. We danced together.

"I need some water," she said. "Let's find another room."

We went back into the hall and through a few more rooms. Nico picked up a bottle of water and I accepted a cup of purple punch that also turned out to have alcohol in it, but by that point I didn't care.

"What do you want to do next?" Nico asked after we'd poked our heads into every open room on the second floor.

I was buzzed and without thinking about it, I said, "You know you can kiss me any time, not just when guys hit on us."

"Really?"

Nico pushed me into the wall and kissed me. We went from zero to sixty in about five seconds: mouths open, her pressing into me, me pulling her even closer.

Someone yelled, "Cylon-lover!" down the hall.

Another voice said, "Get a room!"

Nico pulled away enough to say, "You know, we have a room," three inches from my ear.

"Why aren't we there?"

We ran down the stairs and across the street. Nico got the keycard from a side pocket and managed it into the lock despite the fact that I was kissing the side of her neck. We stumbled into the room. I fell onto the nearest bed and kicked my bag onto the floor. Nico dropped down next to me and we started kissing again.

The flight suits had adjustable belts that we'd both cinched tight. Nico tugged my zipper down until it hit the belt. I shrugged out of the top of the suit so I was in a T-shirt and bra with the upper half of the suit folded down around my waist.

I got Nico's zipper halfway down and she helped with the rest, shucking the top of her suit much faster than I had with mine. I touched the strap of Nico's gray and white *Battlestar Galactica* tank top.

"How can the costumes be both weird and hot?"

"Do you want to slow down?" she asked.

I shook my head. Nico took my hand and put it over her breast.

"Come here, Starbuck," she said.

I shoved up the bottom edge of her tank top until I could get her nipple in my mouth. Her hands knotted in the loose top of my flight suit where it hung around my waist and made the fake leather creak. I spent a long time on her breasts and then kissed all over her flat belly, ridged with muscle.

She tugged on my T-shirt. I pulled it off over my head and threw it somewhere, followed by the bra. She played with my breasts until I was wriggling with the need for more. I reached for her belt at the same time that she reached under mine. Her fingers slid over my boxers, teasing, amazing, and then as she moved down further, I felt the fear, sudden and jagged.

I grabbed her wrist hard. Too hard, from the flash of alarm in her eyes. The off-balance feeling from the alcohol mixed with the pressure of her hand and my body flipped from hot to ice cold.

She used her free hand to pry my fingers off her wrist.

"You can say no," she told me.

I couldn't. I mean, I didn't want to say no.

But I didn't want to go where we were going.

Except that I did—but without the fear. How could I get there without the fear?

"Look at me," Nico said.

I did. Her face so familiar even with the long hair and makeup, even looking like a girl, still always Nico.

"Are you okay?" she asked.

"I think so."

"Do you want this?"

There was an echo of desire, but the fear shoved it aside.

"Maybe?" I said.

She shook her head. "There are no maybes in sex. There's no and yes—maybe is always no."

I twisted the belt of my uniform around my fingers. I had words in there somewhere but far away from being able to say them. I didn't want to say no to Nico. I was saying it to Lindy, over and over again: no, no, no! Not that she'd ever hear me, not even the shard of her stuck in my brain.

I had to stop thinking about that. Blinking hard, I focused on Nico, sitting back on her heels, watching me. The flight suit had gathered around her hips, the white edge of her briefs crisp against her skin. I wanted to get closer again.

I wanted her to push the fear out of my head like Quin had.

"Can I—?" I gestured at her belt area.

"No," she said. "Not tonight."

"Fuck."

I sat up too fast and the room tipped. I put my hands to my head to hold it steady.

"Tucker, how much did you drink?"

"Three maybe," I said. "Unless the Klingon ones count double."

Nico went into the bathroom and came back to press a glass of water into my hand. "I'm going down the hall to get you a bag of chips. Drink that."

She climbed out of bed, dropped the rest of the flight suit and carefully pulled off the wig—and Athena was gone.

I watched Nico's lean, muscled, curvy, angular, beautiful body as yo pulled on jeans and a sweatshirt. I wanted to get up and take all that off again. But the room was wobbly and Nico had said "Not tonight."

I focused on sipping the water. And, when Nico came back, eating a bag of chips.

"You don't drink?" I asked because I was starting to feel stupid.

"Nah." Nico peered sideways at me, shrugged. "I'm eighteen."

"You could. Tonight nobody was checking."

"It never seems like a good idea. And, okay don't laugh at me—Mom would worry. And I like that she trusts me."

"Why would I laugh? That's sweet."

"Uh-huh," Nico said, like I was humoring yo.

"In my family, nobody gives a crap," I said, and it came out way sadder than I wanted it to. Everything was too sad now.

"Do you want me to sit with you?" Nico asked. "Arm around you sort of thing?"

I shook my head. I wanted to want that, but I didn't. I felt the covering of filth over me again, sickness in my gut, layers of awful. I didn't want Nico to touch that.

"Do you want to get up and move around?" yo asked.

"No." If I moved too much I was going to puke.

"Tell me if you need anything else?"

"Yeah," I said.

Nico turned on the bedside light and clicked off the overhead. Yo moved around in the bathroom making splashy, washy sounds, and came out in a T-shirt and boxer briefs. I eventually levered myself up, stripped off the rest of the flight suit, found my T-shirt, took my turn in the bathroom.

I came back to a highly normal hotel room. Nico was tucked into the other bed, a tablet propped on yos knees. I didn't know what to say, so I got into the empty bed and rolled onto my side. I tried to work out what I could've done to keep things from going wrong again. After a while I heard Nico switch off the light and rustle against the sheets and pillows.

"Good night, Starbuck," Nico said.

I wanted to reply, to say everything, but my throat was frozen and aching. Minutes passed and Nico's side of the room stopped rustling. I heard one long, soft breath and another.

I pressed the heels of my hands against my eyes. Teeth clenched, body tightened. Tears forced their way out through the creases where I couldn't shut my eyes hard enough.

CHAPTER TWENTY-ONE

Tucker

In the morning, we got breakfast at the hotel. We talked about all the funny things from the night before and none of the weird things. We seemed provisionally okay. I would have worried about it more if I hadn't had a skull-cracking headache.

In the car, on the way back to Freytag, the sun blazed at me and I kept my eyes closed. What should I say about last night? What were we going to do if I couldn't let Nico touch me and Nico didn't want me to touch yo?

It reminded me of Ella freaking out about Shen before they had sex the first time and I laughed.

"What?" Nico asked.

"I should never have teased Ella so much about all her fussing over sex with Shen."

"Hey, they worked it out."

I wanted to ask if Nico thought we would too, but I was afraid of the answer, so instead I said, "Ella told me you were very…helpful."

"I've been reading sex education books since I was like twelve. My brother left his stash when he moved to our dad's because our dad is a lot more old fashioned about that."

"Was the stash any good?"

"It scared the daylights out of me at first," Nico said. "But the best thing was that I realized you can learn about sex. People don't talk about it and you don't get anything decent in school—but if you're trying to figure something out, you can. Oh and I did end up with a copy of the kama sutra, so I am an encyclopedia of sex positions."

I sat up straighter and stared at Nico.

"I'm not saying I can *do* most of them," Nico said. Yo had a hint of a smile on, eyes crinkling with humor.

"Do you think Ella and Shen can?" I asked.

"Nobody needs all of them. Only the ones that work for them."

I wanted to ask, "What works for you?" but I chickened out.

Nico said, "You know, I should name some positions after *Battlestar Galactica* elements, like 'Viper-on-the-track,' 'the Cylon reincarnation,' and so on."

"What's that second one?"

"You need a bathtub and a lot of Jell-O."

I hadn't seen enough of the show to know what that was a reference to, but the image made me laugh. We went back to talking about nothing in particular and got to campus mid-afternoon. Nico texted Ella, who said she was over at the Union with the crew.

"I'm going to go say hi," Nico said. "Want to come?"

"Yeah, sure. But I need to get the rest of the fluorescent booze taste out of my mouth. I'll meet you there."

Nico headed for the Union and I went back to my room to brush my teeth six times and change into a shirt that didn't stink of alcohol sweat. Could I ask Nico if yo wanted to stay over tonight in my room? My bed wasn't that big, but we could sleep curled up together. I wanted to put my arms around Nico and feel yos body against mine. Maybe even try some of that other stuff again.

I walked to the Union working on a way to ask that didn't involve the phrase "sleep over," like I was twelve.

Ella, Shen, Cal and Tesh were all at our usual table, listening to Nico tell a story. Cal sat at the end of the table, leaning back, with Shen and Ella on one side. Shen pointed avidly toward Nico and Ella beamed. Tesh sat on the other bench, wearing a dark charcoal shirt that deepened the blue of Tesh's hair.

Nico was saying, "…and then this little girl stands up straight and salutes Tucker and Tucker saluted back like she does that every day."

"Adorable," Tesh declared.

I paused at the foot of the table. Nico and Shen were geeking out about cylon number eight. Maybe Ella and I could set up a double date.

I felt someone come up next to me and turned to see Quin. She was in a tight athletic shirt and running pants, hair pulled back. I had guilt vertigo. Like being pulled toward her but being pushed away harder. I crossed my arms to keep my balance, but that seemed too closed off, like I was being a jerk, so I uncrossed them. Then my arms felt weird just hanging off my shoulders.

"Hey, how's it going?" I tried to sound casual.

"Good, usual. You?"

"Good. Just got back to campus," I added in case she was about to do a "why didn't you call me" sort of thing.

"What's going on with you. With us?" she asked. "I thought we were going to get together this weekend."

"I had stuff I had to do," I said.

That went across like the evasive bullshit it was. Quin's face hardened.

"If all that was crap in your room, if you're not into me, just say it," she said. "But don't disrespect me like this. I hear you're dating some guy and then you run off to spend the weekend with him and won't even tell me."

"Fuck no. I don't date guys. What are you talking about?"

Icy cold lightning went along all my nerves as I realized what I'd just said in front of Nico. Did Nico think "fuck no" was my response to anything between us? I caught a flash of pain in Nico's eyes before the mask came down.

Nico pushed up from the table. "I should head back."

Yo gave the group a quick nod, turned away and headed for the door to the quad. Ella jumped up and dashed after Nico. Cal turned from face to face, working it out.

I stared at the doors to the union and wondered how you went after a person you'd made a total ass of yourself in front of.

Tesh met my eyes. "Go after Nico."

Beside me, Quin said, "That's Nico? That's who you were with? Aw, shit."

Only one person on campus was tapped into the gossip lines enough to know I was out of town with Nico—and mean enough to tell Quin I was dating a guy. "I'm going to kill Summer," I snarled.

As if my use of her name called her forth, I saw Summer standing in line at the food counter. How long had she been there? Had she seen Nico walk out?

She'd probably put herself there to watch this scene. She looked like she was gloating. I darted around the tables to the food line, grabbed her arm and pulled her out of line.

"What the hell? Why are you trying to fuck up my life? I didn't go around spreading rumors about you and you know I could—so why are you doing it to me?"

"Oh, does it mess up your life if people know you're dating a guy?" She braced her feet and crossed her arms, making her body seem very solid.

"Nico isn't a guy, Nico's a person," I said.

"Screw that, everybody's got something going on." She uncrossed her arms and started counting off points on her fingers. "First Nico wears a chest binder but said maybe that's to throw people off, okay that could go either way, but then Nico said, and I quote 'everyone is bangable,' and only a bi guy would say that 'cause you have to be into anal—"

I grabbed the front of her shirt in my fists, my arms shaking.

"When did you become such an ignorant shit?" I hissed in her face.

Cal put his arms around me from behind and pulled me so I had to let go of Summer or drag her with us. I jerked against Cal's grip but he held tighter.

"Admit it," Summer said. "You're dating a guy. You like dick."

"That's disgusting. And what the fuck do you care? You need to shut your mouth."

Quin and Tesh came up on either side of Summer. Tesh put a hand on her arm, like if Summer took a step toward me they'd try to hold her back, which in Tesh's case wouldn't be nearly as effective as Cal restraining me.

"Are you going to shut it for me?" Summer sneered at me.

"Both of you shut it," Cal said. "One more word and you're banned from my house for the rest of the year."

It was a strong enough threat for Summer—she loved his parties and they were the nexus of her campus manipulations. She spun on her heel and stalked away.

When she was out of sight, I said, "Thanks, Cal."

He let go of my arms, grim-faced. He nodded in the direction of the doors. Ella and Nico were standing inside; they'd been coming back in. How much had they heard?

How much had Nico heard?

I walked slowly toward them, hands out, open, fingers spread. "I'm sorry," I said when I was close enough to be heard over the general noise of the room without shouting.

Nico shook yos head. "Don't."

Ella put her hand on the front of my shoulder. I stared down at her little, fine-boned fingers, confused.

With a sinking feeling of horror I realized she was trying to keep me away from Nico.

"Nico," I called over her shoulder. "It's not...I didn't mean..."

"No. I don't care what you meant. Don't call me." Nico walked away.

Ella gave me a push in the direction of Cal, so light my shoulder didn't even move, but for Ella that was a huge gesture. It kept me rooted in place as she followed Nico out of the Union.

CHAPTER TWENTY-TWO

Nico

I drove away from Freytag with Tucker's emphatic "fuck no. I don't date guys" and "that's disgusting" replaying in my head a hundred thousand times. *That* was her response to being accused of dating a guy? Yeah we were great together as Starbuck and Athena, but my constellation of gender also included being a guy.

The last two days, part of me had been thinking I could play Athena forever. I enjoyed being a girl in a science fiction future. I'd been wondering if I could do "woman" in a way that showed that current gender roles for women were crap.

I'd been thinking that I could take that option in the upcoming surgery. Do that for Tucker—turn myself into a girl. Be only a woman for the rest of my life. That showed me how deep I was with Tucker, how stupidly much I liked her. No, loved her. Frakking stupid love.

I hadn't loved anyone since Ella. Even then it wasn't the same because I figured we'd never last. Once she got all her surgeries, I wasn't right for her anymore. We worked when we were both outside of cultural gender boxes. But Ella got all up inside my heart and it wrecked me every time she pulled away.

Now my chest felt the same awful, clenching pain about Tucker.

How could I even tell her what was wrong with what she'd said? That I was a guy and wasn't a guy at the same time. The word "nonbinary" confuses people. It puts too much emphasis on the "non." It's about the gender binary, but some people only hear the "non" part. Like it's about not being gendered—instead of being all genders, outside of, beyond them.

I didn't have a good word for all-gendered or beyond gender. There were so many genders to play with: butch guy, pretty boi, artsy girl, emo guy, clever girl, fierce femme, protective dude…I could list them all day. I was working out how to show it in dance for the cabaret and starting to feel like I could.

My sense of gender changed over time. One day I looked in the mirror and the button down shirt was right if I wore earrings. Another day all earrings were wrong because my hair was too long or curling too much.

Was that what it felt like every day for Ella before she transitioned? Did she see a little boy and feel that bone deep shudder of wrongness? I bet she did. But then she knew who she was.

I didn't know who I was. But I knew who I was not. I was not that foolish girl falling for Tucker and getting her heart broken again.

When I got home, I stripped off everything colorful. I put on black sweatpants, a faded gray T-shirt and a purple hoodie because I didn't have any dark sweatshirts.

Yai was at the kitchen table writing longhand on her legal pad. Probably a letter. She wrote a lot of letters: to relatives in Thailand, to theater companies about what she liked in their productions, Letters to the Editor in the newspaper. She saw me in the hall and said, "You're angry."

I poured a glass of juice and sat at the table with her. "It's too hard to explain."

"Starbuck?" she asked.

I folded my arms and slumped down, forehead resting on my forearms. The name that had sounded so cute a day before made me sad. Yai rubbed a circle on my back.

"You'll work it out," she said.

"Doubt it," I grumbled and surprised myself by asking, "Do you think I should pick a gender?"

She took her tea mug into the kitchen for a refill. When she was back and settled into her chair, she said, "You have to answer three questions to answer that one. What do you need? What does the family need? What does the village need?"

"But if I need to be everything but the family needs me to pick one…"

She didn't say anything and I kept thinking. What did the village need? Here in the US where there weren't villages, was the village the city? Or was it my community of people—including the ones I hung out with the most at the Noodle? Or was it the whole country?

If it was the community at the Noodle, that was easy, they needed me to stay everything, to stay fluid and nonbinary, and to show people that was okay. If it was the whole country, did they need anything from me? Was I supposed to be a productive cog in the consumer machine? Make a bunch of money and buy stuff and keep it all going? I could do that better as a man.

"What's the village?" I asked. "And how do I know what it needs?"

Yai looked over at me, her eyes steady and deep. "If you can answer that today, this week even, I'll know you've become enlightened."

I had to grin. She nodded, small smile, went back to writing her letter. I was in no danger of becoming enlightened. What she said got me thinking about the Buddha and the story of how after he gets enlightened, the gods ask him to come back and teach humanity about enlightenment and he doesn't want to.

It was hard to always be teaching people things. It was hard to have a life that taught by example. I got why the Buddha didn't want to teach and I didn't even have something as gigantic as enlightenment to work with.

On the other hand, at least the Buddha got to be enlightened while he had to teach. Maybe if I was enlightened the whole gender thing would get easier. Nah, probably not. It wasn't like the Buddha never suffered again, he just wasn't attached to it.

That was probably the trick of it—not being attached. But non-attachment, not one of my strengths.

Was it easier to be non-attached as a guy? I wouldn't have to worry about things with Tucker. I'd get male privilege. I'd hate it, but I could use it to change things, couldn't I? Or would it always end up using me?

Maybe I should give up what I wanted for a role that was the most useful for everyone else.

"Thanks, Yai. I'm going to dance," I told her. I gave her a quick kiss and headed out to the Noodle.

A few minutes later, Sharani gave me the want-to-talk look and I shook my head. I couldn't repeat what Tucker had said, that whole scene, not even to Sharani. She'd understand, but I didn't want to hear the words again.

I had to move until I didn't feel the hate in my body. The weight of all the judgments, all the ideas that this or that part of me was wrong. Spin and fall and catch myself against the ground until I felt that all of my body belonged to me.

I thought maybe I should block Tucker on my phone again. But it didn't matter, she wasn't going to call.

CHAPTER TWENTY-THREE

Tucker

I slunk back to my dorm room wanting to pound my head against the wall. Made myself lie down instead. The headache from that morning was back, double strength. I hazed out for a while, slipping from hating Summer to hating myself to dozing and then back into the hate cycle.

Knocking woke me. I jumped up in case it was Nico coming back to let me apologize. My brain slammed into the front of my head with blurring pain, but I made it to the door and pulled it open.

It was Quin, grim-faced.

"Hey," she said. "I'm so sorry."

I lowered myself into my desk chair, leaving the door open. She shut it behind her and sat on the side of the bed, elbows on knees.

"We got played," she said.

"Summer told you?"

Quin shook her head. "Nah, I'd have wondered about that. Gal on the soccer team asked if I was with you. I said kind of, because, you know, she might have been asking for Katee, the hot forward and I didn't know what we were. That night and then dinner, we didn't talk about it, but it felt like dating, you know."

I nodded because it had. Because before I heard about Nico's surgery, before we started talking again, I had been thinking about dating Quin.

She went on, "So this girl says how she heard you were away for the weekend with your boyfriend and did I know about that. And I was like: no way because that night when we had breakfast you said guys are gross. But she'd seen a pic of you with this cute guy."

Plausible. There were plenty of pics of me and Nico from over the winter. In some, Nico appeared fairly guy-ish. If you were expecting to see me with a guy in the photo, that's what you'd see.

I didn't know how to explain that to Quin. She stretched up, blew out her breath, put her hands on her knees.

"I figured I should ask about us," she said. "I'm really sorry about when I asked."

"Yeah, that's not on you. That's on Summer. I'm sure she set that girl up to ask you about the boyfriend thing." A long pause. "And it's on me. You didn't know Nico was there. I did."

"I should've waited until we were alone," Quin said. "I just was looking forward to the weekend and seeing you. Then you blew me off and you really were out of town, so that part of the story was true. The more I thought about it…you know, when we hooked up, you never let me touch you."

"I did…" I started to protest but turned it into a question, "I didn't?"

"Tucker, you didn't even take off your boxers. I figured it was a butch thing. But then the dating a guy story got me worried. Though if you weren't really into girls, I figured you'd let me do you, not the other way around."

My head was filling with pressure and heat. Face burning.

I used to…

Back with Lindy, I used to like…

I pushed off the chair and stood up. Stared at the door to the bathroom, wishing I could see through it into Ella's room, and that she'd be there and tell me what to do.

"I am a lesbian," I said. "And I like you. I thought Nico was blowing me off. I thought…but yo wasn't and then I wanted that. I want that. I thought you and me we were rebounding, not really dating yet."

"Could've been," Quin said.

I didn't have an answer for her.

She stood up and walked to the door, then asked, "You still tabling with me at the gym?"

I'd agreed to sit at the Black Lives Matter info table with her before the basketball game.

"You're sure you want a white girl sitting there?"

She shook her head at me. "When it's all black folks we get written off much faster."

"Oh, shit. Yeah, of course, I'll be there. Quin I'm sorry about everything. I—"

She cut me off with an impatient wave. "I'll see you Thursday."

She shut the door hard behind her.

I took some ibuprofen and ate part of an expired protein bar I'd bought on sale at the gas station. It tasted like packing peanuts, minus the peanut. My brain kept circling around to Nico and then looping back in time toward everything I didn't want to remember.

When the headache got less blinding, I went to the gym and hit the heavy bag until my arms were ready to fall off.

CHAPTER TWENTY-FOUR

Nico

I had the data from the girl side of the experiment, time to collect the guy side data. I texted Dad, asking if I could come over. He'd rented a furnished three-bedroom apartment a few miles from Mom's house. A few weeks ago I'd thought that was a pathetic attempt to get me to come hang out. Now I was grateful for it.

"Let's give this a try," I said when I got there. "The guy thing, for real."

He looked me over approvingly, waved me in and got me a pop. "I'm glad you're taking this seriously."

The furnishings were super generic in his living room, like ten shades of taupe. But they centered on a massive flat screen TV, so it worked. Dad had paused a history show, with a bunch of people on screen building some temple.

I dropped onto the couch and took the pop he offered. I told him, "Bring it on. Do it up. Let's do all the guy stuff: monster truck rallies, pro wrestling, maybe we could rope some steers together and then eat twenty ounce steaks."

A bemused grin split the darkness of his beard. "Kenan's coming out tomorrow for his spring break, I'll make plans."

My dad's guy plans the following day did not involve steers or monster trucks. We went to the Science of Big Machines exhibit at the science museum and it was awesome. Dad could explain what all the machines did—how they worked to make bridges and cities. Kenan was into it, which kept him from being a complete douche about every girl within twenty yards of us.

Kenan spent a long time in the cab of the fully assembled crawler 'dozer. Dad leaned in over his shoulder to tell him what the controls did and how much dirt he could move. I hung out by the miniature cranes, moving tiny girders from one side of a mock construction site to another.

Kenan hopped out of the cab when he saw the cute girl we'd passed coming in. Not like he was going to talk to her, though. Kenan had Dad's thick, straight hair, but not the long face. So his eyes were jammed up under a heavy brow and short forehead. This meant that the expression he thought was sexy was, in fact, creepy and menacing.

We'd been through all the big machines and Dad was reading the program to decide what else we should see. I leaned close to Kenan, indicated the girl he'd been stalking, and said, "Ken, stop staring at her, she's not into you."

"What? She's looking at me."

"She's trying to figure out if you're a serial killer. If you want, I'll go ask. In fact, if you don't knock it off, I'm going over to talk to her right now. I'll tell her that you like her but she'd have to work around your Paleolithic manners."

"Asshole," he said.

Kenan didn't get it because he'd never been a girl. Most people who'd never been girls didn't understand the weight of fear that came with being perceived female in our culture. I couldn't explain that to Kenan. He'd never believe me. He'd never believe that half the population spent that much time walking around in fear.

At least when I presented as a guy, he'd listen to me. He stopped staring at the girl. He went over to Dad and they picked our next destination. This was in the opposite direction of the girl.

Afterward I hung out with them at Dad's. We played a snowboarding game and ate spaghetti that Dad made. He wasn't as good a cook as Mom, but he'd mastered a few basics.

Two days later we went to a movie: the new *300* film because Kenan wanted to see it and I didn't have a strong opinion. At first it was fun because Dad's so anti-Greek. We cheered for the Persians. The area that's now Turkey was part of the Persian Empire back in the day.

"The Greeks are not the heroes they're made out to be," Dad grumbled as we left the theater. "They did not invent culture. Turkey was civilized thousands of years before Greece."

"Dad, it's Hollywood," Kenan told him.

"At least they didn't cast a white guy as Xerxes," I offered. "But Artemisia, ugh."

"What? She's hot in that goth girl way," Kenan said.

I spread my hands in helplessness. Where to start? I mean, Artemisia had been the queen of a city and a naval commander— I'm pretty sure she didn't look like the skinniest girls from my college. She'd have had muscles same as the guys.

But that's not what Hollywood demanded. They manufactured cut, muscled bodies to symbolize the pinnacle of manhood. And to contrast, we were supposed to believe that the super skinny bodies were ideal women. That's how you could tell them apart, right? Men were hunks of muscle and women were willowy boob-trees.

These actors all shaped their bodies to fit a cultural ideal. Like the way Dad wanted to alter mine with surgery. Their bodies reinforced the ideal that shaped them.

Like Man and Woman were gods and all the people had to worship at their perfect forms. Do whatever it took to look like one or the other.

And how weird was it that they called a person with low body fat and lots of muscles "cut?" Like they'd done surgery on themselves, maybe cut away parts of themselves.

It made me want to be a guy so I could not be that. So I could put a big signpost in the country of masculinity that said "Here be dragons."

CHAPTER TWENTY-FIVE

Tucker

In my right hand, the notecards for the presentation to Prof. Callander's class. On my left palm, key points written in permanent ink in case I fumbled the notecards. Ella had picked out a shirt for me to wear. It was very blue. I felt phony in this bright shirt and my least-worn jeans.

Sitting in front of the class while Prof. Callander introduced me, the rows of seats seemed to stretch infinitely high. I re-read the writing on my palm so I wouldn't clench my fist and sweat on the notes.

When I got up to talk, I forgot everything. Ella had warned me that could happen. I read words off the cards. My brain slowly figured out what we were doing. The first few presentation slides covered terminology, so they were easy.

After three slides, I glanced up. Half the students sat forward in their seats, curious. A few looked at their books. One was staring around glazed. I wanted all of them focused and listening. I got into the words, let them flow. I felt out of body. The words talked and my body moved while I directed the stream of words one way or another.

I told them about the slur spray-painted on my dorm room door, about the names I was called. I told them about getting harassed in the women's locker room and then—after one girl called her boyfriend—getting jumped and beaten up outside the gym. And I told them how I'd had my pepper spray out, managed to spray both guys in the face and get them kicked out of school.

When I'd practiced this, twenty minutes seemed like forever. Now I got to the end of it really fast. Students clapped and Prof. Callander asked if there were questions.

"How scary was it when those guys attacked you?" one student asked.

"The most scared I've been in life," I said. "But that helped. All the adrenaline kept me focused on finding the pepper spray and getting out of there."

Under my answer was another set of words. The story about what happened weeks later. About how I should have been scared when I was with Lindy, but I wasn't because I thought I knew her.

I took another question, pointing to a girl sitting near the front.

"Okay this isn't going to come out right," she said. "But you're really a girl, I mean, you were in the women's locker room but you're really a woman. And I get if someone's had surgery, she's really a woman too, but what if, like, she…er, um, that person has a penis? That's not okay in the women's locker room."

Prof. Callander said, "We associate penises with maleness, but that's not always the case. There are other physical factors that we don't associate with maleness but that would have health benefits if we did. For example, heart disease can be different in men and women, but culturally we spend very little time talking about that. If a woman with a penis goes into a locker room or public bathroom, what would be the issue?"

"I don't want to see a penis in the locker room," the questioner admitted.

The girl next to her rolled her eyes, "For real? You see one in your bed all the time. Who cares? Like you're staring at everyone's business in the locker room anyway?"

A wave of laughter went through the class. A guy raised his hand slowly and Prof. Callander nodded to him.

"Hasn't testosterone been linked with more violent behavior? And we could assume that a person with a penis is likely to be producing testosterone, so aren't women safer without that? Just last week," he paused and flipped through his notebook, "I can't find the number but overwhelmingly rapists are men."

I should've been able to talk, but I couldn't. My face burned. I turned away to sip from the water bottle by the podium. The words were huge in my mind: some women are rapists too. Billboard-sized. I couldn't say them.

I could stand in front of a class and talk insightfully about getting beat up for being perceived trans, but I could not say a single word about being raped by a woman. Not one word.

"We have a whole section next week examining hormones and behavior in depth, as well as how we assign sex and what we expect because of it. Let's address this question next week." Prof. Callander pushed up from where she'd been leaning against her desk and asked, "What about experiences like Tucker's? Have any of you been discriminated against because of perceived or mistaken identity?"

"People always ask if I'm Mexican or Puerto Rican," one student said. "And I'm Korean."

"I got beat up a lot in junior high school for looking like a girl," said a very muscular guy with a buzz cut.

"I started getting hit on when I was nine because I was tall and people thought I was older," a lanky girl said.

"That's nothing," a girl near her said. "In middle school two guys made me blow them because all the boys said I was a slut. That counts, doesn't it?"

The air in the room got super heavy. Or maybe it was the air in my chest.

"Absolutely," Prof. Callander said. "What helped you move forward from that?"

"This counselor found me a support group for survivors of rape and sexual assault. Hearing the other women talk about what guys had done to them really helped me see that it wasn't my fault and I wasn't alone."

More talking happened after that, but I didn't hear it. My ears roared from the inside. I sat against the desk like Prof. Callander had because my legs were going soft.

This student had been assaulted and she talked to someone and they got her help, just like that. She had a whole supportive band of people with similar experiences to help her get through it. I had none of that.

I had hard stares, confusion, fear, judgment.

I had Bailey saying "I'll fucking kill her" when I needed her to tell me she still loved me, that I was a good person, that she'd help me get okay again.

But I also had Nico saying "maybe is always no" and stopping when I got scared. And I'd screwed that up.

And I had Ella who at least understood what it felt like when your body wasn't your own.

Like now, my body cold and shaking inside. My world narrowing to the points of my breathing, staying upright, not letting the waves of dread and fear show.

The class was leaving. Some stopped to tell me they'd liked the presentation and I went through the motions. As the last students headed for the door, Prof. Callander asked, "Do you have a few minutes to debrief?"

I got my eyes to focus on her but the words were a mess inside me. I must've looked bad because she asked, "Tucker, are you okay?"

I shook my head. "I have to go. I remembered…something. Tomorrow okay?"

"One o'clock?"

I nodded and went for the door. I had my phone out, walking and texting Ella: *my room now?!!!*

On my way, she replied.

I sprinted across the quad and ran up the stairs because I couldn't handle being in the elevator with anyone. And I'd started crying somewhere on the way.

I threw my bag on the bed, continued across the room. I wanted to pace but my legs were shaking. I pressed my hands on the dresser, holding myself up.

I went hand over hand, like a very drunk, very dizzy person, finding my way more by touch than sight from the dresser to the wall. I moved across the closet and more wall to the door between my room and the bathroom I shared with Ella. I unlocked it.

Then I crawled onto my bed, put my back to the wall and pulled my knees up. When Ella knocked, I didn't lift my head from my knees, just said, "It's open."

The door clicked open and shut. Soft steps and the creak of Ella sitting in my desk chair.

"Tucker?"

Head still down, I said, "I need help. I can't do this. I'm cold and hot and shaking and I can't breathe and I can't stop crying. And there's no one…this girl in the class had a support group and there isn't anyone…No one's going to help me. But you said…you keep saying I could get help."

"You can," she said. "There are people who went through what you did. I found some articles online when you're ready."

"How do I stop feeling like this?"

"Can you breathe more slowly?" she asked.

"Maybe."

"Come over here?"

I forced myself off the bed—made myself walk to the side of the desk. My legs that had been feeling like helium balloons were filling up with lead.

"What's this?" She touched the mass of wires affixed to a light and speaker at the edge of my desk.

"Vortex manipulator," I mumbled.

"How does it work?"

I cradled it in my palm. I'd put it back together after many failed attempts to get the light to connect to the buttons. I had it mostly working. I pushed a button and the blue light went on.

I knew what she was doing. And it was good. Nothing hard, only talk about something I know. I traced the metal edges with my finger.

"First button turns the light on, second turns it off," I told her. "I'm working on this last button making a sound come out of the speaker."

"Was it hard?"

"Just figuring out how to split the positive and negative wires to the two buttons, hadn't done that before."

"Show me."

I tipped it toward her and pointed to the circuit from the buttons to the power supply and light.

"I know what you're doing," I told her. "And it's working. What next?"

"You sit on the bed and fiddle with that while I call a place that does walk-in counseling and isn't going to be surprised by same-sex partner rape."

I flinched at the words, but took the vortex manipulator to the bed with my tiny screwdriver. "You think that exists?"

"I know it does," she said. "I called a few hotlines and an anti-violence project until I found someone who could recommend a place. But I thought if I said it too soon you'd brush me off."

"It's like you know me. You've been trying to tell me, I get it."

She smiled and turned the chair half away from me. I focused on the wires going from the speaker to the power and the third button. I'd been thinking I had them wired backwards. Been meaning to switch them, but I got caught up in my presentation prep.

Ella called one number, asked a bunch of questions with phrases ranging from "same-sex partner rape" to "under-insured." When she hung up, she asked, "I want to make you an appointment, can I?"

"No car," I said.

"And you don't want to ask Bailey?"

I shook my head.

She sighed and touched a number on her phone. "Cal, hi, can Tucker borrow your car for a really important errand in another town?…More important than that…Yeah. I wouldn't be asking otherwise. Okay, thanks. I'll text you in a bit and let you know when. You're a hero."

She set the phone down on her leg and regarded me. "There, you have a car, now I'm going to call and get you an appointment. Do you want me to come with you?"

I stared at the tangle of wires in my lap. "Maybe," I admitted.

"Done."

I didn't want to listen to the next call and I hung on every word.

Ella said, "I have a friend, lesbian, who was raped by her ex-girlfriend and she's having trauma reactions she doesn't know how to deal with. Do you have someone who could help her?" After that it was a lot of "oh great" and "yes, when?"

She ended the call and said, "Thursday, four p.m. We'll have to leave here around three. Okay?"

"Thanks," I mumbled.

The bed shifted as she sat next to me. "Thanks for letting me help. It's tough to watch you walking around like you're all shattered glass. This can be a lot better."

I grunted a combination of agreement and doubt.

She leaned against my shoulder and I leaned back into her. We sat like that, talking about things we'd already said so many times before, until my stomach growled. Then she laughed and went to get us food like everything was normal.

* * *

Ella drove because I was feeling shaky. Counseling wasn't a thing anyone in my family did. Shit happened and you got over it, went on. Check another family first off the list: being queer, college, therapy.

The waiting room was beigely bland, but the woman behind the front desk had hot pink pigtails. I relaxed a fraction. Ella introduced us and took a clipboard with paperwork. I let her draw me over to a waiting area with an overstuffed blue-gray couch and two skinny wooden chairs. A sleek black coffee table clashed with the blond wood of the chairs and the cherry wood that curled up the couch arms.

Ella held the clipboard out to me. I couldn't make myself sit down, but I stood against the wall and wrote on the sheet.

The door opened and a woman said, "Jess? Come on back."

She was broad-hipped in dark slacks and a button-down. Tan skin, short spikey brown hair. I glanced from the door in to the door out. I wanted to leave. Maybe I should have gotten a guy therapist. Would he give me the "um…what?" look? At least with a guy I wouldn't be worried that he thought I was a bad lesbian. I mean astoundingly bad. Bad enough to mess up the whole system.

I could make some shit up. I didn't have to tell her.

I followed her into a room with five random chairs. I couldn't tell which one was hers, so I went over to the window.

"I'm Bridget," she said and sat in the official rolling chair. Of course that was hers. I should've known that.

"Tucker," I told her. "I mean, Jess is my first name, but everyone calls me Tucker."

"Have you been in therapy before? Do you have any questions for me?"

"Haven't," I said. "What do I do?"

"You can talk if you want. Or we can sit, do some deep breathing, or not. Do you want to tell me what brought you in here?"

I didn't, but that seemed stupid, having driven all this way. And I was half mad about her asking. Ella had said when she called in what the deal was, but this woman was asking like she didn't know. Maybe they hadn't passed the information on to her so she wouldn't be biased. It wasn't like I knew how therapy was supposed to work.

I couldn't right out say to a stranger what had happened to me, so I went for what I could say, "I'm trying to have this relationship but I keep messing it up."

Outside the window there was a lake with people walking around it and one person running.

"Trying?" she asked.

I shook my head.

"Tucker, do you want to sit down?"

"Am I supposed to?"

"Do you feel better when you're moving?" she asked. "We could go outside and walk."

"You can do that in therapy?"

"Sometimes they let me get away with it," she said.

"Yeah, okay."

We passed through the waiting room where Ella was reading and Bridget announced we were taking a walk. We went around the building and down the path to the lake. There were two joggers now and one walker.

"I can't guarantee confidentiality as well out here," she said. "But you say as much as you're comfortable with."

We got about a quarter of the way around the lake and some words came to me. "It's not about coming out," I said. "Nothing like that. I like being a dyke. I've been out for a few years. And I've had relationships before. Can I tell you about coming out and stuff anyway?"

"Please do," she said.

We walked and I told her about coming out a few years ago and a little about meeting Lindy.

"It was a really bad breakup. And I like this other person but I feel like...I don't know. I screwed it up. This person has intersex traits and I said some stupid things, not to yo, but in front of yo."

Then I had to explain all about Nico and about Summer and by the time I was done we'd made it back to the clinic.

And I hadn't told her. But I felt better anyway.

"I guess I have to come back," I said. "How long does this take?"

"Some people come a few times for help with a specific issue and others come regularly for months or years because it helps them be more effective in their daily lives. Do you want to make an appointment?"

Did I want to? No. But Ella was out there in the waiting room and I knew I needed the help.

"Next week this time?"

"I'll see you then."

Ella didn't ask, but in the middle of the drive back I said, "Thanks for this."

A tiny smile danced across her mouth. "I want my Tucker back."

"Yeah, me too."

I wanted so much back the way it had been, but I wasn't sure I'd get it.

CHAPTER TWENTY-SIX

Nico

Sunday morning I went fishing with Dad. We were out of the house at dawn, which made me feel backwards. Usually if I saw the sunrise, I was on my way in.

We picked up coffee and rolls on the way to a lake with a short beach. Dad got his fishing pole set up and handed it to me. "You remember what to do?"

"Toss it in the water and wait?"

"Over there," he said. "Far out as you can."

I drew the rod back and cast side arm, spooling it out over the water, watching the bait plunk under the surface. The bobber floated happily.

"Leave it or tug it a bit?" I asked. Fishing excursions from a decade ago were starting to come back to me.

"Wait a bit and then small tugs so they think it's alive."

I sat cross-legged on the ground, gripping the pole with one hand, my coffee with the other. Dad sat on a folding chair sewing a split seam on his favorite jacket. I watched his strong fingers maneuver the thin needle through the fabric with grace.

He could construct buildings and down a monstrous steak in no time, but he could also cook and sew. As male role models went, he was pretty good.

We spent the first hour in silence. Me holding the pole over the water and gulping coffee. Him sewing and sorting his lures.

"What if I don't like one better, man or woman?" I asked.

"Then I failed," he said with a long sigh.

"Um, how?"

"I was supposed to teach you how to be a man."

"You've got Kenan for that."

"Two sons," he said. "I have two sons."

"You really don't."

"If I'd fought harder, if I'd been able to take you back from your mother, you wouldn't be like this."

I stared at the red and white bobber on the gray surface of the water. Grow up in California as a guy? I'd probably still be having surgeries on my junk to "fix" it. Wouldn't have met Tucker or Ella and gotten my heart broken. Wouldn't have the family I did now—that I loved.

"I'm sorry that I let you go," he said. "I am sorry for all the time I've missed with you."

I'd needed to hear that so much ten years ago, even five. Now my twinge of hope was overshadowed by so much grief and anger. I wanted to pretend I had a regular dad and everything was okay. If I didn't have Tucker, I needed something else to hold onto.

But I couldn't say nothing. "Then why are you driving me away with this lawsuit?"

"Nico, soon you'll go in for a surgery you should have had many years ago—to remove this potential cancer. What if it had been worse? Your mother, your doctor, let you ignore the risks—"

"No they didn't," I cut in. "We managed the risk. I went for ultrasounds, that's why we caught it. They talk to me, we decide things together. That's how it's supposed to be."

"I should have done better by you," he said. "I should have fought harder when you were young. I have always wanted you to grow up to be a better man than I've been. Or woman, if that's what you choose. My father taught me to be a man. And I failed you. Your confusion—it is *my* fault."

He held his hands palm up in his lap, staring at them, like he was supposed to shape me with them.

I swallowed hard and stared at the ripples in the water. Just a normal guy, hanging out with his dad, trying not to cry.

"I like how I am," I said.

"What about when you go into the world to be an adult, to have a career and a family, and then you discover how hard this life really is? When you want your life to be different, will it be too late to change?"

He had no idea how hard it had already been, how much harder it was with a parent fighting me every step of the way. He'd never seen places that welcomed me and people like me. He'd never been to the Noodle.

No way would he come to the cabaret. He wouldn't fit in at all. Not like Yai, who could be different from everyone there and still be comfortable.

"Do you want to see me dance?" I asked.

"Yes, very much."

I texted Sharani: *Is there a studio open? I want Dad to see me dance.*

She suggested a time that afternoon and added: *I'll be there the whole time.*

Thanks, I told her, more relieved than I could say.

We picked up Kenan from the apartment, went to brunch and then over to the Noodle. Sharani was waiting in the café. She looked very much like a woman with whom you did not fuck. She was in jeans and a loose shirt with a leather vest over it. She was taller than Dad and towered over Kenan.

I made introductions, ignoring Kenan's staring at her. We went up to studio two, which was big enough to set a few chairs in it. I jangled with nerves when I went to change. After I came back and started up the music, I moved and forgot everything else.

I danced through the piece I'd perform at the cabaret, wishing I also had the images to go with it.

They applauded and Kenan said, "Shit, dude, you're awesome." That was stupendous praise from him.

From Dad: "That was remarkable."

I chugged water and toweled the sweat off my face and hands. "It's what I'm doing for the cabaret in a few days. I'd invite you but it's not really your thing."

"How so?"

"All the performers are genderfluid or nonbinary," Sharani told him.

Kenan had returned to a game on his phone and without looking up he said, "Nonbinary means they don't have a gender, Dad. Not identifying as man or woman."

Not exactly, but I gave him points for that last part. I added, "Beyond the gender binary."

"Is that what you want?" Dad asked me.

"I don't know," I said.

He held up his hands and peered heavenward like he was calling for help, but he said, "Nehal, when I see you as a man, I see a beautiful, thoughtful man. And when you are a woman, you're a smart, powerful woman. I hope you'll settle on one of these."

You could've heard a jaw drop in the silence that followed.

Kenan broke it by saying, "If we're voting, I want my brother back so we can complain about girls together."

He was grinning but with a glint of truth in his eyes.

CHAPTER TWENTY-SEVEN

Tucker

For the next appointment, I borrowed Bailey's car and drove to the clinic alone. It looked like a small hurricane had been through the waiting room. There were magazines everywhere, broken pieces of wood and chair parts on the floor.

"I'm sorry," pink-haired girl said. "Don't mind the mess. I'll tell Bridget you're here."

Someone must've picked up one of the flimsy wooden chairs and slammed it down on its neighbor. The bottom chair wasn't in terrible shape, a loose arm hung to one side. The top chair had split along the back and one of the legs was off, another barely attached.

I lifted that splintered chair and set it on the carpet on its back. I put the detached leg next to where it would go and set the dowels of the back into their holes. I examined the bottom chair to see if the dowels could be used in the loose arm. One was splintered and I started working it free of its hole.

A door opened but no one called my name so I jiggled the dowel free. The arm could be glued back into place but it would be better if there was a new dowel.

The door opened and shut again. Bridget bent her long legs and sat on the carpet next to me. She offered me a bottle of wood glue. I held out my hand and she put the glue bottle in it.

"You have a dowel too?" I asked.

"Afraid not," she said. "Laney, do we have dowels?"

Pink-haired Laney said, "Maybe in the back supply room. I'll check if you'll watch the phone."

"Will do," Bridget told her.

The chair back was loose from one side but the dowels were okay so I poured glue into the holes and set it back together. I was holding it, waiting for the glue to set, but Bridget said, "I could do that."

While she held the drying back of the chair, I contemplated the damage to the leg.

"It's not going to be right," I said. "Might not hold a person if we glue it."

"I've been searching for something for my office to put the plants under the window. I was already planning to sneak one of these chairs away when Laney wasn't looking. Would it hold a few pots?"

"Sure," I said.

"I'll take it."

I got the glue on the cracked leg and fit it into place.

Laney came back while we were sitting there holding the chair together and said she hadn't found a dowel—after having to look up "dowel" on her phone because she didn't even know what that was. I had Bridget switch from holding the back to holding the leg and addressed the other leg, the one that was askew but not broken. I squeezed a bit of glue into the gap between leg and seat and gently shimmied it back true.

"Let's take this into my office," Bridget said.

She got up, holding the chair so that she supported its glued legs and nodded toward the door. Laney opened the locked door from the waiting room to the back and I pushed wide the half-open door to Bridget's office. She carried the chair to the window and paused.

"Can I set it on its legs?" she asked.

"Yeah, you should. The weight of the chair will hold it while it finishes drying. Here, let me see."

I crouched in front of it as she set it down and made sure the legs were sitting right in the seat. I put my hand on the seat and pressed down gently. It might never hold a person, but at least it wasn't wobbly and crooked. A few plants would be perfect.

"We should put a little weight on it," I said.

Bridget got two half-dead plants from a short bookshelf and handed them to me. I put them in the middle of the seat and turned their few green leaves toward the sun.

"Thank you," Bridget said.

I shrugged and straightened up so I could stare out the window at the lake. Behind me, Bridget closed the door.

"I'm here because of my ex-girlfriend," I told her. "We were breaking up. I thought she wanted to talk. Maybe she did, at first, I don't know. I wanted to leave, but she wanted me to stay. She pushed herself on me and—I didn't want to, I told her I didn't—she raped me."

I held my breath. Bridget didn't say anything.

I turned around. She faced me, eyes soft with listening. She nodded once. I stared at her boots, at the carpet, at my boots.

"I freak out. I mean, I panic, that's what Ella would say. I don't want to. I was in bed with Nico and I panicked. I gave a presentation to a class, not even about that, and the panic was there. I don't want this shit in my life. I don't want it in my bed. I get this other feeling too, like I'm covered in grime, filth, like it's inside my skin. I don't want to feel that either. I don't want to be like this. I don't know what to do."

"Thank you for telling me," she said and sat down.

I figured what the hell and picked a random chair.

"Are you going to say I'm brave and all that shit?" I asked.

"Do you think you're brave?"

"Nothing about this feels brave. I don't even care. I want to be strong again. I used to be strong. Now I get shaky and I cry and I feel like I'm going to puke. I hate it. It was bad enough… Lindy and…God, I loved her. Fuck. How could she do that to me?"

"Why do you think she did it?" Bridget asked.

I didn't want to think about it. I wanted her to give me an answer. Something quick and easy that made the pain end. But she sat there like we had all afternoon.

"I was leaving. She wanted to stop me," I said. The words came out in ragged clumps. "The girl before me, the one she was dating, Lindy used to complain about how flighty she was, that Lindy had to calm her down all the time. I didn't know that meant she was hitting her. I think, if I asked her about me, about why, she'd give some awful justification like that. That she had to show me…"

I shook my head. Couldn't talk. Balled tissues in my fist and wiped at the tears that kept coming.

"Doesn't matter what she'd say," I said. "She was trying to control me. Like she owned me, like she could do whatever she wanted. Trying to beat me down inside so I'd stay."

"But you didn't," Bridget said.

"Yeah, but I thought she loved me. How could I be so stupid?"

"Would you be that hard on anyone else? If there was another girl in this room who'd been through a similar experience, if she called herself stupid, what would you say to her?"

"Oh, fuck your bullshit questions. I don't know anyone else this has happened to. Just me because I'm the stupid shit who loved someone who fucking raped me."

"There are thousands of women who have had similar experiences to yours," she said.

I was going to argue, but Ella had said she'd found resources online. I hadn't looked. I was afraid I wouldn't find anything. And I was afraid I would. Afraid I'd have to look at it and all the panic and pain would be right there.

I breathed out, let my head hang forward, brushed away more of the tears. I said, "I'd tell her people aren't all good or all bad. You can love someone because of the good in them for a while and maybe not see the bad. Especially if they're working at hiding it from you, if they act like they love you too. I'd tell her it wasn't her fault."

Bridget let me cry. Held out the box of tissues when mine got all soaked.

"How do I stop feeling so bad all the time?" I asked.

"Let's make a plan for that. How was your anxiety level with Nico when you panicked—on a scale from one to ten?"

"Like a seven. But the week before with Quin it was a nine and I was afraid it was going to be like that again."

"Can you stop at five?" she asked. "Are there actions that don't push your anxiety level higher?"

"Yeah, making out was great…oh, you mean *really* stop at five?"

I couldn't imagine wanting to stop that night in the hotel, except for the fear and hurting Nico. How did a person do that? Any time action stopped in the past it was the other person stopping.

Bridget had both feet on the floor, hands resting on the arms of her chair, no clipboard or notebook or anything. I thought therapists always had those. But she was just sitting, open and relaxed. I uncrossed my arms and tried to breathe more evenly.

"Does Nico know what happened?" she asked. "Can you ask to keep things at a level where you're never above a five?"

"Yeah, I told Nico what happened. But I want to have sex."

"Stopping at five is for now," she said.

"Oh. I ask Nico—assuming yo will even talk to me—to keep it where I feel five or less or whatever?"

"Whatever?" She repeated the word with curiosity, like it was a whole bunch of questions at once.

I turned enough to see the broken chair by the window and said, "I feel messed up. I feel like Nico shouldn't have to deal with all that."

"What if Nico was asking you to keep the action at a five or lower because Nico was afraid?"

I didn't have to think about that. "No problem. Oh shit, yeah. I see what you did there."

She grinned at me with a flash of mischief that made me like her more.

She said, "What you experienced is stored in your body as a traumatic memory. We don't remember trauma the way we remember ordinary events. It's not linear. That's why it feels like parts of it keep coming back at you. It's what we call a trigger. Your body is trying to protect you from something like that happening again."

"How do we tell my body it's not going to?"

"You practice feeling safe. I'd like to teach you a breathing exercise and one or two other ways to bring yourself into the present moment. You can try them and see what works best for you."

"I'm going to feel stupid doing them," I told her.

"As long as you're feeling self-conscious in the present, not the past, you're in good shape."

Bridget had me breathe with a focus on exhaling, slowly, most of the air in my lungs. She had me pay attention to the sensations in my body. Feel my body and my feet on the ground. Tune in to my heart beating. Put a hand on my stomach if I felt weird or nauseous. And she wanted me to do this self-hugging, hand-squeezing thing that seemed ridiculous, but did make me feel better.

For the first time in months I had a way to manage the damage in me. I wished I'd had that before the convention and freaking out with Nico. Even if I couldn't figure out how to get us back the way we were, I had to find a way to apologize.

* * *

On the drive back to school, it dawned on me that I knew people who were smart about having a relationship with gender complexity in it. I'd met Emily and Claire two years ago at a convention, not the kind with costumes, the kind with an academic track that I was avoiding.

Emily had come out as trans and started her transition while dating Claire in high school. From Claire's perspective, her boyfriend turned into her girlfriend. They'd stayed together until they went to college in different cities. After a few years apart, Claire asked Emily out again and now they lived together.

I video-called them.

"Tucker," Claire answered, cheerfully peering into the screen. Black hair was coming out of a messy bun, wisping around her face. "I thought you might be too busy to call. That was a great pic you sent. Is that Nico?"

I had to remember all the way back to the convention weeks ago. I'd sent her the photo of me and Nico in our Battlestar flight suits. Before all the stupid stuff. I propped my phone on my desk and rested my head in my hands while I talked. Thinking about Nico made my head a lot heavier.

"Yeah, that's Nico in costume."

"Are you an item now?" she asked.

"That's what I'm calling about. What do you do if you like someone but maybe their body isn't…you know, what you expect?"

Her forehead creased, mouth a thoughtful frown. "Tucker, when you love someone they become beautiful to you."

"Seriously?"

"Every year I'm with Emily, she's more beautiful. You don't love someone because they're beautiful, loving them is what makes them beautiful to you."

She turned away from the screen and called, "Isn't that right?"

Emily's voice came from across the room. "You were always beautiful."

"You're not helping," Claire told her. "Come say hi to Tucker."

A chair leg scraped on wood and then Emily's voice sounded closer to the phone. "She's right," Emily said. Her face appeared in the screen as she leaned over Claire's shoulder. Brown hair curled to her shoulders, wild and loose.

Emily said, "Looking at Claire makes me happy even more than back when we were in high school. I think it's the weight of all the good times together and deeply knowing each other."

I had to groan. "Ugh, you two are so sappy."

A knock on my door and Ella's voice called, "Hey, is that Emily?"

I opened the door. Ella slipped past me and stole my desk chair. "Hey you two, how cold is it up there?"

"Minnesota cold," Emily said. "So we're fine and you'd be a block of ice."

I shifted from foot to foot behind Ella. Harder to tell them the story of what I'd said in front of Nico now that Ella was here. I let them go through the basic catching up while I tried to figure out what to say.

"Tucker, you're pacing," Claire said.

I stopped in the middle of walking back from my dresser. I hadn't realized I was moving that much.

"You want to tell them what happened?" I asked Ella.

"Oh, no way, this is all you," she said and got up from the chair.

I dropped into it and made my stammering, halting way through the events from the convention to my stupid mouth in the student union. I managed not to out Nico. I didn't have any right to.

In the middle, Claire seemed perplexed. She opened her mouth and asked, "How—?" but Emily touched her shoulder and said, "We get it."

"Yeah," Claire agreed and waved for me to continue.

At the end I asked, "How do I fix it?" looking from the screen to Ella so she'd know she wasn't off the hook for answering.

"I don't know," Ella said.

"You have to apologize," Claire insisted, leaning close to the screen.

"Hon, Nico said not to call," Emily reminded Claire. "That makes it quite a bit harder."

"Oh, she can figure it out. Our Tucker's smart. Phone's not the only way to communicate." Claire turned back to the screen, staring at me hard. "But don't go off half-cocked. Take your time and think about this. What would show Nico that you get it?"

I laughed bitterly. "I could run naked down the street."

"I am not advocating public nudity," Claire said. "Not much at least. But that's a start, being willing to be awkward. You're on the right track."

Ella was staring at the Evolution of Life poster that she'd hung at the start of the year when the room was empty. I'd never taken it down because it reminded me of her. She raised a finger and traced a curve that ended in the mammals.

"We've got to go," I said. "Thanks a ton."

"Keep us updated and take care of yourself," Claire said.

Emily put her arms around Claire's shoulder and added, "Hugs."

Turning the chair away from the desk, I asked Ella, "What are you thinking?"

Still facing the poster, she said, "Can you imagine what it's like to want someone and when you take off your pants they say—this person who was totally into you a minute ago—'what the fuck is that?' and laugh at you?"

I imagined Quin saying that when we'd been in bed. A shudder went the length of my spine. Being naked in front of someone already felt much more vulnerable to me than it used to. How would I feel to always be a hundred times more vulnerable? I crossed my legs and leaned forward.

Had that happened to Nico? For sure it had happened to someone Ella and Nico knew. How many people had to have amazingly careful conversations with prospective partners or chance hearing awful words at their most vulnerable?

I leaned an elbow on my knee and put my face in my hand. How betrayed did Nico feel when I said "fuck no" about dating a guy?

"What I said in the Union, I didn't mean it like that, can you tell Nico? It was all Summer trying to get at me."

"And your pride," Ella said.

I raised my face. She was watching me, arms folded.

She said, "You're very proud about being a lesbian, and that's great, and Summer went after your identity. I get that. But you know that's not what Nico heard."

"Because sometimes Nico is a guy too, right?"

"I think inside Nico's always both. But walking around in the world, that gets pretty exhausting to explain. Sometimes Nico plays boy or girl so that it's all easier for a while—or at least easier on the outside. And doing it with cosplay, with characters, that's how Nico says, 'Hey, I'm pretending, don't think this is the real me.'"

What did it feel like to always be both in a world that split male and female apart so consistently and harshly? I might be dykey and walk around tough and act like a guy in some ways, but I never wanted to be one. I knew I wasn't.

Ella held up a picture of Nico on her phone: yos hair gelled forward in the front, as much like spikey bangs as curly hair could be; the long, blue military coat I'd seen in the café; a pressed blue oxford shirt and suspenders showing under one side of the coat. Nico was smirking and tensing the muscle of yos jaw to make it more square.

"That's the full Jack Harkness outfit," Ella said.

I scrutinized the bold masculinity of it. I compared it to the image in my mind of Nico as Athena—hard to believe they were the same person. I tried to upload this new image to my mind, this aspect of Nico.

"If you want to be with Nico, you have to like all of this," Ella said.

"I think I do. But I'm not bi. I'm not attracted to guys at all."

"Then maybe you have to change your definition of lesbian," she said.

How? By definition that was women with women, right? Except I'd learned that for some cisgender women, that meant no trans women, only cis women with each other, and that wasn't my definition. Could I keep expanding it? Could it include people who were part woman?

"Part" didn't sound right. Maybe people who were women but also men? Or nonbinary people who had woman in their repertoire?

If I did end up fixing this and dating Nico, I didn't care what people called me as long as it wasn't misleading or insulting. The real thing wasn't the labels. I might be proud about being a lesbian, but hey I'd be proud about being any kind of queer.

The thing was: what if below the belt Nico had a penis and balls and the whole kit? I felt like a jerk to be thinking about stuff Nico hadn't chosen to share with me. But once I started, I couldn't stop thinking about it. I got up and paced, which in a small dorm room didn't help much. Ella stayed near the poster, arms folded, watching me.

If Nico had a penis, would I want to touch it? That night in the hotel when we were making out, if Nico had let me into yos pants and it was a penis down there, would I have felt turned off cold?

How shit would that have been for Nico to go from ultra-hot to nothing? No wonder yo didn't want to go there.

My experience with penises was limited to exactly one that belonged to a guy I went to high school with. Curious, I offered to give him a hand job one day and of course he said yes. I was shocked about how soft it was. I mean the skin of it because as soon as he got it out and I started touching it, it was hard. But the way the soft skin moved over the hard interior was kind of amazing and I got what straight girls liked about that.

And yet, I felt nothing for him. Inside my head was like a scientist observing an alien species. Afterward, when I was home thinking back on it, it felt gross. It was wrong for me.

Would I feel that way about Nico? I didn't think so. I'd never been attracted to that guy in high school and I wanted to be with Nico more than I'd ever wanted to be with anyone.

Assuming that at some point I could even have sex again.

I started laughing, a dry, barking sound, and had to go drink out of the bathroom faucet. Catching myself in the mirror, I flashed to Nico as Athena in the women's bathroom putting on mascara, yos shoulders broad and strong under the flight suit, yos body masculine and feminine and graceful.

Nico did cosplay to show that all yos gender was performance, maybe to remind us that all gender itself was performance. But that's not all cosplay could do. Claire had suggested I do something awkward. I felt darned awkward in costumes.

I asked Ella, "Do you think Shen would help me with some cosplay?"

"He will levitate with joy. I'll text him. What do you have in mind?"

"Showing Nico that yo's not the only one who can communicate through costumes."

She stared at me and a smile pried up the corners of her mouth. "You might be on to something," she said.

CHAPTER TWENTY-EIGHT

Tucker

The next afternoon I got started on the costume for Nico. I walked over to the Math & Science dorm where Shen and his cousin Johnny lived. Last semester they went everywhere together, but now that Shen and Ella were intensely dating, I hadn't seen Johnny around much. I met them in the gaming common room.

"What if someone likes cosplay and I need to dress up in something complementary—can you help me out?" I asked them.

"Give us more to go on," Johnny said. "Saying someone likes cosplay is like saying someone likes television."

"Um, *Battlestar Galactica* and…" I paused trying to remember the names of the other stuff Nico liked.

"Is this for Nico?" Shen asked.

I nodded.

He thought for a while and he and Johnny said a bunch things to each other that I didn't follow. I heard Athena and *Battlestar Galactica*, plus Captain Jack Harkness and *Torchwood*.

Finally Shen turned back to me and said, "Ianto Jones."

"I don't know what that is but can you help me make one?"

Shen was more soft-spoken than Johnny, at least when they weren't gaming, but he laughed just as loud.

When they got done laughing, Johnny said, "I don't know. Ianto is kind of a wuss."

"On the first season. He improves," Shen told him. To me he said, "He's a character on *Torchwood*. He dates Jack Harkness."

"For real? Gay-dates him?"

"Yep," Johnny said. "He does other things too. I mean, he's part of the team."

"I don't know if you call it gay dating because Jack is bisexual," Shen added.

"But they kiss on screen?"

Shen nodded. I hugged him. He patted me on the back like he wasn't sure what to do, but he was chuckling.

"You're a genius!" I told him.

"He knows," Johnny said and slapped his shoulder. "Come on, we'll show you what Ianto looks like."

I followed them to their dorm room. On Shen's laptop, they called up images of a clean-shaven, baby-faced guy with a predilection for suits, ties and vests.

"We can get you the ID badge and tactical earpiece," Shen said. "Can you do the clothing and hair?"

"Sure can. Thanks a ton."

I lit out of there and over to my room where I called Bailey.

"Not again," she said.

"I don't need the car," I told her. "I need a haircut and dye. What's your day like tomorrow?"

"I can get you in. What do you have in mind?"

"Short and boyish. I'll show you a pic tomorrow."

"Jess, when are you going to let me do purple?"

"Next after this, I promise," I told her.

* * *

I met Bailey for dinner near campus and showed her a picture of Ianto. She drove me to her salon and did my hair like his: short, spikey in the front, and brown. She got creative and shaved the back closer than his hair, but it worked great.

"Why you want brown escapes me," she said around the clip she held in her teeth.

"I'm trying to get a date," I said.

"That's valid. Which girl? Hold still."

"The person you saw with the car. We had a…I said something wrong, this is the apology."

"Good luck. How's that therapy going?"

I'd set up to borrow her car for it again next week. "Actually helpful."

"Huh, who knew?"

"Yeah."

When I got back to my room, Ella's light was on. I tried on the purple shirt, dark gray vest and striped tie that I'd picked up from a secondhand store. Then I texted Shen and asked when he could bring the other stuff. He was heading over to Ella's in a few and said he'd swing by.

When he saw the outfit so far, he nodded. "Good color on the shirt. Here's your badge and earpiece."

The laminated plastic badge said: "Torchwood Institute, Ianto Jones, General Support." The earpiece looked awesomely science fictiony.

"Where'd you get these?" I asked.

"I made the badge. We have a laminator just for such emergencies. The earpiece was from a costume Johnny had a few years back."

He helped me get the earpiece in place and texted Ella to come across from her room. She opened the bathroom door and leaned in.

"Why is my boyfriend texting me from *your* room?" she asked. And then in a much higher pitched tone, "Oh my God, your hair."

"I'm Ianto Jones," I said.

"Who?"

I was glad that she didn't know who he was either. Hanging around so many geeks was making me feel culturally out of step.

"He's the boyfriend of Captain Jack Harkness," I told her.

Her head cocked to one side and she got this huge grin on her face. "Being vulnerable too so Nico sees it's not one-sided. Tucker, that's really clever."

"It was Shen's idea. At least the Ianto part."

She turned to Shen who flashed her a smile that got bigger the longer he looked at her.

"If this doesn't work, I'm going Klingon next," I told Ella. "Do you think it will work?"

"I'd go out with you," she replied. But then she took Shen's arm and pulled him through to her room.

"Sweet," I said in my empty room. I took off the pieces of the Ianto costume. When could I use it? And how?

CHAPTER TWENTY-NINE

Nico

Ella came down on Thursday with Shen to have a long weekend in the city. My cabaret performance was Saturday night. She and Shen were staying over at her place, but she left him at the house and came out to dinner alone so we could talk.

Walking to the restaurant from my car, I caught our reflection in the window. A flash of bitterness rose in me. Ella was pretty, petite, her fine, blond hair caught up on one side with a cute barrette. I was in another crisp button-down shirt, khakis and suspenders. Curls oiled tight to my head, my jaw more square from the anger I'd been carrying around.

We looked like the perfect heteronormative pair. We looked the way Ella had wanted us to be when we were dating.

I picked a chair with its back to the window so I wouldn't have to see my reflection behind her. The server brought breadsticks as we went through the basics of what we'd been up to.

Me: dancing, Dad, destroying the patriarchy from the inside, pending surgery, deconstructing gender.

Ella: Shen, Shen, Shen, biology class, Shen.

When I got sick of the romance, I made a circle with one hand and a Vulcan symbol with the other. I bumped them together and asked, "Are you two still living long and prospering?"

She was used to me pantomiming sex with a variety of weird hand signs and got the idea right away. She put her hands over mine, pushing them down to the table.

"Cut it out," she said.

"But it's good, right?"

"Yes, it's super good. Listen, Tucker wants to apologize to you."

My heart jumped at the mention of her name. I hated that. I tore a breadstick in half and then in half again. Ella pulled the fluffy middle out of my fingers.

"You know she was reacting to Summer," Ella said. "Summer set her up because she's pissed at Tucker."

"Why?"

"Apparently Women's and Gender Studies is in love with Tucker and Summer feels like she stole her spot," Ella said. "And she didn't mean for all that to happen in the Union like it did. She was just jabbing at Tucker. I think even Summer feels awful about you getting caught in it."

"Oh." I got back to the core problem. "Yeah, but Tucker said 'disgusting.' About me."

"She said it about an idea. She didn't mean *you*."

I tore another breadstick in half. Put a bite in my mouth and chewed and swallowed before replying.

"What would you have done if you came out to Shen and he called you disgusting? Or not even you? What if he called the idea of trans women disgusting?"

She sighed. "You know what I'd have done. I'd have cried for weeks. And then I'd get someone else to talk to him because I'd be too chicken to do it."

I waved the torn half breadstick at her. "And you're supposed to be that someone else in my situation with Tucker?"

"I could be. If you want that. Nico, she really likes you and she's great like ninety-nine percent of the time. Plus, with everything, she's so off balance. I don't want to see you two fall apart over something Summer did."

Fall apart? We'd hardly been together. We'd barely kissed at Cal's before she panicked. And then I'd blocked her on my phone for weeks, which hadn't been at all fair to her. Despite that, she drove down right away when she heard about the surgery. She came to a convention and played Starbuck with me. Making out in the hotel, panicking in the middle, how hard that had to be for her.

What she'd said in the Union hurt deep, but she was struggling too, confused, broken apart. She hadn't been trying to hurt me. Maybe I wasn't being fair.

"Invite Tucker to the cabaret," I told Ella. "But I'm not promising anything."

She bounced in her seat and grinned at me, but got from my tone that we were done with this topic. She asked, "How are you feeling about the surgery?"

"Freaked the hell out," I said. "I'm afraid I'm going to have to write 'don't take the boobs' on my chest in permanent marker. *If* that's what I decide."

"Couldn't hurt. I'll do it for you if you want it more legible," Ella said. I fell in love again with her and her serious, lost elf face.

"I can't decide if I want them to do anything else," I admitted. "They could make me look all girl or more dude or whatever. But it feels like I'm giving in. To all the people who people who fought so kids with intersex traits wouldn't get a random gender…"

I had to stop and blink hard and try not to cry. I didn't tell her about the nightmares where I was walking through wards of hospital beds of mutilated bodies. Ella had heard this before, about all the babies who got assigned genders and operated on before they could even talk, about the people like Sharani who were forced into the gender their parents wanted them to be.

"You don't have to pick anything now," Ella said.

"But Tucker. If we don't…I'd like a relationship one of these days. What does it even feel like to know you're one gender?"

She stared into the distance, eyes unfocused. "I always assumed I'd grow up to be like my mother," she said. "I saw myself like her. When I was really young, people would say boys don't do that and I'd wonder why they were telling me. Mom was always going on about different world cultures, so I didn't get a concrete set of expectations about what I was supposed to be. I didn't freak out about it until Amy got her period. I realized that when I was her age, I'd be hairy and gross and smelly instead."

"Does Shen know that's how you think guys are?" I asked, smirking.

"That's different. It's cute when it's someone else."

"Even the gross parts?"

"Yes."

"I cannot understand how culturally you are considered less weird than me," I said.

"Who did you want to be when you grew up?" she asked.

I sighed. It wasn't a simple answer.

"When I was little? Both my parents. I look like both of them, why not be both of them? I liked how strong Dad was, how he could pick me up and carry me on his shoulders all day, and I liked how thoughtful mom was, how she knew about everything and how well she listened.

"I still want that. I want strong and sure and that protective thing—that thing you see when a big guy cradles a baby. And I want complex and intricate, deep and receptive. Like when you talk about biology and it's all these layers on layers of thought. And I want things that aren't gendered or are genderfluid. I want to be at home in the performative culture of the kathoey. I am at home there. Gender is so messy and complicated, like nature. Nature loves diversity. And I was, I got there, I found it the last few years…and now they're going to take it away."

Ella put her hands on mine and squeezed. She looked down, thoughtful.

Was she thinking about her body? Because she'd taken drugs to block puberty, she'd never be able to have kids. Trans women who transitioned later could freeze their sperm, but Ella never developed enough along the male pathway to produce viable sperm.

She got rid of what she didn't want, what wasn't her, but she had to give up so much to do it. Was I about to do the reverse of that? Give up what I wanted to become something I didn't?

CHAPTER THIRTY

Tucker

Ella texted that I was invited down to the cabaret on Saturday night. At least I'd get to see Nico dance. Cal was driving down with Tesh and her girlfriend Alisa. I got the last space in the car. Summer wasn't going anyway, but if she were, no way would she cram herself in a car with Tesh and Alisa.

I half paid attention to the conversation: Tesh obsessing about whether they should run for leadership of our LGBTQIA+ group when Cal's term ended. Mostly I worried about Nico. Ella had had dinner with Nico but she didn't say anything about it. The lack of detail was frightening—like she didn't have anything good to say.

We pulled into the parking lot of the Noodle with enough time to use the bathroom and buy tickets. The long performance room had a stage at one end and rows of theater seating—mismatched castoffs from old movie theaters. There was a sound booth in the back on a raised platform and space to stand around it.

Everyone else from Freytag went to sit with Ella and Shen, as close to the front as they could get. I found a seat in the back. The distance and my new hair color would hide me.

As my eyes adjusted to the diffuse light, my brain un-adjusted to the people I saw. Two tall women in dresses passed up the center aisle. As they moved by me, I figured they were drag queens, then that they were trans women, then that they were cis women dressed as drag queens, or trans women dressed as drag queens, and around in that loop of gender guessing again. I wanted an "off" switch. I thought that I was cooler than this, but every person I saw triggered an attempt to understand their gender, their body.

The announcer hopped onto the stage, opened the show and quickly made way for the first act. A trio of masculine-appearing people bounced and spilled onto the stage. One was tall, two stout. They danced and lip synced to a song I didn't know, stripping off their jackets so they were in sleeveless T-shirts, suspenders, men's trousers and heavy boots. They all had facial hair. On two of them it was hard to tell if it was makeup or hormones. The handlebar mustache on the third was hopefully fake.

Handlebar Mustache looked like a drag king to me, but the other two could have been trans men. They could've been cis men with wide hips. My brain kept switching its opinions.

My attractions shifted too. The tall one with the mustache was hot. She? They? My mind thought of her as a woman and I corrected myself to the neutral because I didn't know what gender they identified as. They had broad shoulders but also broad hips. I could imagine wanting to kiss that person, even with the mustache on. But the other two, even the one whose hips were wider than the tall dancer, seemed male to me. No interest there.

The three guys finished their song and bounded cheerfully off stage. The next performer came out from behind the curtains already singing, or lip syncing, to the music. She looked like a Disney princess with a long gown and a curtain of auburn hair half covering her face. After a minute of singing on stage, she descended the front steps and walked into the central aisle of the audience.

In fast, fluid moves, she unzipped the dress and stepped out of it. The wig came off, dropped onto the pile of the dress.

The performer, still singing, was now a slender boy in a tank top and bike shorts, with slicked-back brown hair. He turned back toward the stage and climbed onto it without breaking his lip syncing.

He brushed a hand through his hair, spiking it up in a faux hawk women's style, pulled off the shorts to reveal panties, and stripped out of the tank top to a strapless bra—back to female. She was beautiful in either form, I thought, because of the way her personality came through all the changes, the emotion of the performance, the courage it took to keep stripping off appearances. And she was again completely convincing as a woman even though a moment ago in the tank with the slicked back hair he'd looked male.

"Beautiful," someone whispered next to me. A very tall, strikingly attractive woman had slipped into the empty chair on my left.

The performer took off the bra and the panties. Under this they were wearing what looked like black electrical tape, though I hoped it wasn't that, over their nipples and crotch. They had no breasts, but they seemed not to have male genitals either. They pulled out a makeup removing wipe from thin air as far as I could tell, and rubbed it furiously across their face, removing most of the makeup and smearing what was left in a colorful blur across their fine features. They'd stripped down to the bare essence of human. I couldn't see this person as male or female.

I grinned. If I could see neither in this performer, I should definitely be able to see both in Nico. I held on to that idea through the next few acts: a belly dancer, a burlesque group, and a comedian/poet.

Then Nico came out. Yo wore dark gray pants that fit closely in the thighs but loose at the ankle with a tight, black T-shirt. It was the least colorful I'd ever seen Nico. It reminded me of the

Battlestar tank top and of breasts. I ached to run to Nico and apologize again and again until yo heard me.

Nico danced modern with flares of ballet and hip hop. Yo leapt and landed, held sculpted poses with yos body, spun, rippled, flashed across the stage. I watched the powerful quad muscles bunching in Nico's legs, strong shoulders and arms— thick enough to be male but not so heavy as to be outside of the realm of an athletic woman. The "package" in the front of yos pants could have been real or fake or some combination of both. I could see Nico as all genders. The physicality of Nico's performance throbbed in my gut like a drum.

The dance was about constraint and freedom. Nico lunged and spun, fell forward and caught yoself at the floor, crawled painfully, climbed agonizingly up to yos feet and then leapt, spun and flashed across the stage again. Nico said more to me than I'd ever heard in words before—about wonder and life and gender and the crazy things people do. About what it was like to be more than most people would ever understand.

The whole time, on the bare wall behind the stage, a projector showed images of people. First naked bodies, medical photographs with graphs behind them, eyes covered with a black line.

The woman beside me sucked in a breath and whispered, "Oh, Nico."

"Who are they?" I asked.

"Victims," she said.

The medical photos changed to black and white and color images of people. Most of them were clearly presenting male or female but a few weren't so easy to pigeonhole.

The woman pointed and whispered, "She had her clit removed because doctors thought it was too big and would make her lesbian; now she can't have orgasms. He had his penis 'corrected' so he could pee standing up. The infections nearly killed him and he still has to sit to pee. He was raised as a girl after his micropenis was removed; he killed himself. She was beaten by her father every day for being a 'freak' instead of the son he thought he should've had."

I was shaking. I wanted to get up and run, toward Nico or out into the parking lot, both. I wanted to put my body over Nico's, so the people who'd done these things could never touch yo.

The images shifted again. This time showing groups of people laughing together.

The woman's whisper was less pained. "Kathoey people of Thailand," she said. "Two-spirit people in Canada, hijira in India."

The last image was an official document. I had to puzzle it out: lines of blue and black writing, a photograph of Nico, a signature. A passport. The line indicating "sex" said "X."

I turned half toward the woman and she said, "Australia. They're one of the few countries that includes X as an official sex or gender."

Nico stood in the center of the stage, under the X.

The music held, rose, faded. Nico bowed.

The audience was on its feet instantly, the room ringing with applause and cheers.

As Nico left the stage, I slipped out of my seat and through the short hallway to the doors outside. In the heavy night air, leaning against the side of the building, I closed my eyes. I wanted to see Nico over and over, nothing else. But I saw everything: the medical photos, the people whose lives had been irreparably damaged when they were babies, the cultures that had more space than mine for gender, the X glowing on the screen above Nico's beautiful face.

* * *

Cal texted me that the performance space was being set up for a party. *Come back, I want to dance*, he said.

I wanted to talk to Nico so much. And I didn't know what to say. I could hang near Cal and let Nico decide if yo wanted to talk to me.

The front part of the audience area was fixed seating, but the folding chairs that made up the back six rows had been picked up, leaving space for dancing. I found Cal amid the moving bodies. We danced as the crowd thinned. I was getting thirsty and too sweaty.

In another song, Cal had worn himself out. "Come on," he said. I followed him across the hall to the coffee shop. He got a cold water and handed me one.

Ella and Shen sat at a table with Tesh and waved us over. Tesh was glowing. I sat in their shadow, sipping water. Nico appeared in the doorway, beaming and radiant, one arm around the waist of a tall, pretty person with big hoop earrings and a slouchy hat.

Ella hopped up and hugged Nico. I sat and burned with jealousy. Nico had no trouble attracting people—was this my replacement? Had I already spent too long figuring out my apology?

Nico glanced at me, did a hard double-take and stared.

"Tucker? Hair? What happened?"

I braced myself and said, "It's, um, for a cosplay project."

Nico cocked yos head, "Who?"

"It's a surprise."

"What con are you wearing it to?"

"Haven't decided yet."

I was cuttingly aware of everyone staring at us. I didn't know what to say. If we were alone…oh screw it.

"I'm sorry," I told Nico. "So sorry for what I said. I'd like to talk sometime if you want."

"Yeah," Nico said, but non-serious, already looking away. Yo addressed the group, "Everyone, this is Kaj." And then went around introducing everyone.

"My pronouns are she/her," Kaj said brightly. She pulled up a chair and sat near Ella while Nico went to the counter to order, like the gallant boyfriend.

Were we all supposed to say our pronouns?

Tesh pointed around the table as if we did this everyday, "She, he, they, he, she…and Alisa's dancing but she's also she." I was grateful for that. It made us seem cool, but it also hurt my head. Or maybe that was from seeing Nico bouncy and boyish with this lanky, fashionable girl.

The group discussed all the awesomeness of Nico's performance as yo returned with two mugs of cocoa and a plate of cookies. I spaced out, trying get my insides to feel less like I'd swallowed a handful of nails.

I came back into the conversation when I heard Cal say, "I keep getting stuck on the dating thing. I get that in the day-to-day, if we're friends, it's none of my business. But we're some pretty hot people here and I like to know who's got my favorite kind of junk in case Kendrick dumps my butt."

"He wouldn't," Ella said.

Cal shook his head. "I don't know, he said his momma doesn't give a damn if he's gay, but she doesn't like him dating a white guy."

"You can get to know someone without needing to know what their genitals look like," Tesh said.

"Is that fair to me and my hypothetical person?" Cal countered. "Wouldn't you be disappointed if you and I spent some evenings flirting and then it turns out there's some deal breaker? Isn't it worse if we've got a vibe going and then I'm all, 'oh honey, I don't roll that way?'"

"That could be anything," Ella said. "That's what dating is, finding out if you've got deal-breakers. It could be that one person smokes or hates cats or loves cats, and you can't handle that. Why are private parts any different?"

"It's the treacherous transsexual narrative," I grumbled. "It's bullshit. It's just because people are afraid they're being turned queer."

"Or straight," Nico said.

"Yeah," I agreed, face burning, staring at my hands under the table.

Into the awkward silence, Shen said, "I think if I am attracted to a person, she is a woman."

"Huh?" Cal asked.

"I'm a straight man, thus attracted to women. Therefore if I'm attracted, she is a woman. What I mean is, the body isn't what breaks a deal. If a person is not being woman in some way, I won't have enough attraction for it to go anywhere. I trust my attractions."

"But what if you saw someone you thought was super hot and they turned out to be a guy?" Cal asked. "Wouldn't you think you might be a little queer?"

"I can find a man hot," Shen said. "But you mean what if I'm shopping, let's say, and I meet a kathoey woman and she is very beautiful, do I stop being a straight man? I don't think so. What I'm attracted to in her is her womanliness even if she has parts of her body that people would call male."

"Kathoey?" Tesh asked.

"Thailand's third gender," Nico said. "Also, seriously, girls can have dicks. People need to get over that. And guys can be guys without them. Dicks are not automatic maleness."

"Then how do we even know who's male or female?" Cal asked.

"Genetics?" Shen suggested.

"Nope." Ella rested her hand on his arm. "There's XXY and all sort of genotypes. That's not a reliable measure. And when you consider all the intersex variations, the size of your gametes doesn't work either."

I didn't know what the heck a gamete was, but I figured that was similar to the picking-by-genitals method. What if you couldn't find male or female in the body? Where was it?

From what I'd read, science wasn't doing so well at finding it in the brain either. There were slight differences if you looked at huge populations, but they had so much overlap that if you gave the smartest scientist in the world a brain, they couldn't tell you definitively if it was male or female.

"Maybe it's what they say," I suggested.

"Who?" Cal asked.

"Each person. That's the only definition I can think of that works: a woman is a person who says they're a woman, a man is person who says they're a man, and so on."

Everyone was quiet. Ella played with Shen's sleeve. He was trying not to grin too foolishly at her. Nico's foot tapped in time to the music from the other room. Kaj broke off a piece of cookie and slipped it between her glossy lips.

Tesh said, "I can't find a hole in that."

Cal leaned forward, thick forearms on the table. "So if I see someone across the room, I go up and ask 'Hey, hotness, what's your preferred pronoun?' and whatever they say that's what they are? And then I know if I can hit on them or not?"

"Sounds like it works," Kaj said.

Cal turned to Nico. "Hey hotness, what's your preferred pronoun?"

Nico laughed. "It's yo and yos."

"And so I remain confused," Cal said.

"But you weren't hitting on me," Nico told him. "You're not actually into me."

"You got me. The only person I find hot at this table is Shen."

Shen smiled and muttered, "Thanks."

"See, your sexuality is safe," Ella said. "Shen's 'trust your attractions' theory is standing up to the test. And you keep your bear paws off my man."

I watched Nico slide out of yos seat to get water. Did that mean that being as attracted to Nico as I was, automatically Nico counted as woman enough to keep my lesbian status? Could it be that simple?

CHAPTER THIRTY-ONE

Nico

I caught up with Tucker as the Freytag contingent was walking to Cal's car. I could not get used to her hair being short and brown. It looked good, not epic like the Mohawk, but darned handsome. Who had short brown hair? Far too many people in the whole Sci-Fi/Fantasy universe for me to figure out what cosplay project she had in mind.

I did want to talk to her. Now seemed like a good time. I was in full boymode, armored up, buzzing on the adrenaline of dancing and the applause. No idea what I'd say. Let her apologize again, I guess, and talk through things. Tell her I might live as a guy for a while so maybe it wouldn't work between us anyway. Find a way to let her go.

Maybe in the morning, though.

When she turned to me, I asked, "You said you wanted to talk. Do you want to stay at my house and I'll drive you back tomorrow?"

"Yeah."

She told Cal she wasn't going back with him and followed me to my car.

"You'll have to sleep on the couch because the girls are both home," I warned her.

"That's fine."

"Mom gets up at dawn. That's only a few hours away."

"I'll live. At least I've got a shot at getting something tasty."

The weight of all the things we had to talk about pressed down on us. The ride was silent and heavy under that shroud. In the house, I retrieved blankets from the hall closet and a pillow from my room for the couch.

Tucker kicked off her boots and got under the blanket with all her clothes on. I wanted to crawl under it with her. I thought I'd gotten more distance from her. That dressing as a boy, being a boy, would make it easier. Now that she was here…

That thing she'd said about gender: that you were the gender you said you were, was so clear and elegant. I wanted to press against her and kiss her and smooth the troubled look off her face.

"Good night," I told her.

"You too. Sleep well. Really great performance."

"Thanks."

I snuck up to my room and paused in the doorway. Almost turned around. Made myself step inside and shut the door.

When I turned to the mirror, the wrongness of my reflection hit me in the chest. The young man I saw was so bound up and constricted. Caught up in trying to be what he wasn't. Playacting the saddest script ever written. That wasn't me.

Especially tonight after the performance, after getting to be as fully myself as I'd ever been.

I tore off the shirt, buttons popping, and ripped the binder off, throwing it across the room. The pants came down, kicked off so I was in boxer briefs and bare-chested. I ruffled my hair with my fingertips, breaking the gel, making the curls perk up. I held onto the edges of the mirror, staring at myself, eyes wet.

I couldn't be that man all the time. I couldn't wrap those metal bars around me until they crushed me.

A soft tap on the door and another. Tucker's whispered voice, "Nico? You okay?"

I grabbed a T-shirt and shrugged into it, jerked the door open. Seeing my face, her eyes went sad. I stepped out of the way. She closed the door behind her.

"What's wrong?"

I pointed at the button down shirt and binder thrown half across my desk. "Not me."

Okay." Her word was soft and full of openness. She sat on the bed.

I sat next to her and leaned in. She put her arms around me. I cried and she held onto me saying, "It's okay," over and over again.

I got cried out and went for glasses of water for both of us. Tucker waited, sitting on top of my covers, propped up against the headboard.

When I got back, she asked, "Can I say some things?"

"Yeah, I guess." Bracing for anything, still standing, I leaned against my desk.

"I was royally pissed at Summer, but I don't mean that like an excuse. I was so wrong to say what I did. And I don't…I'm not saying I understand what it's like, but I can learn and I've been…" She took a huge breath in like it was a monster big deal what she was going to say. "…seeing a therapist."

I bit my cheek so I wouldn't laugh at her adorable discomfort.

"Is it helping?"

"I think so. I won't know until I end up in bed with someone again."

"End up?"

"Don't distract me," she said, the faintest smile playing across her lips. "I'm trying to tell you something here."

Climbing onto the bed, I settled next to her. I leaned back against the headboard, but sitting far enough away that we weren't touching.

She said, "I had to go twice before I could even tell her what had happened. And my third time, a couple of days ago, we talked about it a bunch more. I got to wondering why it had been so hard to talk about."

As she spoke, her hands rubbed together, like her fingers really wanted to fiddle with anything but had to content themselves with counting over her calluses.

She said, "When those guys jumped me on campus and beat me up, it was so easy to say what had happened. I told the cops and the Dean of Students. I told everyone in our queer and trans group. I told my sister Bailey the next time I saw her. I told my mom. Why was it different being raped?"

"What was it?" The question breathed out of me, curious and worried.

"It was shame. That's the feeling that's haunted me since it happened. I couldn't name it, only knew that I felt filthy. It was just shame. And I let it shut me down completely. Because I've grown up with rape being something that made the victim… disgusting. Nico, I'm afraid I did that to you, shamed you. I never want you to feel that, not for a second."

She glanced sideways at me, eyes full of tears. I was almost crying too.

"That is by far the best apology I've ever gotten," I told her.

"Second best," she said with a faint grin. "The best will be when you see my cosplay."

I pushed off the bed, grabbed a box of tissues and got back into my spot.

"When *am* I seeing that?" I asked.

"I thought maybe after your surgery, while you're recovering. You might need some comic relief. If that's okay?"

"Uh, it's perfect."

"If I can say one more thing—"

I shrug-nodded.

"I don't care if you have a clarinet down your pants, I want to go out with you."

I chuckled, but had to ask, "How would you know, never having met my clarinet?"

"Because I can't imagine anything that would make me change my mind," she said. "If you're still single and all."

"Why wouldn't I be?"

"Kaj."

"She's got a girlfriend."

"Oh, thank God. But, you know, even with the therapist, I'm not sure. You might not want to go out with me. I don't know if I can stand to be touched…" She waved a hand down her body.

"Genitally?" I offered.

"Yeah."

"It's okay," I said, an echo of how she'd comforted me. "That's normal for what you went through."

I didn't know a lot of people who'd been raped, but I knew more than enough people who'd had their bodies violated surgically. Trouble with being touched ranked high on the list of outcomes from that. I didn't have that, but I could understand how a person got there.

With Tucker, though, I also felt afraid for me. How long would it take her to heal? Would I know what to do to help her? How hard was this process going to be? Would I screw it up? At least I knew how to talk about sex.

"What did the therapist say about not wanting to be touched?" I asked her.

"To think about my fear on a one to ten scale and I'm supposed to stop at a five and we'll work on it. And I'm supposed to breathe and stuff." She was bent away from me, head and shoulders down.

I wanted to let her know she wasn't alone. Give her something to hold onto. Maybe I wanted to give her everything.

"I learned to dance," I said.

She turned back toward me, puzzled. "I know."

"When I was four, after my dad took me in for surgery. I was terrified after. I panicked a lot. Mom took me to a somatic specialist for medical trauma in kids and he taught me to dance."

"Nico," she said, the soft sadness heavy in her voice.

"The interesting thing is that it wasn't the surgery that was traumatic. I was out for that. It was the way they thought they had to fix me. The way they all treated me. They took away my selfhood. They made me into a non-person."

Tucker whispered, "Lindy…yes, that's how I felt. I wasn't a person to her anymore. I wasn't a person at all, anywhere in the world. She wiped me out. Nothing was safe anymore because I wasn't a person. Because anyone could come in and take my self away from me. Do you still get scared?"

"Some now with this surgery coming up. I'm super afraid of surgery. I'm afraid I'll go in and wake up and not be real anymore."

She held her hand palm up on her thigh and I put my hand in hers. Her fingers closed hard on mine.

She said, "You'll always be real. If you forget, if you feel like that, I'll remind you. I promise."

"Me too, for you."

It got super intense in the room. If I didn't keep talking, I was going to try to kiss her. I said, "What if it's an oboe, not a clarinet? What's your stance on oboes?"

She gave me a half-grin. "What if I don't know the difference?"

"Well, you're obviously not an oboesexual."

"Sometimes labels suck. I like you. Whatever you've got, oboe, cello, I'll like it."

I wanted wrap her around me and never leave this space. I asked, "Do you want to sleep in here with me?"

"Will your mom freak out?"

"A little, but I can handle it. Come get in bed. And take off your pants, you're not sleeping next to me in jeans. Unless you're commando, in which case you can borrow my shorts."

"I'm good," she said and stripped down to boxers and T-shirt. She deftly worked her way out of her bra without taking off her shirt. Under the covers, I took her hand and rolled away from her, pulling her toward me. She put her arm around my stomach and spooned behind me.

I told her, "My dad and brother want me to be a boy. I was trying it this week, being a boy all the time. I thought I had it, but tonight in the mirror I looked so wrong to me."

"Yeah. That's happened to me the few times I've put on a dress. Sorry, that's probably not the same."

"I think it's close. I might be able to do girl. It's less restrictive than boy in a lot of ways, but you get treated shittier."

"Why do you have to pick?"

Her breath was tickling the side of my ear. I turned my head a fraction away so I wouldn't laugh, but pressed back against her more. Her arm tightened around me. We fit together really well, at least with her behind me. I loved her warm weight along my back.

I told her, "When I was a kid, they thought I'd pick at three years old or thirteen or whatever. And I still don't want to, but I'm so sick of everything, the questions and the pressure and the quiet, sinking disapproval like needles all through me."

"You don't have to pick with me," she said.

"Don't you want a girlfriend?"

"I think I need a person who's at least somewhat a girl, but that doesn't have to be exclusive. Girl plus boy plus whatever else works for me. I'm not completely inflexible. You'll see when I show you the cosplay."

I reached behind me and ruffled her short, darker hair. "Are you a boy?"

"Yep."

"I for sure want to see that."

"You will."

She didn't say any more, but her breathing was too fast for sleep. Did she regret her bold words or was something else keeping her up? I couldn't ask, too much to think about already. Neither of us fell asleep for a while.

CHAPTER THIRTY-TWO

Nico

We ducked out of my house fast so we wouldn't get the third degree from Mom and Yai. Stopped for breakfast on the way up to Freytag. Talked about the cabaret. Tucker rested her hand on my leg as I drove, which made me crazy but in a great way.

When we got to campus, Tucker asked me back to her room. I was dying to make out with her, but I wasn't going to push it. Her room was a more make-outable space than any other on campus. But when we got there, she sat in the desk chair. I perched on the edge of the bed all by myself.

"About this dating thing?" I asked.

"Do you want to? I mean, I'm asking you out. I want to go out with you, oboe or no. If you want me to prove that…I don't know how to."

I was running on five hours of sleep and a residual high from the performance the night before. I felt light-headed and filled with wanting to be closer to Tucker, pressed against her.

Some small voice in the back of my head was telling me to be careful, but my mouth said, "Why don't we both take off our pants and get it over with. See if it's a deal-breaker."

"What?"

I'd never seen her eyebrows go quite that high before.

I said, "If you're going to have issues, questions, whatever, I'd prefer that you have them across the room from me, not, like, on top of me. So let's both take off our pants right now and see where we're at."

"You're not kidding?"

"You have a better idea?" I asked.

"Honestly, no."

If it turned out that me having a dick was a deal-breaker, I could at least crawl next door to Ella's room and cry in her bed until she got sick of me. I loved Tucker's brave talk of the night before, but I wasn't a hundred percent sure she could live up to it.

Tucker stood and glanced at both doors, locked and locked. She unbuckled her belt, unzipped and dropped her trousers, kicking them to one side. She pulled off her boxers and stood by her desk.

"Hey, at least I can do this without messing up the anxiety scale," she said.

"Where are we at?"

"About a three. I'll have to let Bridget know standing around with no pants works."

As she talked, she unbuttoned her dress shirt and pulled it off so the shirt tails weren't covering her. She was in a white undershirt, bunched up at her waist. I could see her bare hips and legs and everything.

"Undershirt too?" she asked.

"Uh," was all the reply I could manage, watching Tucker, tough and vulnerable, with most of her clothes in a pile on the floor.

She said, "You don't have to do this. I don't want you to do anything you don't want to. I mean, I deeply do not. But, you know, if it helps I'll stand around with the wind blowing on my ass as long as you need."

I laughed. "There's no wind."

"Feels like it."

"Yeah, I know." I'd been in similar enough situations in doctors' offices throughout my life. I knew how exposed it felt. I loved that she was willing to go first. Too many people thought they should know about me, get access to me, without being willing to be vulnerable themselves.

Tucker sat backwards in the desk chair. Her legs were open around the chair's narrow spine. I could see all sorts of intimate landscape. My brain was a city grid losing power—lights winking out block by block the longer I looked at her. If I kept standing there, I wasn't going to have a shred of power left for higher thinking.

I turned away and undid my pants fast. Might as well muscle through this while I had the brain power to get myself out of the room if she freaked out. I pushed pants and boxer briefs down to where I could yank them back up fast and turned toward her.

Her mouth was half-open, eyes intense, looking and looking before flicking up to my face.

"Nico," she said. "Will you please go out with me now?"

"Um?" Lights blinking out in my brain.

She got up, knocking the chair flat on its back. Took a step, stopped, "Can I?"

"What? Touch it?"

"Kiss you?"

"Oh, yeah—"

The attempted kiss turned into a wrestling-style smackdown. I stepped toward her, forgetting my pants were around my knees, and fell forward. She grabbed for me and tried to lurch us onto the bed, but it wasn't wide enough. I ended up half across the bed with Tucker on the floor.

I thought she was laughing, but when I bent over the side of the mattress I saw that she was crying more than laughing.

"You hurt?" I asked.

"Why can't I make anything work?" Her words came out muffled because she had her knees up, arms folded over them, face tucked into her arms.

"Dtao, why don't you put your boxers on and come get in bed?"

"Probably work better if you call me Starbuck," she grumbled.

"Starbuck, put on your boxers and come here."

She crawled across the floor to snag her boxers and jackknife into them, asking, "Does that make you Athena?"

"Did you want Athena?"

"She's hot, but I like you better."

"I could have the surgery to go that way, to make me more traditionally a girl." The words fell out. Now that we'd gotten through the worst part, I was babbling with relief. "That's the deal with this surgery, they can change things, you know, remove the clarinet and all that."

"You don't have to say clarinet," she said. "I'm not going to run screaming if you say 'dick.' What do you say?"

She'd scooted back to sit against the side of the bed with me belly-down on the mattress, our faces close and level. Looking into her sea-blue eyes, I said "Dick, usually, or clit or junk or cletis."

"Cletis," she grinned. "I like that. I was afraid you were going to say 'Little Jack Harkness.'"

"Huh, I'm going to have to think about that."

"I don't know my way around dicks," Tucker said. "Is it okay that you'll have to tell me?"

"It's better that way. Mine's not the most average. And the undercarriage isn't guy-standard. There's labia and a vagina."

"Oh, I've seen some of those," she said with a smirk. "Not that yours aren't special."

"Hah, thanks. You want to come up on the bed?"

"Not yet. It's easier like this, to talk. I'm kind of fucked up."

"Trauma and fucked up are not the same thing," I told her.

"What if we can't have sex? What if I can't do what you like and you don't want me to—"

"I do," I said. "Me and Little Jack are in complete agreement about that."

"Oh wow, no."

I was laughing because she was right, that sounded awful. I said, "Sorry. Can I come down to the floor with you?"

"Sure, it's posh down here."

I pulled up my boxer briefs, kicked off my shoes and jeans. Then I slid down to the floor and rested my shoulder against Tucker's.

I asked her, "Now that we're going out, do we swap varsity rings or letter jackets?"

She turned and kissed me. The last illuminated city block of my brain winked out into the soft darkness of my closed eyes and Tucker's lips.

The kissing went past breathless into panting and horizontal. I only got conscious thought back when my shoulder, jammed against the bed leg, became painful.

"Can you move over?" I asked.

"Let's try the bed," she suggested and climbed onto the mattress.

Back to kissing, but awkwardly because every time I started to roll onto her, I backed off again. Reflex from the night of Cal's party when she panicked and left.

"I think I'm okay," Tucker said.

"Let's not rush it."

"You don't want to?"

"Oh, I want to, but…you asked me out and everything, maybe we should have a date."

Confusion crossed her face, a hint of frustration, a wash of relief.

"Like movies and holding hands?" she asked. "To make up for the part where we stood around with our pants off?"

"Exactly like that."

"There's a theater a few blocks away. Can you stay over? Do you want to?"

"Yeah, I'll text Mom."

So we went to a movie. Got dinner. Somehow managed to be back in Tucker's room with most of our clothes off, in the bed, not making out.

She curled into me and I wrapped an arm around her and prayed that this was going to work.

CHAPTER THIRTY-THREE

Tucker

I had a late morning class that Monday, which I offered to skip. Nico said to go, that yo had homework to do anyway. We went to Mill's for breakfast. Then I gave Nico the key to my room and went to class. All I could think about was Nico in my room and how I wanted to get back there.

When finally I did, Nico was cross-legged on the bed reading from yos tablet.

"What do you usually do Monday afternoons?" Nico asked.

"Study or go work out."

"Let's work out. Can I get into your gym?"

"I can swipe you in. Let me change."

I got on my running clothes and loaned Nico an extra pair of sweats and T-shirt. The gym was nearly empty. Nico found an open dance studio room and sent me to run. I did two miles but that was all I was in the mood for. I wanted to get back to Nico.

I went down to the studio and looked through the glass door. Just stood there for a long time watching Nico move.

Nico saw me and opened the door. "What are you doing? It wasn't locked."

"I could watch you all day."

Nico laughed. "Boring."

"Let's go shower?" I suggested.

Nico followed me out of the gym and we walked across the quad together. "You know I'm showering alone, right?" yo asked.

I'd been thinking about how awesome it would be to be together under the hot spray with the soap and all that, but then I realized how exposed that could make Nico feel.

"Oh, yeah, do you want the first or second?"

"First," Nico said. "I smell like an ox."

"No you don't."

I tried to slip an arm around Nico's waist, but yo danced away. "Seriously, I do."

We got back to my room and Nico showered. I paced. I knew what I wanted, but I wasn't sure that I had the guts to do it. When I got out of my shower, Nico was sitting in my bed reading on yos tablet, like earlier in the day. I liked seeing Nico there.

I'd thrown on a clean T-shirt and shorts, with nothing underneath, and I climbed into the bed next to Nico. The two of us barely fit. I kissed the side of Nico's neck, up to where yos wet curls dampened the tip of my nose. Nico reached across me to put the tablet on the nightstand and then we were kissing hard, Nico on top, me pulling yo down against me.

When Nico rolled to the side I pulled off my shirt and dropped it by the bed. Nico did the same. I said, "Wait," and got up to turn off the overhead light.

Nico pushed up onto one elbow. "Tucker, should we talk about things more first?"

I'd been talking things to death with therapy. Wasn't it enough to admit I needed help and to get it? Did I have to keep being the broken one?

"I don't particularly want to," I said.

"But, how do you picture this going?"

I got back into the bed. Nico wrapped yos arms around me and kissed up my cheek to the corner of my eye. I traced a finger down Nico's collarbone and felt yo shudder.

"Smoothly," I said.

"That's only in movies. Let's try something, okay?"

I remembered grabbing Nico's wrist in the hotel, the flash of alarm in yos eyes. I thought about what Ella had said, what I knew about Nico's life, all the opinions about yos body, all the weight Nico operated under.

If I panicked again, it would be hard for Nico not to take some of that personally. Maybe Nico was as scared as I was. Maybe this wasn't Nico trying to fix broken me. Maybe it was a circuit—wires running from me to Nico and back again—that could carry fear or safety like a current.

Nico was trying to make our circuit feel safe.

Could that be true for Ella too? Maybe people weren't trying to fix me out of pity, but because we were all wired up together. When I was in better shape, good energy came through me to them.

"Yeah," I said with real enthusiasm. Now I was curious about what Nico wanted to try instead of insulted. "What it is?"

Nico grinned, the tension around yos eyes melting away. Better energy in the circuit.

Yo said, "I'm going to ask you three questions that sound random."

"Go for it."

"Do you like lima beans?"

I stuck out my tongue. "Yucky."

"Good. Do you want to do go to Sandusky?" Nico asked.

"Maybe, if it's with you?"

Nico kissed me. I felt the upturned, smiling shape of yos mouth in the kiss.

"Are you a feminist?" yo asked.

"Fuck yes!"

"Perfect," Nico said. "How did that feel when you said that?"

"What do you mean?"

"In your body, how did you feel?

"Warm," I said. "And like my chest was expanding fast."

"And the other answers?'

"Lima beans was a gross feeling in my gut," I said. "And Sandusky, nothing really."

"That warm, fast, expansive feeling is what 'yes' feels like to you—an enthusiastic yes. Lima beans is what 'no' feels like and Sandusky isn't a strong no, but it's a pause, okay? If you're not feeling the 'fuck yes I'm a feminist' feeling with me, I want you to press pause. And pause or stop if you get the gross-yuck feeling or anxiety, fear, panic, any of that. We don't have to do a hard stop, but pause and see where we're at. Will you do that?"

All the energy going through me was warm, glowing, happy. Nico wasn't trying to fix me. Yo was making sure our connections were good, no loose wires, no short circuits.

I smiled. "God, Nico, how do you know this stuff?"

"I read books. Where did your therapist tell you stop?"

"At five."

It didn't suck to say that out loud now. I heard it as information, not a confession of how screwed up I was. I pressed closer to Nico.

"If we get to five, or above that, tell me 'five' and we'll figure it out," yo said.

The circuit transmitted both energy and information. I said what I was really thinking and feeling, "Now I'm a little scared, distracted about this five thing, I don't even know where to start."

Nico pushed me down onto the bed, slowly, watching with yos steady brown-green eyes. I wrapped my hands around Nico's shoulders. The muscles felt good, dense, and imbued with the magic of Nico's dancing. Nico leaned half on top of me and kissed down the side of my neck.

I gasped. "Okay, good start."

Nico made it down to my breasts and peered up at me. "Yes?"

"Oh, yes."

A while later, Nico tugged at my shorts. "Yes?"

My breath caught. I wanted it but I was afraid, but less than five. Nico waited, watching my face, paused like a video recording of that moment, smiling, completely focused on me. It was okay to say yes now because if it got bad I could pause us again. And Nico had said "pause" not "stop" so it didn't mean my choices were only go full steam ahead or stop everything.

I nodded but Nico shook yos head and asked, "Yes?"

If I thought about wires and circuits, the words were there behind my lips, not locked down in my chest.

"Yes," I said.

I helped Nico pull my shorts down and over my legs. Nico's fingers explored. I rocked my head back and stopped thinking for a long time, until I felt one finger slip between my inner lips.

I grabbed Nico's wrist, but not as hard as the last time.

"Wait. Five."

Nico pulled slightly away, putting yos other hand on top of mine. Not to take my hand off yos wrist, but comforting, my hand pressed between skin and skin.

"Do you want to say no?" Nico asked.

I had the word in my mouth, a burning in my throat and eyes. I pushed the word out, whispered, "No."

Nico rested next to me, extending an arm so I could curl into yos side.

"See, it's okay to say no."

"No," I said, louder, and then I couldn't stop saying it, tears rising in my eyes, my mouth repeating, "No, no, no."

"I've got you," Nico said while I cried.

When I'd settled into a wet mess, Nico asked, "Do you want to go get dinner?"

"No," I said and started laughing because that was the only word I'd said in a while. "I don't want to get out of bed with you. Are you starving?"

"I'm okay, but you…"

"Nico. Fuck."

"I need more words than that. You want to keep going?" Nico asked.

"Yes, but how?"

"What worked with Quin?"

"When I, you know, did her."

Nico peered into my face and sighed. "Starbuck…Let's try that. But you promise never to say that you 'did' me or anyone else ever again."

"Scout's honor."

"I am not into Boy Scout roleplay," Nico said with a wink and kissed me.

We kissed and writhed against each other. I felt the hardness in the front of Nico's boxers but Nico was angling away from me to keep me from feeling all of it. And I thought: *screw that.*

I ran a hand down Nico's belly to the waistband of the boxers and said, "Should I make you say yes every step of the way?" I moved my fingers a fraction of an inch.

Nico groaned and covered my hand with yos palm. "I'm a blanket yes," yo said. "Are you going to freak out?"

"Only if you *don't* let me in your boxers."

We went back to kissing. I held Nico close, slid my hand into yos boxer briefs. I felt the soft and hard length against my palm, in my fingers. Under that lips, thick and wet, familiar, and a cleft between them that it was too soon to explore.

I roamed back up, felt the length, the textures. Tried to discern what kinds of touch Nico liked best. It wasn't like: *omg I'm touching a dick*. I was touching Nico, who was pressing into my hand, groaning, yos head thrown back on the pillows. I was touching Nico the way I'd wanted to since winter.

All that build up, the fear, the identity questions, and this wasn't strange at all. Soft and hard and wet, different shapes than I was used to, but everyone was different from everyone else. Learning what someone liked was part of the fun.

I kissed Nico's neck and collarbone. Pulling far enough away to look at Nico, I saw the worry and desire in yos eyes.

"Take off your damn boxers," I said.

Laughing, Nico pulled them off and threw them over the foot of the bed.

"Are you going to tell me what you like or do I have to do this by feel?" I asked.

"Can we do both?"

Framed by the pillows, naked in my bed, I saw Nico, a person, playful and grinning, still worried, vulnerable, bare, beautiful. I lowered my body over Nico's, one hand sliding down between us and said, close to yos ear, "Yes, a very enthusiastic yes."

CHAPTER THIRTY-FOUR

Nico

I got one more weekend with Tucker before finals and the surgery. It wasn't nearly enough.

I told Dr. Peace what I wanted done. Then it was out of my hands.

Being put under anesthesia felt like being tipped backwards further and further beyond the bed and the floor, until everything disappeared. When I got conscious again, I was dizzy-nauseous. A nurse handed me a bucket because apparently patients hurl all the time after anesthesia. I kept spitting in a disgusting, drooling way. I sipped fizzy, clear pop until I was sure I wasn't going to puke. Then I gave the nurse the bucket and kept the pop.

Everything from my sternum down hurt like the worst cramps ever and like I'd been kicked by a horse a time or six. Mom and Matt and Hazey and Deena and Yai all crowded into the room as soon as they heard I was up. After twenty minutes, I had to close my eyes and rest. Mom ushered them all out again, saying that they'd be in the waiting room if I needed anything.

I dozed and woke to find Sharani from the Noodle sitting near the foot of my bed, reading. In the tiny hospital chair she looked very tall, quite wild, and every inch the martial arts expert I wanted watching over me post-surgery.

"You doing okay?" she asked.

"Yeah."

"I heard your doctor talking to your mother. The surgery team didn't do anything you didn't ask for and everything you wanted went smoothly."

"Thank you," I breathed.

I stared at the ceiling, tears of relief leaking out of my eyes. After I wiped them away and focused on Sharani, she said, "Ella made me promise to tell her when you're up. You want me to get her?"

"Sure," I told her and dozed again. I liked the idea of Sharani and Ella talking. I thought I could hear them chatting about the cabaret, but I might have dreamed that.

When I came fully awake, Ella sat in the chair where Sharani had been. We put on some bland TV. Mom and the girls cycled in. Mom said she was taking them down to get a late lunch in the cafeteria.

The next time the door opened, I couldn't figure out what I was seeing. A familiar-looking person stepped into the room wearing suit pants and a vest over a pressed shirt and tie. They wore an official badge I couldn't quite read. My brain disgorged the words "Tucker" and "cosplay."

"Hi, Jack," she said.

She meant Jack Harkness?

"What drugs am I on?" I asked.

She pulled up a chair to the other side of the bed from where Ella sat, took the badge off her vest and handed it to me. I saw the tactical earpiece over her right ear and a thick leather wristband. I focused my bleary eyes on the badge: "Torchwood Institute, Ianto Jones, General Support."

I peered back at Tucker. Her short, brown hair made sense now. She looked uncomfortable with the shirt buttoned all the way up and the tie—and she looked great. I read the badge again because I couldn't quite believe it.

"You remembered *Torchwood*?" I asked.

"We watched those two episodes. And then I went through all of seasons one and two over the last few weeks," she said. "I'm watching it at night when I miss you."

I'd have asked her to kiss me except that my mouth tasted like a garbage-burning facility.

"You can take off the tie," I said. "He sometimes wears an open collar."

She undid the tie and pulled it off, popped the top button on the collar and relaxed a bit in her chair.

"How are you doing?"

"It hurts, but it's not awful. The nurses have been great and I have more visitors than the room can hold. I might be able to go home tonight unless I start bleeding from my ears."

She ducked her head so I was looking at the top of it, the short brown, freshly-dyed hair standing up in clumps.

I turned my face to Ella. She cocked her head toward the door, silently asking if she should go, and I nodded.

"I'm going to go, uh, check on the cat," she said and left the room.

"There's a cat?" Tucker asked.

"No, it's a thing we made up years ago, an excuse to get up and leave."

I reached across the bed. She took my hand, rubbing her thumb over the back of my knuckles.

"You look amazing," I told her. "Will you wear that to a convention with me?"

A smirk stole across her lips. "I hear you get a lot of action at conventions."

"We don't have to leave the room."

"And keep the world from seeing our cosplay? You're joking," she said. "Hey, I made a better vortex manipulator for Captain Jack."

She unbuckled the wristband and carefully buckled it onto my left wrist. Then she snapped open the top and pressed a button. A little blue light went on. Another button made a buzzing sound.

"That's so much better than my old one," I told her. "You made this?"

"Learned a few things about electronics," she said, grinning.

I squeezed her hand and wondered if it was too soon to say *I love you* out loud.

A nurse popped in to check on me. I was getting hungry so she came back with a cup of broth, some crackers and more pop. While I ate, very slowly, Tucker told me about how Johnny and Shen came up with the Ianto Jones costume and helped her get it together.

Then my Dad walked in.

I was not ready for him.

The last times we'd been hanging out together I was doing "son" hardcore. He had all kinds of expectations. The whole "I failed" and "it's my fault" conversation still rang in my head.

The pressure radiated from him like heat. He was checking me out to make sure I was okay, but I had a shudder of paranoia that he was trying to see if my chest was bandaged, if it was flat now.

He came to the open side of the bed and asked, "How do you feel?"

"Some pain, okay though, it went well."

"You let them fix you?" he asked.

I closed my eyes.

"Nehal, this has gone on much too long. Tell me you let them make it right."

After going fishing with him, taking him to see me dance, I knew I wanted him in my life more—but not like this.

Tucker cleared her throat. With a surprising amount of authority, she declared, "Sir, the patient needs to rest. This phase of recovery should be as free of stress as possible. If you'll go to the waiting room, I'll tell the Doctor you're here."

She said "Doctor" with the right amount of stress, the capital letter, the implication of Doctor Who. I opened my eyes enough to see Dad stare at her like he hadn't even noticed her in the room until that moment.

He read the name badge and said, "Torchwood Institute, what is that?"

Tucker took a breath to speak, but I saw the uncertainty in her eyes. I said, "Advanced Studies of Gender Endocrinology."

"You're not a doctor," he said to Tucker.

"Ianto Jones, General Support. I'm a glorified secretary but I work with the Doctor. Now I have some questions I need to go over with Nehal and I think it's best that we go over those privately."

He'd stepped back from the bed, but didn't look convinced. Tucker's use of my given name made her sound official. But there was the genderqueer feel of Tucker's whole outfit: the crisp button-down shirt and vest over her big chest.

"Does Mom know you're here?" I asked him.

"She wasn't going to tell me you were having surgery, so I don't see a reason to share information with her," he said. "When will your doctor be in? Will you give her permission to talk to me?"

Tucker stood by the bed, obviously uncomfortable, even afraid. But she wasn't moving for anything. When I'd met her last fall she was tough. Now that toughness had cracked away and reformed into a deeper strength that could be flexible or, as now, unmoving.

She'd come here cosplaying Ianto Jones just to make me grin. She was willing to feel weird and out of place to make my world more familiar and safe. If my dad were to scream in her face, I had no doubt she'd lean into it, push him back by force of will.

I could live into the future she was creating.

I might be a kid in my dad's eyes, but my choice had been enough for my doctor. I didn't have to know everything to know what was right for me.

And I didn't have to decide for my dad if he could be in my life or not. I could tell him how it was and let him decide if he'd meet me on equal ground, if he'd respect me as an adult.

"No," I told him.

"What?" Dark eyebrows drew close, his frown creased his cheeks.

In the past I might have told Tucker to go get Mom or my doctor, but I didn't need them here. My body shifted inside, like learning a dance move, getting it solid so it became automatic. This new move was speaking from a core of certainty, not feeling I had to manage the worlds of the people around me.

"No," I repeated. And then, slowly and clearly, "You will *not* talk to my doctor about my medical care."

"Nehal?"

I drew on the cocky assurance of Captain Jack, the deep competence of Athena, a million other characteristics, gendered and non-gendered. I rooted deep in myself.

"Here's my offer," I told him. "You withdraw the lawsuit and I will come visit you in California as your son. I will be a man when I'm with you. You may call me your son and use he/him pronouns for me all the time. You can teach me everything you wanted to about being a man."

I paused for that to sink in, then said, "But when I'm here, home, I am Nico: queer, genderfluid, nonbinary, everything I choose to be. I will play your son for you so we can be a family and you will leave me alone to make my own choices."

I added, "You have no need…no right to know what I did or did not choose for my body."

His face reddened above his beard. He glared at me and at Tucker. I think if she hadn't looked like an official person, he'd have said a lot more to me. Instead, he left.

I glanced at Tucker's face and away, unable to sort out her expression and everything I felt. "That better not be pity," I grumbled at her.

Her fingers curled around mine. "I love you," she said.

"Dammit."

"What?"

"I was about to say that like fifteen minutes ago," I told her, shifting my hand in hers so I could feel all the places where our skin touched.

"So say it."

"Now it's going to sound all contrived."

She stared at me, fierce and costumed and amazing. I grinned back at her. I didn't need my costumes to be all the shades of me with her or with my dad or anyone. Not that I planned on giving them up any time soon.

"I love you too," I said, hearing the full fluidity of the "I" and the "you."

EPILOGUE

Tucker

I spent as much of the summer as I could down in Columbus. When I wasn't there, Nico was at Bailey's with me. Sure, my room in her new apartment was an old pantry and barely had room for a bed, but we made it work.

Sex felt like a big, huge thing for most of the summer. Not on Nico's side, that was fun, learning and exploring and enjoying. But for me, parts of my body felt like a minefield of panic and anger.

Nico let me take the lead for weeks, until I was the one grabbing Nico's hand and putting it where I wanted. Even then I had a bunch of "pause" and "no" moments. Nico was great at backing off, touching or not touching, holding me, letting me cry, being patient minute to minute as things changed.

Over time, the spikes of fear came less often, further apart. We talked more than I've ever talked in bed, more than I ever thought I could. Nico suggested some things that made me blush but we did them anyway. We repeated anything that was awesome and non-fear-inducing. Nico even got me to read one of yos stash of sex books and I made a few suggestions of my own.

I wasn't eager for school to start because we'd only see each other on weekends. At least it was a short drive and I'd be back in the dorms. This year the administration didn't give Ella her own room, but they let us stay roommates. As a junior, Shen had a room to himself, and Ella said she'd spend the weekends there or visiting her family, so Nico and I could have our own space.

The room thing wasn't my top worry. Summer was a senior this year. Neither of us got the work study position she was so mad about, but she still blamed me. Plus me being with Nico and her not being with Tesh made her meaner. I'd already heard nasty asides about how I wasn't trans and now I wasn't a lesbian, so maybe I should pick an identity I could stick with.

She'd been elected to lead the LGBTQIA+ student group. She was popular and the larger group wasn't aware of our core group drama. This meant she had first crack at the incoming students and no doubt a bunch of them were enthralled by her outspoken politics. Problem was, most of her politics were about coalition building and were great—so it was hard to notice the jabs and twists.

"I'm afraid to ask Nico to drive up," I told Cal and Ella as we moved boxes into the room Ella and I shared. "Not like Summer's going to do anything big, but she'll get one of the first years to say something. Even if it's just about how she doesn't think I can still call myself lesbian, which I totally can, that's going to make Nico feel bad."

"I could threaten to ban her from the house," Cal said. "But I think she's planning some big campus parties. She doesn't need the house as her nexus anymore. She's got Quin and Katee on her planning committee. Those two are running the Black Student Union together."

"I guess we could avoid hanging out in the union," I said. "Nico and I can stay in the room."

Ella shook her head. "That's not fair. We need to educate the incoming class, not avoid them. Besides, Tesh."

"How are they doing?"

"Rough," Ella said. "Their mother lost it and threw away all their non-feminine clothing. They had to grow their hair out and listen to female pronouns all summer."

"Maybe I will keep my hair like this," I said, rubbing my hand across my head. "Tesh needs to see people support them."

"Yeah." Ella's eyes got that sparkly, faraway look like she was up to mischief. "Let me know when Nico's coming up."

The first week of classes felt immensely long. Nico drove up Friday afternoon. Yo only had morning classes and my last was done at three, so we'd have almost half the day, plus Saturday and most of Sunday.

Ella wasn't in the room when Nico arrived. But she texted me insistently in the middle of our damn-I-missed-you making out. After the fourth buzz, I looked at my phone.

Ella had texted a series of messages:

Bring Nico to the Union for dinner.

You and Nico dinner, Union.

Where are you?

Omg put your pants on and come to the Union, both of you. Pants! Now!

I showed Nico the screen and typed back: *Are you sure? Isn't Summer there holding court?*

I've got this, she wrote back.

Reading that, Nico shrugged and said, "If my babygirl says she's got it, then she's got it. Let's go."

Sure enough in the student union, at the table where we usually sat, there was Summer and Quin and a bunch of other people I didn't know. Summer glared at me and Nico. A furious round of whispering went around the table.

I wanted to grab Nico's hand and leave at a run, but I heard Cal yell, "Over here!"

He stood by a table on the right side of the eating area, the mirror-image of the table with Summer and her crew.

And he was wearing a dress. A loud, red dress with spaghetti straps.

Beside me, Nico said, "Cylon Number Six" and broke into a huge grin.

"Oh, yeah," I said. It was a similar dress to the one worn by the beautiful blonde Cylon in *Battlestar Galactica*, albeit very different on Cal's towering, barrel-chested frame.

Nico bounded over, me in yos wake.

Shen and Johnny wore leather jackets over women's blouses—and girly makeup! They had name badges for Gwen Cooper and Toshiko Sato from *Torchwood*. Ella was in the full blue dress uniform from *Battlestar Galactica* and Tesh's girlfriend Alisa wore a dark man's suit with her hair tied back. Cal's boyfriend sported a woman's suit jacket and a red wig.

"Can I guess?" Nico asked. Seeing the nods, yo pointed to Cal's boyfriend. "You're President Laura Roslin, that's easy. Ella, are you Apollo?"

"Yep."

"Alisa is Gaius Baltar, Cal, you're a spectacular Number Six. Where did you change?"

Cal put a broad hand on Nico's shoulder. "Nico, my friend, I walked all the way from my house in this dress. That is my level of commitment to being fabulous for you. But I did change my shoes."

Tesh was the only one dressed as themself at the table, and they looked as surprised as I felt.

"This is amazing," I said. "If you told me, I'd have dressed up."

"And ruined the surprise," Ella replied. "You tell Nico everything. And anyway, this was your idea when you cosplayed Ianto."

I glanced back across the Union. It was on the early side for dinner, not half full. At the other table, Summer was on her feet, staring at us, talking quickly to the people around her. Quin blinked and rubbed one eye with her finger. She and the stocky woman next to her had turned around in their seats to fully look at us.

I brushed Nico's arm. "Can I kiss you?"

"Here? Yeah."

I was jittery about it up to the point where I put my hands on the sides of Nico's face, drawing yo close to me. Then there was only Nico and me. Well, and seven of the best friends in the world standing behind us.

Cal whooped, which got the rest of the group cheering. That made me self-conscious again. I broke off, feeling Nico's hands warm and steady on my waist.

The room went silent. Students who had nothing to do with any of this stopped in their tracks, looking from Summer's angry face to the two of us. Waiting to see how the drama played out.

A chair scraped against the floor.

Quin marched toward us. I braced myself. Of everyone in this room, she was the one who had the most legit right to be mad at me.

She walked up to Cal and said, "You got anything for me to wear?"

He pulled his fall jacket off the back of his chair and held it out. She shrugged into it. It was an unremarkable navy windbreaker, but in the group with Ella's uniform it could pass.

Nico saluted and said, "Commander Adama, welcome aboard."

Quin grinned and gave Nico a nod.

"Me too," a voice behind me said. I turned to see the light brown, sunburned face of the stocky girl who'd been sitting next to Quin. "I'm Katee," she told the group.

Shen pulled his name-badge lanyard off and got a marker from his bag. He crossed out "Gwen Cooper" and wrote in, "Owen Harper," then handed it to Katee.

Putting it on Katee asked, "How do I do Owen?"

"He got a surprising amount of action," Nico told her. "So mix swagger with eccentric genius and you're all set."

"Sweet."

I turned back to the former table to see Summer stomping away, trailed by three fresh-faced students. The few others from the table were drifting toward us, slow and uncertain, until Katee hollered, "Get over here!"

"What are we doing anyway?" she asked Cal.

"Cross-gender cosplay to show Nico and Tesh that we love them. And that we'll do whatever we've got to in order to make this a safe campus for them," he said.

"Damn, that's epic. These the people you were telling me about?" she asked Quin.

"Sure are. Nico here stole Tucker from me."

"Thank God for that," Katee said with a big grin. "You two look happy."

I put an arm over Nico's shoulders. "We are. Whether we're Athena and Starbuck, or Jack and Ianto, or especially when we're Nico and Tucker."